HOW WE FALL APART

Also by Katie Zhao
The Dragon Warrior
The Fallen Hero

HOW WE
FALL
APART

KATIE ZHAO

BLOOMSBURY

NEW YORK   LONDON   OXFORD   NEW DELHI   SYDNEY

BLOOMSBURY YA
Bloomsbury Publishing Inc., part of Bloomsbury Publishing Plc
1385 Broadway, New York, NY 10018

BLOOMSBURY and the Diana logo are trademarks of Bloomsbury Publishing Plc

First published in the United States of America in August 2021 by Bloomsbury YA

Bloomsbury books may be purchased for business or promotional use.
For information on bulk purchases please contact Macmillan Corporate and
Premium Sales Department at specialmarkets@macmillan.com

Library of Congress Cataloging-in-Publication Data
Names: Zhao, Katie, author.
Title: How we fall apart / by Katie Zhao.
Description: New York : Bloomsbury Children's Books, 2021.
Summary: Nancy Luo, Krystal Choi, Akil Patel, and Alexander Lin,
juniors at Manhattan's elite Sinclair Prep, are forced to confront their secrets
after Jamie Ruan, once their closest friend, is found dead.
Identifiers: LCCN 2020056156 (print) • LCCN 2020056157 (e-book)
ISBN 978-1-5476-0397-8 (hardcover) • ISBN 978-1-5476-0398-5 (e-book)
Subjects: CYAC: Murder—Fiction. | Secrets—Fiction. | Preparatory schools—Fiction. | Schools—
Fiction. | Friendship—Fiction. | Asian Americans—Fiction.
Classification: LCC PZ7.1.Z513 How 2021 (print) | LCC PZ7.1.Z513 (e-book) | DDC [Fic]—dc23
LC record available at https://lccn.loc.gov/2020056156

Book design by Jeanette Levy
Typeset by Westchester Publishing Services
Printed and bound in the U.S.A. by Sheridan, Chelsea, Michigan
2 4 6 8 10 9 7 5 3 1

To find out more about our authors and books visit
www.bloomsbury.com and sign up for our newsletters.

For those who aspire to greatness,
no matter the personal cost

In inceptum finis est.

AUTHOR'S NOTE

Please note that this book contains depictions of abuse, self-harm, violence, parental neglect, panic attacks, drug use, mental illness, an inappropriate student/teacher relationship, racism, and suicidal thoughts. I understand these themes may be triggering and would suggest proceeding with caution.

MY MOTHER ONCE TOLD ME

My mother once told me I had to get into a top university, or die trying.

You have to be the best, Nancy. Remember: my sacrifices for you. Remember: everything we toiled for in this strange and foreign country.

You cannot let it be for nothing.

I thought Mama was joking. Immigrant mothers often made impossible requests of their high-achieving children.

Like: practice piano every day until you're good enough to play at Carnegie Hall. Like: take tennis lessons under the best coach and become the national champion.

They had achieved miracles, and so they asked us to do the same.

My mother once told me to take the most advanced courses. Earn the highest grades. Become the best.

Or else.

Back then, I did not understand what Mama was asking for, what granting her wishes would cost me. Then, I did not know a debt of life could only be repaid with life. With blood.

And so I promised, and so I vowed. For family. For everything we sacrificed.

I would die trying.

CONFESSION ONE

J.R. is so perfect, it pisses me off. I wouldn't mind if
she disappeared. Permanently. —Anon

★ ★ ★ ★ ★

It was easy stepping into her skin. Wearing it as well as she did
was another matter.

Jamie Ruan. A name—a legend—to which nobody could
ever live up. In the eleven years I was friends with her, I'd known
Jamie to have no weaknesses.

Everyone feared her. Everyone wanted to be her. Of course
they did. She was top of the elite junior class at Richard Sinclair Preparatory School, or Sinclair Prep for short. Class president. Captain of the girls' volleyball team. All that in addition
to being wealthy, beautiful, ambitious, and smart.

I could match Jamie's ambition and intelligence. Slip into
her skin and pretend I was her. But I could only wish, like so

many other girls, to be as effortlessly perfect as her. That the stars would align for me as obediently as they did for her.

Because in the end, I was no Jamie Ruan.

Jamie could get away with anything, do away with anyone. Could ruin your life with a single whisper to her wealthy, influential father.

There was Pam Jensen, who got the solo in choir over Jamie during sophomore year. Jamie bullied her into leaving before she could sing it. The year before, Karen Outa made varsity volleyball instead of Jamie, but mysteriously had to switch schools before the season started. Countless more in middle and elementary and Chinese school, names and faces we'd long since buried like ghosts in our memories.

Tonight, I'd hoped that for once, maybe Jamie wouldn't be the center of attention. Tonight, in Sinclair Prep's century-old auditorium, over a hundred pairs of eyes were trained on the brightly lit stage. Trained on me, and the students sitting behind me.

Principal Bates was taking his time getting the sound system and projector set up. But in the lull, the whispers rose up and surrounded me. Everyone wondering the same thing.

"Where *is* Jamie?" Two seats to my left, Louisa Wu huffed to Kiara William. "I haven't seen her since AP World, and she hasn't even read any of my texts."

"Maybe she fell asleep. You know how stressed she's been," murmured Kiara. Louisa and Kiara were Jamie's latest hangers-on-slash-BFFs.

"This is Jamie Ruan we're talking about," piped up Isabel

Lim, who sat right behind Kiara. "I don't think she *ever* sleeps. Maybe Jamie's too ashamed. I wouldn't show up to give a speech in front of all the parents either if everyone knew my father was an embezzling, low-life, no-good crook—"

"Students, please!" Principal Bates turned around with a glare, raising a finger to his lips. The whispers quieted, but didn't stop. Here at Sinclair Prep, the whispers never stopped. That was why some students liked to theorize that these archaic halls were haunted, inhabited and troubled by ghosts.

My cell phone buzzed in the sliver of space between the waistband of my skirt and my skin. Students weren't supposed to have electronics on stage. This meant, of course, everyone around me texted subtly in their laps.

Once Bates turned back around, I slid my phone out.

Krystal: *Nancy! Best of luck with the speech* ☺
Akil: *Break a leg bro*
Alexander: 👍
Nancy: *Thx guys. Just wondering why Jamie didn't show up to give the speech herself*
Krystal: *It isn't like her to not show up for a chance to show off . . .*
Nancy: *Yeah I'm worried. Remember how earlier she asked us to meet her at Bethesda fountain cuz she wanted to tell us something, and she didn't come to that either? It's really not like her*
Alexander: *Maybe Jamie needed a day off. I mean we've all been cramming for AP tests this entire month, plus*

the girls' volleyball team won states. I wouldn't blame
her if she sleeps until graduation lol
Akil: *Or maybe Jamie's dead. Like on top of her dad being*
an embezzler, he's a murderer too

I shuddered at Akil's text. All the whispers traveling around me, and these auditorium lights creaking above like phantoms, and now this talk of death. It was enough to spook anyone.

Nancy: *Omg don't even joke about that.*
Alexander: *Mr. Ruan's been in jail for months tho.*
There's no way he could do anything to Jamie.
Akil: *Ask Louisa Wu, maybe she knows. Isn't she BFFs*
w/ Jamie now?
Nancy: *Louisa doesn't know either, heard her saying that.*

"Nancy!" The principal waved me over, an invitation to join him at the podium.

I stood and took a deep breath, shaking my head to clear my thoughts. *Focus. Concentrate. Nothing matters except this speech.* I tried desperately to channel Jamie's powerful aura as I left my seat and stepped up to the podium in her place.

"Welcome," Principal Bates announced, "to the ninety-second Junior Honors Night of Richard Sinclair Preparatory School, the preeminent private high school in the United. States, home to a centuries-old tradition of the very highest academic excellence. Here at Sinclair Prep, our students strive to uphold our values of earning a merit-based education, celebrating our differences, and together exploring the achievements of mankind. I am proud to introduce this evening's student speaker—distinguished honor student Nancy Luo."

Polite applause followed the principal's introduction. Per tradition, the privilege of speaking at honors night went to the top-ranked student of the grade. For our class, that had always been Jamie. But tonight, Jamie wasn't here, which meant that responsibility fell to me.

Principal Bates passed me the microphone and PowerPoint clicker with a tight-lipped smile. Behind me, the giant projector screen flashed with the opening slide of the presentation Jamie had painstakingly prepared for this night.

WE'VE MADE IT, CLASS OF 2023! read the title slide. Below it, the subtitle of Sinclair Prep's motto: *In inceptum finis est.*

And below that, our junior class photo, which had been taken in the fall. The deadened eyes and glazed smiles of my classmates stared back at me from the slide.

When she'd originally emailed her PowerPoint to Bates weeks ago, the principal had forwarded it to me, so I'd taken a look at it before tonight and had an idea of what to say. Still, it was impossible not to be nervous speaking in front of *this* audience. The families here were among the wealthiest and most powerful in the country: CEOs, film directors, political leaders. Their kids would go on to run the country five, ten years from now.

Located at West Ninety-Sixth Street and Broadway on the

Upper West Side, Sinclair Prep was a three-story, gray-bricked elite high school that ranked number one in every area imaginable: university entrance rates, debate championships, number of alumni who went on to become U.S. presidents.

Whispers, loud, from the students sitting behind me. Whispers, from the walls, from everywhere. Saying I didn't belong up here, didn't deserve to give this speech. After all, I was a lucky scholarship student attending this elite high school. The daughter of two immigrants who'd fought tooth and nail to make it to the States, only to spend years struggling to make ends meet.

Tendrils of my long, straight black hair clung to my neck. A bead of sweat trailed beneath the gray collar of my black, long-sleeved shirt, down the black skirt that came down to my knees. I wore this uniform every day to class, but now it felt uncomfortably hot and stiff.

Jamie would ignore the whispers, if she even heard them. She would own the floor.

So I envisioned myself as Jamie: top of the class, confident, unbreakable. I envisioned the look of envy that would've replaced her usual smugness if she could see me now, taking *her* coveted place. The nerves melted away. The whispers quieted.

Like I'd practiced in front of my bedroom mirror, I slid Jamie's confident, perfect smile onto my face. "Good evening. It's been a long journey to this night."

Three years, to be exact. Three years of exhausting work and misery. Of clawing our way to the top academic ranks at America's top private high school.

We'd worn ourselves to the bone to make it to this night. Sacrificed hobbies. Neglected personal health. All for the chance to call ourselves the nation's top students. All for the chance to have everything.

I clicked through to the next slide. SINCLAIR JUNIORS OUTRANKED 97% OF THE NATION IN STANDARD-IZED TESTING! "This year, our academic achievements . . . ," I started, then faltered. What was the point of me getting up here to regurgitate a bunch of statistics? All this information was no doubt already on the school website.

Silence permeated the auditorium. Principal Bates turned toward me with a nervous look.

Whispers, louder. Whispers, urging, in my head. *Tell them how you really feel.*

"Junior year hasn't been easy," I blurted out. I didn't know exactly where this speech was going now. But I held the microphone. I controlled this moment. "Over the course of the year, we've . . . said goodbye to several classmates."

Faces swam before my vision, replacing the actual audience. So many classmates who'd succumbed to the pressure. Left with their heads hanging in shame. I didn't know whether Sinclair had created their depression, anxiety, or other mental illnesses, or if this place and the competition exacerbated it in anyone without the iron will and drive to cut it here. Jamie hadn't put *that* information in her presentation.

My fingers gripped the microphone so tightly that my knuckles turned white. I wouldn't let that happen to me. Wouldn't disappoint Mama, who'd struggled balancing odd jobs for years so I could stand on the stage tonight. Wouldn't disappoint myself.

"The accomplishments we celebrate tonight represent all of us juniors. We've worked hard. We've earned our places on this stage. And as we finish out the school year and apply to colleges, we'll continue excelling into senior year." I clicked the button to move to the next slide, which was about our class's extracurricular achievements. "Besides academics—"

A collective gasp from the crowd drowned out my voice. And the whispers, the whispers grew to a crescendo.

"What—what is the meaning of this?" roared Principal Bates.

My heart thudded when I looked—really looked—at the slide. I remembered this slide to show the picture of our varsity debate team holding a first-place trophy from the state championship a couple of weeks ago. I remembered sitting in the center when that photo was taken—me, secretary of the debate team, worn to the bone from juggling extracurriculars and academics, but still managing a painful smile. A smile full of relief that I'd ended the debate season with awards to pad my résumé.

Now, instead of showing the varsity debate team, this slide showed a scanned photo of a pink page. It appeared to have been torn out of a notebook.

On it was an alarming message scrawled in bold red ink.

The whispers grew louder. The noise reached me as though from a distance, my mind at a time and place far from this auditorium.

These hands, picking up that blood-red pen.

These hands, carving those sentences, as if doing so would tattoo them into my own skin. Hissing each word, like a promise of revenge.

Splitting myself open to bleed an oath onto the page:

I WILL END YOU. JAMIE RUAN.
MARK MY WORDS.

CONFESSION TWO

@ The person who played a HUGE prank at Juniors
Honors Night: lmk who you are so I can send you
flowers —Anon

* * * * *

Principal Bates swooped down to grab the mic and clicker from my limp hand. He moved swiftly, shutting off the projector.

He couldn't shut off the whispers, though. Couldn't stop the shock from traveling through the audience.

"Th-Thank you, Nancy! What a wonderful speech." Bates spoke into the microphone with forced calm, and the whispers died down somewhat. "I'll close out this ceremony with the motto of our wise founder, Richard Sinclair, who envisioned this fine institution over two centuries ago." A pause for dramatic flair. "*In inceptum finis est.* In the beginning, is the end. The promise our students have shown at Sinclair, at the beginning of their lives, foreshadows great things for the rest of their days." Bates inclined his head out of respect for the school's ancient motto. "Now please, everyone, enjoy the refreshments out in the hall. And congratulations again to the Junior Honors Class of 2023—who, in the upcoming fall, will become the top *seniors* in the school!"

Scattered, halfhearted applause followed his pronouncement. Murmuring audience members stood to queue for the exit.

"Nancy, did you tamper with Jamie's PowerPoint?" demanded the principal, whirling on me with accusation in his eyes.

I shook my head. "N-No, sir."

Principal Bates gave me a long, hard look. I stared right back. I hadn't tampered with Jamie's presentation.

But I was hiding the small fact that *I* was the one who'd written that threatening message, months ago. In my wildest dreams, or maybe nightmares, I couldn't have imagined it would show up here.

Principal Bates rubbed his head and sighed. "Must've been one of the tech guys, thinking it'd be a funny prank. I'm going to have a word with them. Excuse me." The principal stormed behind the stage curtains, ready to ruin a tech guy's day.

Chairs scraped the floor as students filed off the stage past me, but I barely noticed.

Those words. That page. There was no mistaking it—the page had come from *my* journal. My old journal, my secret journal. My "Diss Diary." A compilation of my darkest, angriest thoughts about anybody and everybody who annoyed me—mostly Jamie.

I kept it locked tightly in a drawer in my bedroom. Who could've possibly taken the journal, scanned that page, and uploaded it to Jamie's PowerPoint?

Whoever had it now held the power to ruin my life. I had to find the culprit. Had to get it back.

Louisa bumped into me in her eagerness to leave, her sleek brown ponytail smacking me in the face. She didn't apologize before rushing to catch up with Kiara.

I glared at her—not that she noticed in her rush.

"Kiara, you *need* to check Tip Tap right now. Someone posted about Jamie . . ." Louisa spoke loudly enough that everyone in the vicinity heard. The two girls pulled out their phones. I followed suit, opening Tip Tap, a gossip app where users could post anonymously about anything they wanted.

Ever since the Ruan scandal had broken about two months ago, when Jamie's father was caught embezzling millions from the Matsumoto Technology Corporation, there'd been at least a couple posts about Jamie and her family every day.

The ones tonight were no less vicious.

I def don't blame Jamie for ditching the ceremony tonight lol

If my daddy got busted by the cops for embezzlement and my family lost face, I wouldn't be able to call myself an honorable person, much less an honors student.

Does this mean Jamie's stepping down as class prez?

Bruh . . . who cares about the embezzlement, that's old news now. What was that creepy message on that last slide??

My curiosity burned. *Did* Jamie's absence tonight have something to do with her father? And if so, was she in serious trouble?

Outside the auditorium, students and their families gathered around the refreshments table, which even had a chocolate fountain. Limited-edition jewelry, diamonds, pearls, and emeralds flashed on the earlobes and necks of the other girls and their mothers. Rolexes glinted on the wrists of sons and fathers.

Middle-aged mothers laughed and air-kissed one another. Fathers shook hands as though they were at a business function instead of a school honors night. To them, this probably *was* another networking night.

I spotted two of my friends near the refreshments and started toward them, but stopped when I saw they were with their families.

Krystal Choi, a tall Korean girl with chin-length black hair. One of Sinclair Prep's fashion icons, she was usually sporting either Max Mara or Zimmermann outside class. She was the heir to a family fortune made through a pharmaceutical empire, and the president of our school's volunteer club.

Akil Patel, an equally tall Indian guy with thick, curly

brown hair. Heir to the wealth of Patel Ventures, which domi-nated the market of luxury hotels, and the star of Sinclair's boys' track team.

Their parents were talking, probably negotiating some partnership. During our freshman year, the Patels, Chois, and Ruans had all done business together, which was how Akil and Krystal got close to Jamie.

I guess even the Ruans' fall wouldn't stop the Patels and Chois from moving forward with their deal. Even if they no longer associated with the Ruans in the aftermath of the scandal.

Even if, like everyone else, like me, Akil and Krystal stopped being Jamie's friend.

Mr. Ruan had been arrested late this winter. And Jamie's world turned upside down with swift, vicious speed.

For weeks, the story was on the media, Facebook, Tip Tap—everywhere.

Despite our class difference, the Ruans had been, if not friends, at least family acquaintances for many years. But that didn't stop Mama from resigning her part-time job as the Ruans' housekeeper. Didn't stop Mama from warning me to stay away from Jamie and her family. Didn't stop me from obeying, despite the guilt that twisted my insides.

Occasionally I had dreamed of it, dreamed of seeing myself at the top of the school, instead of Jamie. Dreamed of being the one who had everything, instead of Jamie.

But I'd never actually expected Jamie to fall. Never thought *she'd* be the one to shatter into a million pieces.

I yelped when my phone buzzed in my hand. A text from a restricted number lit up the screen. It was accompanied by a gruesome photograph of a pale hand dripping with blood.

It's the end of Jamie's era, and the beginning of MY reign. Lesson number one, Sinclair Prep students: betrayal will haunt you from the grave.
—The Proctor

DECEMBER, JUNIOR YEAR

Jamie's penthouse, which was located a short walk away from Columbus Circle, offered one of the most breathtaking views of the city. From my seat at the mahogany dining table, I stared through the huge glass window in the dining room at the pristine buildings that created Manhattan's famous skyline.

A city of over eight million people. A city of extremes, of the cruelest and kindest, of the wealthiest and poorest. Sitting way up here, in a luxury penthouse, I could pretend, for a moment, that I'd made it to the top, ruled over everything and everyone.

"Nancy, what're you looking at?"

I tore my eyes away from the window. Jamie peered at me, her glossy lips pursed. Her fingers played with the silver heart toggle Tiffany necklace she wore.

"Nothing." I returned to reality, which was staring at my AP Lang assignment, and then sighed. "Ugh, this sucks," I groaned, banging my head against the table. "I'm never going to finish this essay in time."

"Well, you should've started earlier," Jamie said loftily. She shuffled the papers in front of her, arranging them into a neat pile. "I'm finished."

"What?" I gaped at her. "That was so fast."

Jamie flashed me a prim little smile. Her signature I'm-better-than-you smile. "And you call yourself the writer."

I shrank back at the dismissal in her tone, the arrogance. And the guilt that sparked at her words.

I couldn't call myself a writer these days, not really. The stress of junior year, everything piling up on my plate, had kept me too busy, too drained to write my poetry. At Sinclair Prep, those who didn't keep up with the workload would be crushed by the others, become the steps of the ladder the elite climbed to the top.

I was determined not to be crushed. No matter what.

Jamie reached for the bowl of cut peaches between us and plucked out a slice. She chewed it delicately, closing her eyes. "Your mother did a great job cutting the fruit."

I clenched my jaw. It was a barb, disguised as a compliment. Jamie's specialty.

To help make ends meet, my mother had been working for the Ruans as their housekeeper ever since we were kids, as far back as the days when Jamie and I attended Shuang Wen Learning Center, a weekend Chinese school on the Lower East Side.

Back then, Jamie had avoided me like the plague—when

she wasn't busy teasing me for being poor. Even as a kid, Jamie knew she was a step above everyone else, knew it and used it. But one day, she saw me playing with a Barbie. Mrs. Ruan had banned all toys from their household, but Mama rewarded me with dolls when I did well in school or behaved myself.

Jamie wanted to play with my Barbie. So I let her, because what Jamie wanted, she got. And that Barbie, of all things, was the reason Jamie and I became friends.

Normally, I would let Jamie's comments pass. Let Jamie split me open again and again, without a word of complaint.

But enough was enough. The stress of the essay assignment, or the combined stress of junior year, maybe, or anger finally got to me. I snapped, "Yes, my mother has many useful skills. How about your mother, Jamie?"

If Jamie wanted to throw a barb at me, I was going to throw one back. We both knew, at this moment, Mrs. Ruan, a house-wife who spent very little time actually in the house, was out in the city. She was probably at one of her favorite haunts, Korea-town or Chelsea, having early drinks with her girlfriends.

Jamie held my gaze. A stare. A challenge. Her expression revealed no emotion.

She picked up another peach slice. Slowly raised it, eyes never leaving mine. Then, when it was inches from her lips, Jamie let the peach drop to the floor. Deliberately. She did this again. And again. In moments, several peach slices lay on the otherwise spotless floor at our feet.

Still those eyes seared into mine. "Oh, Mrs. Luo, Nancy dropped some of the peaches onto the floor. Can you come clean up the mess?" Jamie said in that sickly sweet voice she liked to use around adults.

Mama, who'd been busy tidying in the next room, came rushing over with a broom and dustpan. "Nancy, don't dirty the Ruans' floor!" she scolded. To Jamie, she gave an apologetic smile. "Sorry, Jamie."

"That's okay, Mrs. Luo. It's not your fault." Jamie tilted her chin up at me, indicating that she'd won our challenge. Then she went back to rereading her essay, as though already the matter was behind her.

Shame flooded through me. I hated seeing my mother like this, at Jamie's beck and call. Hated that there was nothing I could do, nothing I could say, to change anything, no matter how hard I tried.

The message was clear. The message was always this: the Ruan family—Jamie—stood far, far above me. If I dared step out of line, Jamie would crush me.

I focused on my essay, not saying another word, the moment of rebellion gone. One more word would put me out of Jamie's good graces. And at Sinclair Prep, being out of Jamie's good graces spelled a death sentence.

The tense silence was broken when the door opened. Jamie stiffened at the sound, and it was the only time I saw a flash of apprehension, of fear, in her eyes.

My mother rushed to greet him first. "Mr. Ruan! Welcome home."

Jamie's father, sweeping into the penthouse swiftly and quietly as a ghost.

Jamie's knuckles, clenching into fists so tightly they turned white.

Mr. Ruan entered the dining room. Anger in his eyes, so like his daughter's. But he was quick to disguise it, quick to give us a smile that didn't reach his eyes. A smile that revealed white, perfect, sharp teeth.

Jamie turned slowly, ever so slowly, toward her father. And now she wore the same face I'd made earlier when she'd dropped those peaches onto the floor, one by one. A mask, carved like an ice sculpture, on the verge of cracking.

"Welcome home, Daddy."

CONFESSION THREE

Legend has it that if you touch the Richard Sinclair
statue at midnight, you'll see all the ghosts that haunt
this school . . . —Anon

*****

The eerie text must have been sent to everyone in our class. Students stared at their phone screens, their parents looking over their shoulders. The celebratory atmosphere had turned heavy with confusion and fear. Shivers—of apprehension, of adrenaline—traveled down my spine.

A current ran through the crowd, setting them to whispering and murmuring. Everyone talking about what the text meant, discussing theories, some even as far-fetched as death. Jamie's death.

It's the end of Jamie's era.

That made it sound final. Made it sound like Jamie was gone. But that wasn't possible. Was it?

Families all around me left the school building, bumping into me on their way out, but my mind was elsewhere. First, Jamie's disappearance today. Then, the stolen Diss Diary page dropped into the PowerPoint. Now, this eerie text, this person calling themselves "The Proctor."

And whispers, whispers of Jamie, Jamie's end, Jamie's death . . .

A hand clamped down on my shoulder, jolting me out of my thoughts. I gasped.

"Nancy! It's me."

"Alexander," I breathed in relief at the familiar voice. My gaze met a pair of dark brown eyes framed by long lashes. Alexander Lin tugged at the gray uniform tie around his neck, which topped off the black blazer, white shirt, and black dress pants of the boys' uniform. He pulled it off well with his mussed mop of black hair. A chunk of his bangs stuck to his forehead with sweat.

The sight of Alexander usually put me at ease. There was comfort in being friends with the other come-from-nothing scholarship kid in a school full of rich elite. But tonight, nothing could calm my nerves.

Alexander frowned. "Are you all right? You look like you've seen a ghost."

"I'm worried about Jamie. I mean—you got that strange text too, right? Doesn't it seem like someone—I don't know—*harmed* her?"

"We don't know anything," Alexander said, but his grim expression told me what we both already sensed: Jamie was in trouble. Something was really wrong. "Let's get out of here first."

As if agreeing with that suggestion, a large man shoved into me in his eagerness to leave, bumping me right into Alexander's chest. "Whoa!" Alexander draped an arm around me protectively, and my heart rate sped up. "You okay?"

I nodded and followed Alexander out, squeezing past the crowd. The cool evening air was a balm on my warm cheeks. As soon as we'd gotten away from the bulk of the crowd, Alexander let his arm drop and moved away from me.

"I'm sure she's okay, right?" The words came out almost without me meaning to, like muscle memory. Almost like I'd said them before. Like I needed them to be true, needed to convince Alexander—and myself. "I mean, this is Jamie we're talking about. Nothing bad could ever happen to her."

Alexander bit his lip. *You're right,* I wanted him to say. *Jamie's fine, and this is all some weird collective nightmare we're having, and honors night went without a hitch, and everything will go back to normal tomorrow morning.*

Alexander said, "Which train are you taking?"

"The Two."

"That's on my way. I'll walk you."

"Oh, that's okay," I said automatically. "You don't have to—"

"Don't be silly." Alexander's voice was kind but firm. And I realized I was glad to have his presence beside me after that chilling text we'd received earlier. The silence between us wasn't exactly comfortable, though. There was too much unspoken in that space.

Feeling the need to say something, anything at all, I said, "So, um, what's new with you? Everything good at home?"

The moment those words flew thoughtlessly out of my mouth, I wished I could stuff them back in.

A muscle worked in his jaw, but other than that, Alexander didn't give any sign that the mention of "home" had bothered him.

I knew it must have, though. To Alexander, "everything at home" meant only himself. But it wasn't always like that.

Once, Alexander had lived with his brother, Eric. Before his brother was taken down by this school, by all the whispers. Before he became a cautionary tale to those who didn't watch each step they took at Sinclair Prep.

Eric Lin had been three years ahead of us. Like us, he'd been on scholarship, and by his junior year, was ranked fourth in the class. He'd been treasurer of his class, captain of the swim team, and on track to get into at least a few of the Ivies.

Then, Eric was caught red-handed with the answer key to the AP World History final exam. And he'd been turned in by none other than a few of his best friends—Richard Li, David Kim, and Peter Shui, the top three students in their class, known as the Golden Trio.

For a scholarship student, getting caught cheating was the end of the road. As Principal Bates would put it, cheaters tarnished the name of the Richard Sinclair Preparatory School. Eric was stripped of his scholarship, stripped of his chance to graduate with a high school diploma from a top school. And he fell—all the way down the ladder.

After, Eric was spotted getting into fights in K-town. There was a rumor he beat up someone badly enough that the other guy had to be hospitalized. Then Eric vanished, and with him, the whispers.

I'd never heard Alexander speak about his brother again. I wanted to kick myself for bringing up his home life, something that had always been a sore spot for him. The tension of the night had gotten to me, and I hadn't been thinking clearly.

"I'm doing fine. You know, hanging in there for AP exams." Alexander's voice was far too light to be casual. I let him steer the conversation toward comfortable waters. Let him pretend that we were everything we appeared to be on the surface: two friendly, maybe a bit competitive Sinclair Prep students, sharing nothing more than a walk to the train station. "How are you, Nancy?" The question sounded a bit stiff. As though Alexander knew his role, knew he had to play along in this facade, but didn't like it.

"Oh, you know. Same old, same old. Haven't changed."

"You aren't the same old Nancy, though. You haven't been for a while."

I stopped walking so suddenly that an older couple swerved around me to keep from hitting me. Alexander moved off the sidewalk and gestured for me to do the same. "What do you mean, I'm not 'the same old Nancy'?"

"I mean, you've . . . changed."

A silence between us that lasted a moment, a year. Then it was broken by a kid who ran shrieking up the sidewalk as his mother chased him, bumping into Alexander's side on his way.

On reflex, I reached out to grab Alexander's arm and steady him. He ruffled the spot on his uniform where the kid had bumped him.

"Be careful," I said.

"Yeah, let's stop lingering where all the kids can bulldoze us."

"Be careful," I repeated, and only then did Alexander look at me, really look at me. Only then did he realize I wasn't talking about watching out for random passersby.

There were some topics we had to be careful about. If Alexander wanted to dig out those memories, if he wanted to touch the flame, it was my job to remind him it would burn him.

We lapsed into easy, familiar conversation. In no time, we reached the subway station. Alexander and I stopped near the entrance.

He jerked a thumb over his shoulder and said rather sheepishly, "My train's actually that way."

"Wait. You're not heading home?" I asked, confused. "What did you walk all the way over here for, then?"

With a slightly sly smile, Alexander said, "Get home safe, okay? And don't forget we have that AP Lit practice test tomorrow." Then he turned around and loped away, navigating the crowd with the ease of a born and raised New Yorker.

Leave it to Alexander to remember our schoolwork in the midst of the chaos. I watched his retreating back as he disappeared into the throng of people. He'd come the opposite way to walk me to the station. The thought filled me, for a moment, with a warm, tingly feeling.

"Good night, Alexander."

———————

My thoughts were so far away that I didn't react in time when the train screeched to a halt, causing me to practically careen into a stern-looking businessman. I'd arrived at my stop.

After weaving through busy Chinatown dinner crowds and ducking around trash for two blocks, I turned onto Orchard Street, and I was home. "Home" was a small, two-bedroom apartment on the Lower East Side, where Mama and I had lived for ten years.

"I'm back!" I yelled as I opened the door, slipping my shoes off and stepping into the apartment.

"Le-Le." Mama came out of the kitchen, a weary smile on her face. She was already dressed in her sleepwear, a simple floral gown. Quite a contrast to the parents dressed lavishly at honors night, who'd waltzed around in designer labels like they were about to hit the red carpet. "Nǐ chī fàn le ma? I have leftovers from work."

"I'm not hungry," I said. The smell of fried dumplings wafted from the kitchen. Normally the food from Lucky Jade Kitchen, the restaurant where she worked, was irresistible to me. But after tonight's events, I had no appetite.

"You'll be hungry later," Mama warned.

"I'll eat some granola bars." It was a habit now. My mother

31

was so busy managing the restaurant that she didn't cook much anymore. Since Baba wasn't around either, I'd stopped caring about what I ate, as long as it kept my stomach from growling.

"Le-Le! You can't always eat that junk food!"

Ignoring Mama's scolding, I skirted the coffee table in the living room and turned on the TV to the news channel. A blond news anchor reported the weather.

I headed into my cramped bedroom. The walls were bare except for some old ribbons left over from science fairs and Chinese speech contests. I slept on a twin-size bed. There was a bookshelf next to the closet, filled with textbooks and extra workbooks Mama had bought so I could get ahead in school. A small blue crate served as my doorstop.

I made a beeline for my white writing desk, which stood across from my bookshelf. I reached into the bottom drawer. Dug through old papers and notebooks. Pulled out everything until the whole drawer was empty.

My pounding heart nearly stopped. This was the confirmation I'd been scared of: my Diss Diary—the rest of that letter—was gone. Stolen out from under my nose.

But *how*? No one but I knew that journal existed. Not Jamie, not Alexander, not Krystal, not Akil. Not even my own mother. I'd never brought it to school, never carelessly left it where someone could have picked it up.

"Mama," I shouted, trying to keep the rising panic out of my voice, "have—have any of my friends come over lately? When I wasn't here, I mean?"

"I haven't seen any of them," my mother yelled back. "Lái, gāi chī fàn le."

"I said I'm not hungry!"

I checked all my other drawers, between the books on my bookshelf, under my bed. Everywhere. No Diss Diary in sight.

I sank to my knees on the floor, stunned. Who could have taken it? It must've been months since I'd last had anyone over at my apartment. I didn't like having friends over. Nothing screamed "I'm not one of you" like inviting your rich friends to your dumpy apartment.

I raced out of my room, only to be brought up short by the sight of Mama leaning against the counter, hand covering her mouth, transfixed by the TV. "Oh, no. How awful."

The solemn reporter was saying, ". . . tragedy strikes the Upper West Side. The body of a teenage girl was found in an empty apartment. The cause of death is still unknown, but police advise . . ."

There was no name, no face, no age, no identifying information whatsoever. The news report revealed nothing about the deceased, except the fact that she was a teenage girl.

And still a voice whispered, whispered. . . .

It's the end of Jamie's era.

And I knew, with near certainty, that Jamie Ruan was dead.

CONFESSION FOUR

When the upperclassmen said AP exam week was going
to kill us, I didn't realize they meant it literally —Anon

* * * * *

Secrets never stayed secrets for long at Sinclair Prep. Even the
best publicist in the world couldn't spread the word faster than
our student body.

By the next morning, my entire Tip Tap feed was filled with
students panicking and discussing far-fetched theories about
that strange text from the Proctor. Many reached the same
conclusion I had, linking Jamie's disappearance to the dead
girl discovered last night. It was guesswork at best, since there
had been no official announcement from the school or the news
outlets.

Yet somehow, everyone seemed to know.

A sense of surreality settled over the school. Jamie Ruan

was . . . Jamie Ruan. Class president. Shoo-in for an Ivy League education.

Unbreakable. Invincible.

The perfect daughter, Mama always liked to say. *Why can't you be more like Jamie?*

Jamie couldn't be *gone.* Not when she'd had so much going for her. Not when she'd never known what it felt like to be inferior—or anything less than perfect.

In first hour, students buzzed over Jamie's empty desk. A few looked teary. Some sat in their seats in shocked silence. Others whispered to their neighbors.

In the hallways between morning classes, in the cafeteria at lunch, students put their heads together. And the whispers, the *whispers,* they seemed to come from everywhere, seemed to come from the very walls of the school.

"I can't believe Jamie Ruan of all people . . ."

"I *swear* I saw her in the library this morning, though . . ."

"Well, I thought I saw her in the girls' bathroom . . ."

"Maybe it's her *ghost* . . ."

To try to escape them, I took my lunch outside to the small courtyard behind the school. The bench in front of Richard Sinclair's statue was empty, and I claimed it before anyone else could.

The bronze figure of Sinclair Prep's founder stood tall with a book in one hand, his shoulder-length hair in curls. The other hand pointed toward a spot on the horizon. The plaque at his feet, slightly weathered from years of rain and snow, bore the inscription of the school's motto: *In inceptum finis est.*

I'd heard, even from my first week at Sinclair, that this statue was haunted. That these grounds were haunted, that there were ghosts trapped within the walls of Sinclair Prep. They said you could hear them whispering and groaning. Most likely, those noises were the old pipes creaking. Or the living students gossiping and moaning about homework.

Sinclair Prep was no stranger to death, though. Four years ago, a senior who'd failed to get into his first choice college had jumped from the top of the building. Two years later, there was a death in my year.

Spirits, now. Ghosts trapped within these walls, for eternity.

———

By midafternoon, it was official. During my AP World History class, Principal Bates came over the loudspeaker to make the announcement most of the school had been waiting for.

"Good afternoon, students of Sinclair Prep. Earlier today, we received the sad news that a student at our school, junior Jamie Ruan, passed away last night. At this time, we do not have further information regarding the circumstances surrounding the event. Further, we would ask that, out of respect for Jamie Ruan's privacy and the integrity of this school, you do not seek out information from her family or friends."

The loudspeaker crackled as Bates drew a deep, shuddering breath. Nobody in the classroom moved a muscle. "I know we are all saddened by Jamie's sudden passing, and send our condolences to her family and friends during this very difficult time. For any students who wish to speak with a counselor, we will have crisis stations located throughout the school today and tomorrow. We will provide information about the funeral for Jamie Ruan when it is available, and students may attend with parental permission. Thank you for your time and attention."

Another crackle, and the announcement was over.

Jamie's era was over, just like that.

———

"Hey." Alexander slid into the seat in front of me as the bell rang, signaling the start of sixth hour. Two hours since Bates's announcement. Since we'd found out Jamie was dead.

"Hey," I said in a feeble attempt at a greeting. I wasn't sure how I'd passed the last two hours. The words from the mass text we'd received last night kept looping in my head.

The end of Jamie's era.

I wished I knew who had sent that text. But there was no way to trace it; it had come from a restricted number.

This was it. The end of an era. The start of someone else's— maybe mine, if I wanted it to be. The thought brought me no joy. Only made me sick to my stomach that it was even a thought I had.

Alexander turned to face me, and I noticed dark bags under his eyes. He'd slept about as much as I had last night, I guessed. "You holding up okay?"

I shook my head and rubbed my temples, as if that would somehow make the numbness go away. As if I could wake up from this nightmare where Jamie was dead. Never to walk down these halls. Never to narrowly beat me on an exam again.

Alexander reached out a hand and then seemed to reconsider what he was doing. He left it there, hovering in midair, in the space between us.

Maybe it was the incredible sadness that pressed on my chest. Maybe it was the need to feel that *something* was real in this situation. Whatever the case, I reached out and grabbed Alexander's offered hand.

"Pass up your homework, class," came the sharp voice of our AP Chemistry student teacher, Mr. Shui.

I looked up, and dark brown eyes met mine from across the room. Mr. Shui. Peter Shui. Jamie's cousin, and one of the infamous Golden Trio who had graduated three years ago. Peter's eyes were red and puffy, but otherwise he appeared the same as usual: neatly groomed, handsome, cold. We shared a look that contained a world of grief. A world of secrets.

Alexander dropped my hand and pressed his lips into a thin line as he stared hard at Peter.

I broke away from Peter's piercing gaze, a warm flush creeping up my neck. Nobody could unsettle me like Peter did. Even after all these years, that would never change.

As the papers reached the front of the room, Mr. Delaney, our short, gray-haired teacher, rose from his desk. "As you all know, the AP exam is coming up. We'll be reviewing in class until then." In the absence of his star pupil—Jamie—Mr. Delaney looked meaner than ever, his eyebrows drawn together, a frown plastered on his face. His eyes flicked to Jamie's empty desk, and his expression drooped with sorrow. "Although one of your classmates has tragically passed, we'll move forward with our curriculum and do our best in her memory. Remember: there are only three days left until the exam."

As Mr. Delaney continued his lecture, my mind drifted. I couldn't focus. I thought of Jamie dead and gone. Jamie, lifeless, with blood pooling beneath her, long brown hair fanned out on the floor.

A loud cough from the front of the classroom startled me back to reality. "Nancy," said Mr. Delaney. Heat flooded my cheeks when I realized he'd picked me to identify the diagram on the board. "Your answer?"

"I . . ." Peter's eyes bored into mine. Challenging me. Around me, my classmates' whispers grew louder. Laughing at me. Waiting for me to fall off my pedestal. Waiting to pounce on my spot as one of the academic superstars of the junior class.

I wouldn't give these snobby students what they wanted. I'd fought tooth and nail to make it this far, to get into this elite school. To live up to what Mama and Baba had always wanted for me: to become, as of today, the number one student at Sinclair Prep.

And nobody was taking that from me.

Nobody.

"The answer is D," Alexander said.

"Excuse me?" Mr. Delaney snapped.

"The answer is D, Mr. Delaney," Alexander repeated, louder this time. "A double bond contains one sigma bond and one pi bond."

Mr. Delaney's face turned red and splotchy, a sure sign that he was about to lecture us both. Peter said nothing, but I didn't miss the scrutinizing look he gave Alexander.

The bell rang. I'd never run out of a classroom as fast as I did then. I was in such a rush that I bumped into Alexander as we both passed through the doorway.

"Thanks for earlier," I said to him. "You saved my life."

"No problem." He stopped in the middle of the crowded hall, backpack slung over one shoulder, turning to me. "Scholarship kids, we have to look out for each other, you know?"

I flashed Alexander a grateful smile.

"Still, you gotta clean up your act a little," he teased. "The number one student can't be zoning out in class."

Number one student. The title should've felt like a prize. And I *was* happy, but not satisfied. I hadn't beaten Jamie to earn that title. She'd died. And in dying, she'd made it impossible for me to ever win against her.

As Alexander and I walked past a group of freshmen who'd been huddling over their phones, one of the girls choked while drinking from her water bottle.

"You okay?" Alexander asked her.

"It's them," a boy murmured. "The ones from the Tip Tap post."

The group scattered down the hall, away from us. Alexander turned to me and shrugged, looking as confused as I felt. "That was weird."

"Is someone saying something about us on Tip Tap?"

"Dunno. Haven't checked."

Curiosity getting the best of me, I opened the school's gossip app on my phone. My eyes were drawn to the first post. For a split second, I thought I was looking at an SAT problem.

Jamie has four former friends. Each friend has a secret. One day, Jamie goes missing. Which friend is guilty and deserves punishment?

    a) the one who sunk the lowest to get highest
    b) the one who ruined a girl three years ago
    c) the one hiding a criminal
    d) the one who traded conscience for grades

Happy testing,
The Proctor

Worse still was the image attached to the post. I recognized the picture of the five of us—Jamie, Alexander, Krystal, Akil, and me—sitting together at the honors luncheon last year. As the full realization hit me, my head grew dizzy.

Four friends. Each with their own secrets. Their own demons.

Someone was accusing one of us of hurting Jamie.

A loud voice spoke from the intercom. "Would the following students please report to the principal's office: Alexander Lin, Akil Patel, Krystal Choi, and Nancy Luo."

Trying to ignore the prying stares, Alexander and I rushed past shuffling bodies toward the principal's office, the whispers surrounding us, following us.

"We're not really in trouble, are we?" I couldn't imagine

how the anonymous poster knew our secrets—unless the person behind it was Jamie. And that was impossible because Jamie was dead.

Alexander sped down the art hall. I almost had to jog to keep up with his long, loping stride. "No, we can't be. I'm sure it's nothing."

The flip-flopping in my stomach told me this wasn't nothing, though. It couldn't be a coincidence for the principal to summon the four of us to his office, especially after the post on Tip Tap had shown up.

We turned the corner. At the same time, a pair of police officers left the principal's office, walking the opposite way down the hall toward a back exit. The sight of the police unnerved me, and Alexander swore under his breath. When we reached the black door with a gold nameplate stamped with Principal Bates, Alexander pushed it open and made his way into the room. I followed.

Principal Bates gave us a solemn look from behind the stack of papers on his desk and gestured toward a pair of open chairs next to Akil and Krystal, who'd gotten here first. Their clueless expressions told me that they didn't know why we were here, either. That they were as shocked by Jamie's passing, as fearful about that Tip Tap post and what it meant for us.

I sat gingerly in a seat.

"Looks like we're all here," said Bates with a feeble attempt at a smile. He correctly interpreted the horror on our faces and added, "Don't worry. You're not in trouble. I wanted to ask you some questions." He closed his eyes and pressed his fingertips together, forming a pyramid with his hands.

"I'm going to cut to the chase. You're aware that your friend, Jamie Ruan, has died. May she rest in peace." He inclined his head, a mournful expression on his face. "Jamie was a star student, truly the embodiment of Sinclair Prep's values. The school will feel this loss for a long, long time."

We sat silently, unsure if we should speak. I didn't even know if I *could* speak, still numb with disbelief.

"In my conversation with the police, I learned they're still determining the exact cause of death." Bates paused, the wrinkles lining his face deepening, as though he were torn about which cause of death was worse. He cleared his throat and continued. "In any case, aside from the *tragedy* of all this, of course the interests of the Richard Sinclair Preparatory School are front of mind for me. I've become aware that all of the students have received an anonymous tip with a strange"—he hesitated— "*riddle*, and a picture. The tipper claims that the four of you might be involved in Jamie's death."

The Proctor.

"The police are very interested in this tip, as well as any clues that might point to suspects in this case, which they've ruled a homicide," Bates said. "They'd like to speak with the students referred to in the post, but I cannot grant them permission to interrogate Sinclair students or search our student roll. I cannot deny I think they'll be back, though, as soon as your identities are confirmed." He leaned forward, and now he took turns staring each of us dead in the eye. It was impossible to look away, and yet holding the sharpness of his glare was like trying to gaze directly into the sun. "So I need to consult you four privately. I need you to be honest with me, and I need you to give me your word that whatever information we discuss within the walls of the office will stay within these walls. Do I have your word?"

We all nodded.

Bates exhaled. "Good. Now, then. Please answer me honestly. Were you or were you not somehow involved in Jamie Ruan's death?"

CONFESSION FIVE

You know how they say you can't spell "studying"
without "dying"? Well I figured out that you can't spell
"Sinclair Prep" without "sin" either . . . lmaooo guys
we're in the Bad Place for real —Anon

* * * * *

The stunned silence in Principal Bates's office was broken
only by the sound of the ticking clock on the wall. Probably
the only thing more shocking than learning about Jamie's
death was hearing the police thought it was a homicide . . .
and that, because of the Tip Tap post, we might actually be
suspects.

*Were you or were you not somehow involved in Jamie Ruan's
death?*

The shock was evident on my friends' expressions.

None of us were involved in Jamie Ruan's death.

But, of course, all of us were involved in Jamie Ruan's death.

"No," whispered Akil. His body trembled, as though rejecting the news. "No, none of us were involved. A—A homicide? It's . . . it has to be a mistake."

"Mr. Patel, I assure you I wish all of this were an error," said Principal Bates with a grimace. "The exact details of Ms. Ruan's death are classified while the police investigate, but yes, I'm assured all signs point to this being a case of homicide."

"What?" Krystal squeaked. "Wh-Why would you call us here, then? Aren't you going to find out who did it?"

Principal Bates swept his cold gaze across the four of us. "That's the question, isn't it? I was hoping, by bringing you to my office, you'd help me answer it. I need to know what I need to know to protect our school and its reputation. Sinclair Prep has an image to uphold. Can't have law enforcement swarming our grounds, nor nosy news reporters buzzing about in hopes of tarnishing our reputation." He shook his head. "And I have reason to believe one—or all—of you might be able to help me decipher the meaning of this note." He held up his phone and read the Tip Tap post.

Jamie has four former friends. Each friend has a secret. One day, Jamie goes missing. Which friend is guilty and deserves punishment?

 a) the one who sunk the lowest to get highest
 b) the one who ruined a girl three years ago

c) the one hiding a criminal

d) the one who traded conscience for grades

Happy testing,

The Proctor

The one who traded conscience for grades.

A chain of memories stirred in my mind. *Traded conscience for grades.* That choice referred to me. Someone knew what I'd done. But how could anyone have found out about my secret?

And how could Principal Bates, who'd watched me deliver that speech last night on behalf of the junior class, who'd watched with pride, now gaze at me with suspicion?

"Principal Bates, you *know* us," I said. "We're some of the best students in the junior class. You can't possibly think that— that this anonymous tipper can be trusted? That *we* had something to do with Jamie's death?"

Bates regarded me with a calculating expression. "I don't have any other leads. Do you, Nancy?"

"I . . ." I scrambled to think of something, anything, and then an idea struck me. That strange text message. "Get out your phones," I told my friends. "That text we got last night— that's the proof of our innocence."

Realization dawned on each of their faces. In a flurry of movement, in unison, we took out our phones, opened our recent text messages, and showed Bates our screens. He leaned over, frowning.

47

"Everyone got this weird message last night from a restricted number," I explained. "We thought it was spam at first—"

"—but it isn't," Krystal gasped. "Someone—the true culprit—was warning us about Jamie's death. 'The end of Jamie's era.' See?"

"This proves we aren't the criminals," Alexander said. "Why would we spam ourselves with a weird warning like this?"

"I'll have to investigate this matter further myself. I'll ask one of you to give me your phone, please." Bates held out his hand toward Krystal, who drew her phone back protectively.

"No way. I *need* this. You can't—" She faltered under Bates's stern gaze, and meekly dropped her phone into his outstretched palm.

"You'll get it back by the end of the day," Bates reassured her with a stiff smile. "I'll be taking a look, but I'm sure that message is unrelated to Ms. Ruan's unfortunate death. And speaking of phones, the anonymous tipper also sent in an enlarged photograph—of you four with Jamie."

Bates slid a piece of white computer paper in front of us and flipped it over. It was that picture of the five of us, the same one that'd been posted to Tip Tap, blown up to show more detail. To show that it was unmistakably us.

"We're obviously being framed," I said quickly. "The real culprit is the one behind the texts, who tampered with the presentation last night at the—" My voice faltered as a horrifying realization punched me in the gut.

The point of including my revenge note in the presentation

wasn't to threaten the school with Jamie's death. The point was to threaten *me*. What I'd written about Jamie in my Diss Diary was enough to make me look guilty of harming her.

Maybe enough to frame me for the crime.

"That picture doesn't prove anything," Alexander interjected, saving me the challenge of coming up with words when my mind had gone blank with panic.

"No," admitted Bates. "But it gives us a place to start our investigation. If my memory serves correctly, the four of you are some of Jamie's closest friends." His eyes bored into ours, as though trying to see right through our souls.

I tried not to let my terror show in my face. Clenched my shaking fists in my lap. I had to find the true culprit. Had to get my Diss Diary back.

Otherwise, I was sure whoever was behind this would blame Jamie's death on me.

"Actually, we . . . we haven't been close to Jamie in a little while," Krystal admitted in a whisper, staring at her boots.

"Have you questioned the girls' volleyball team for information? They might know. Jamie was their captain," Alexander suggested. "Or . . . Quiz bowl?"

"We plan to investigate all potential leads," Bates said matter-of-factly.

I turned toward the three faces that had grown so familiar to me over the years, almost as familiar as my own. Alexander. Krystal. Akil.

Alexander was like me. A poor scholarship student. Murder was the last thing that'd be on his mind. Krystal and Akil were clean, perfect rich kids. I couldn't imagine either of them doing what Bates was insinuating.

"Well, you know there's no way we could have done this, Principal Bates," Akil said, as though the idea were ridiculous. "Yesterday afternoon, right? I'm sure we all have alibis. I was—"

"Wait," I cut in. "We were together. Jamie asked us four to meet her after school yesterday afternoon. We went, but she never showed up. Maybe by then she already . . . she . . ."

"In other words, nobody can confirm your whereabouts yesterday afternoon?" asked Bates.

We exchanged nervous looks. Out of the blue, Jamie had asked us to meet her, and despite everything, we'd gone, of course we'd gone, because something had seemed *off.* Had she known something was about to happen to her? Had she been calling for our help, and we'd been too late to save her?

"Well, nobody at school can confirm our alibis, but maybe someone who saw us in the park yesterday can verify that we were there?" Akil put in feebly.

"How can you be so sure a student murdered Jamie?" Alexander asked. "What if it was a stranger, or—or someone else? An adult?"

"Let's not conjecture any more, please," Bates said. "If any of you uncover additional information, please report it to me immediately. You're dismissed. And please, don't speak of this meeting to anyone else."

I shot up from my chair, heading for the door.

"Oh, and when further news goes public—which it will,

despite my efforts," I heard Principal Bates call after us, "please . . . be careful with yourselves."

I fought the strangest urge to laugh. As if we, of all people, didn't know how to be careful. As if we hadn't spent our entire existence crafting the careful, perfect lives our parents had mapped out for us.

A lot of people had been angry with the Ruans after the embezzlement scandal had broken. What if one of them had been angered enough to murder Jamie? Who hated her— and wanted her out of the way—that much?

Too many names came to mind. Too many bridges Jamie had burned, classmates whose spines had snapped under her Burberry leather boots as she climbed her way quickly, mercilessly, to the top. Peers who'd waited for her to fall apart in the aftermath of her father's arrest.

I could still picture Jamie's sometimes sweet, sometimes gleeful smile. Eyes, burning, when she spiked the volleyball and scored a point. Eyes, glittering, as she snatched the top score out of someone else's fingertips.

Maybe someone in this school—even one of us—really did have the motivation to get rid of Jamie.

If Bates had asked if we'd ever thought about getting rid of our friend, we would have said no.

We would have been lying.

FEBRUARY, JUNIOR YEAR

I was always lying. Pretending to be someone I wasn't in order to fit in. Pretending was so much easier than being who I really was. Because the real me, the real Nancy Luo in all her imperfect glory, wasn't allowed to exist in the rules of this world.

No matter where I went—school or Chinatown or even home—I could never quite shake the feeling of being different. Foreign and unwanted and unwelcome.

But I'd never felt as out of place in my life as I did at Jamie's seventeenth birthday party. Hanging back behind a car, I stared up at the huge, imposing home that was the Ruans' family house in the Hamptons. My hands fidgeted absentmindedly with the beads of the pearl necklace I wore. It belonged to Mama, one of her few treasured pieces of jewelry that she'd brought with her from China.

I watched Jamie's guests, some I recognized as my classmates, and some older-looking strangers. They mingled in front of her house, admiring the garden before heading inside. They were all dressed to the nines, the girls donning designer gowns and the guys sporting fancy suits. I wore a simple black Vera Wang dress, which Krystal had given me when I'd confided in her that I had nothing to wear to Jamie's party.

My free hand gripped the wrapped present I'd brought for Jamie. A warm, fuzzy beanie that I'd knit myself. It had taken me over a month to complete, and I'd accidentally poked myself with the needle too many times to admit. Now, I felt like a fool for even bringing it. Jamie was bound to get tons of flashier, expensive gifts. What if she opened mine and laughed in my face?

I knew my friends were inside that huge house somewhere, but the urge to leave overwhelmed me. I shouldn't have come. I didn't belong here. I turned on my heel, already composing an excuse to text Jamie about being too sick to attend her party.

"Nancy! You made it."

Too late. Cursing my heels for impeding me from a speedier escape, I winced and turned around. A sinking sensation filled the pit of my stomach at the sight of Jamie Ruan walking toward me. Wearing a long, strapless green gown and a pair of huge emerald earrings, she was the picture of elegance, a model who'd stepped outside the pages of *Vogue*. The scent of her Dior J'adore perfume wafted from her body.

Next to Jamie, I must've looked like a frumpy little girl. Still, I mustered a smile and raised the present toward Jamie. "Happy birthday."

Jamie accepted the gift with a wide smile. "Thank you. You're late, though. Everyone's already here." She linked arms with me and forced my immobile body forward. "I want you to meet my extended family. You've never met them before, right?"

"No."

"Get ready, 'cause there's a lot of them. They flew in all the way from Shanghai for my birthday, can you believe it? Usually my parents and I have to go visit them for my birthday every year."

"Every . . . year?" My heart sank. I grew more aware than ever of the ocean of different that existed between us, as vast and intimidating as the ocean that separated my relatives from me.

Jamie could visit her family, the place she'd come from, every year. Hell, her family was so rich that she could visit whenever she wanted, unlike me.

If Jamie noticed my sour mood, she ignored it. She squealed, "Oh, look—there's my uncle!" She all but steered me up the polished front steps and through the doorway of her huge house, where the sound of chatter and laughter overwhelmed me. Jamie tossed my present, my hand-knitted gift, haphazardly onto a table right inside the entrance.

Silver candelabras decorated staged tables straight out of a Conde Nast magazine, and high above our heads hung a glittering white chandelier. Everywhere I turned, reminders of Jamie's family's wealth. Everywhere I turned, reminders that I was different.

Growing up in America, I'd always been too different. I'd never *really* fit in. Here was no different. I didn't belong in Jamie's world. And the people who didn't belong in Jamie's world—they ended up forcibly removed.

People like Em.

No. No, I didn't want to remember that. I blinked the memories back. Took a deep breath.

Jamie placed me in front of a smiling, balding man who looked like he was in his fifties. She introduced me to so many of her relatives, my head was spinning. There were at least a dozen aunts and uncles, and five or six cousins, most of them older than we.

For a moment, I could almost feel what it would be like to have her world, her life. My anger ebbed as I allowed myself to pretend that these were *my* relatives. That they'd flown in to celebrate me and my birthday.

When Jamie's uncle smiled at me, I almost fooled myself into thinking he was *my* uncle.

"This is Nancy. She's my friend. Her mom's the housemaid," Jamie said brightly in crisp, perfect Mandarin.

The light in my—no, *Jamie's*—uncle's eyes dimmed a little, as did his smile. That smile, I knew. That smile, recognizing that I was beneath him.

The brief bliss of stepping into Jamie's life was replaced by mortification.

As if Jamie's family would ever accept me. Not when even my own hadn't. I wanted to sink through the marble floor. Why did Jamie have to mention that Mama was her housemaid?

Was it to make me look bad? To show her relatives that I was some poor charity case of a girl, some fool who'd bring a hand-made gift to a lavish party?

Someone who would never belong?

I took a few deep breaths. This was Jamie's birthday party. I couldn't make a scene here. Couldn't give them more reason to think badly of kids like me, kids who came from nothing, who had nothing but their own grit and nobody but themselves.

As Jamie continued speaking to her uncle, I glanced around, trying to spot my friends. The Ruans had pulled out all the stops, naturally. Bright, colorful lights were strung along the walls, and servants bustled in and out of the room, carrying an array of Chinese and American cuisine on their platters: Peking duck, veggie platters, dumplings, cherry pie.

There, near the fruit plate at the end of the table. I locked eyes with Alexander, who was standing next to Akil and Krystal. Part of me had hoped that he'd look and feel as uneasy as I did, as the only scholarship kids at a gathering for some of the wealthiest families around. But his suit and tie fit his form so well, and he lounged in a state of perfect comfort.

Alexander waved me over. Gladly, I navigated through the crowd to join my friends.

"Nancy, where've you been?" Krystal said. She was the height of fashion, sporting a gold and white Zimmermann dress. She clutched a Birkin bag in one hand and a plate of fruit in the other. "The rest of us got here a while ago."

"Um . . . traffic," I lied.

"Well, at least you look great." Krystal gave my outfit an approving look. "Doesn't she, boys?"

When Krystal glared at him, Akil choked on a piece of fruit. "Oh . . . y-yeah. Yeah, that's . . . that's a dress." I swear I could hear Krystal rolling her eyes.

"You look really great, Nancy," said Alexander.

I beamed. "You, too."

"That's how you compliment someone," Krystal said, clucking her tongue at Akil. "Take notes, Patel."

Akil let out a nervous laugh, and then promptly dropped his plate, where it shattered on the floor, scattering food and glass everywhere. Squeals erupted around me. We dove out of the way.

"No worries—I've got it." A nearby butler pushed past us, broom and dustpan already in hand.

"Akil, are you okay?" Alexander asked.

Akil's hands were shaking uncontrollably. His eyes were wide and sunken, with dark circles under them. "Y-Yeah, fine. Probably had too much coffee earlier." There it was, that nervous guffaw. Coming out shakily. Coming out wrong.

After a moment, Krystal spoke in a voice of forced normalcy. "Anyway, I got some good news today." She smiled, but it wasn't her true smile. This one didn't show teeth. "I got my acceptance email into the James Hale Summer Law Internship Program."

"That's great, Krystal!" Alexander said, and we congratulated her.

"Yeah, my parents were really happy when I told them," she said. And it was a weary smile, a smile of relief, that painted her face.

"Are *you* happy about it, though?" I asked before thinking.

57

Krystal's lips parted, and she stared, just stared. A brief silence, interrupted by a familiar tinkling laugh behind me— Jamie's.

"Nancy's on an academic scholarship," Jamie was saying.

I whirled around at the sound of my name to find her speaking to a group of her relatives.

"Isn't that great? Sinclair Prep is *so* generous to its poor students. Plus, Daddy pours so much money into the school, I bet we're funding part of Nancy's scholarship too."

"Your father is so generous," a middle-aged woman echoed. "He's always been." Nods around her, murmurs of confirmation.

"Daddy is proof that if you work hard, you can do anything. Anyone can make it to the top in the States, as long as they aren't lazy."

And Jamie's smile, the smile that could cut you open, flashing amid her crowd of admirers. Jamie's smile, finding me, and widening.

I couldn't take it any longer. The lights, the chatter, the fakeness. Jamie shoving her superiority in my face. Jamie's whole family flying to the States to celebrate her birthday.

In that moment, I wished I *were* Jamie. Wished I could slip inside her skin, even if only for a day. To know what it was like to be handed everything on a silver platter. To be *allowed* to "make it."

I didn't want to be Nancy Luo anymore. I, who couldn't afford an actual gift for Jamie. I, always below, gazing up at the impossibly faraway top, no matter how hard I worked.

Tears, tears were falling. Blurring the faces of the partygoers.

"Nancy?" Jamie's blob-like face turned toward me. "Something wrong?"

"Get away from me." A voice, a growl, that took me a moment to recognize as mine. Our classmates' eyes snapped toward me. And the whispers rose once more. But I didn't care if Jamie's and my fight became the source of school gossip.

I only cared about this burning fury balled up in my chest. This fury that had been smoldering for months—maybe years—waiting for its moment to explode.

Jamie seethed. "*Excuse* you? It's my birthday. So if you want to throw a temper tantrum, at least throw it somewhere—"

"You'll never understand what it's like to be me," I snapped. "You—you have everything." *You can erase anything—anybody—unpleasant from your life.* "Your life *is* the American dream. And I—"

I have nothing but shards, the shattered remains of an American dream that would always lie beyond my family's grasp. That was what I wanted to say, but the words stuck in my throat. Instead I choked out, "I'm leaving."

I stormed out of the party, Jamie's shouts of anger following me out the door.

At home, I went straight to my room, straight to my drawer.

These hands, lifting my Diss Diary, crafting a final entry, the only entry that mattered.

These hands, tattooing a promise onto the page, tattooing it on my skin.

Red ink running, red ink bleeding.

I WILL END YOU, JAMIE RUAN.
MARK MY WORDS.

———————

And then, it turned out, the world would grant me my secret wish.

Not long after, Mr. Ruan was arrested for embezzlement. And Jamie's American dream shattered in a spectacular explosion.

Jamie was stripped of everything. Friend after friend abandoned her, many of them gleeful about it, as though they'd been waiting for this to happen.

I wish I could say that I would change things if I went back in time. That I'd be the bigger person, stay by Jamie's side as her world fell apart around her.

But in all honesty? I wouldn't change a damn thing.

The flames burning down Jamie's world were far too grand a sight.

CONFESSION SIX

Student teacher P.S. is so dreamy. Damn, I miss
the days when the Golden Trio ruled Sinclair Prep . . .
—Anon

* * * * *

Since my first day attending Sinclair Prep, I'd attracted whispers and stares. Instead of carrying designer backpacks and
Gucci purses, I used a plain blue backpack that Mama had
bought from a street vendor. Instead of wearing Doc Martens,
I sported a pair of old, cheap boots.

It was impossible for me to fit in here. Impossible to catch
up to my classmates when my starting point was miles behind.

Now, the eyes of the student body followed me more
closely than ever. The other students watched all four of us
with a mixture of fear and morbid curiosity in their eyes. They
watched us as though we were the ones who'd killed Jamie.

We gathered around a table in a study room inside the school library, nestled behind towering shelves of books in the test prep section. Normally it was next to impossible to snag a room in the middle of exam season, but after taking one look at us, the group of mousy freshmen practically bolted out of their seats. I guess that was one perk of being accused of murder by anonymous people on an app.

"Is the door shut?" I asked.

"Yeah," said Krystal, who was the last one to come in.

"Good. We have a lot to talk about."

It'd been a while since the four of us had hung out like this. Guilt, at dropping Jamie, had wrenched us apart. Guilt, hanging thick in the air, mingling with the dust in this ancient library, even now.

And Jamie was here, too. Even though she was dead, her presence lingered. Hovering over us, suffocating us.

Walking these halls, whispering from behind the bookshelves, following the living students around. I believed those stories now. Believed Jamie was still watching.

"We need to be careful. More careful than usual." I paced the short length of the floor, and the others watched me go back and forth, back and forth. "People are going to be *scrutinizing* us now. If you have secrets that you think this person somehow knows, I think it's possible they're really going to come out."

Akil's eyes tracked me. In his intense stare, there was a burning question. I stared back defiantly.

"Nancy's right. I don't know which of those multiple choices applies to you all. I'm not sure what's true, and I'm not going to ask. But we have to stick together. And we can't doubt each other, guys. I don't believe any of us is behind Jamie's death," Alexander said. He looked us all square in the eyes— first me, then Krystal, then Akil. His eyes were black and lifeless, surrounded by dark shadows that told me he hadn't slept well in a while. "We have to work together. It's the only way we'll be able to clear our names and catch the true killer."

"Don't worry. There's no way we'll let the Proctor blame their schtick on any of us," Krystal said.

Akil said nothing, arms crossed over his chest, eyes still narrowed at me. Finally, he looked away and ran his hands through his thick, curly brown hair. "Thing is, we shouldn't even *have* to clear our names. We already gave Bates our alibis. Jamie really did ask us to meet her in the park."

"Unfortunately, there's no proof of us being there," I said.

"Maybe not, but still, it's not like there's hard evidence tying us to the crime. There wouldn't be, since we didn't do it!"

"But everyone, even Principal Bates, knew we used to be close to Jamie," Krystal pointed out. "And we got called down to the office *right* after that Tip Tap post went up. No matter how you look at it, things look bad for us."

"So who the hell did it and wants to frame us?" Akil snapped his fingers. "I'll bet you anything it was Sharon Siu. She was *pissed* when Jamie knocked her out of the Volunteer of the Month spot a few weeks ago, remember?"

"If we're suspecting everyone Jamie has ever pissed off at Sinclair Prep, we're going to have more suspects than there are residents in the entire Upper West Side," Alexander said.

"And how are we even going to find the time to catch a killer with exams going on, anyway?" Krystal sighed. "It's hopeless."

"We need a lot more time," Akil agreed.

I shook my head. "No, we don't need more time. We need more manpower. People who're good at sticking their noses where they don't belong—" As I was speaking, an idea struck me. "Wait. People who stick their noses where they don't belong. The newspaper club!"

Krystal's eyebrows shot up. "You want to get the newspaper club involved in a murder investigation?"

"Don't you think that's more interesting than another article ranking the cafeteria food? Plus, I'm sure they've got resources we could use, like camera equipment—"

"—and coffee," Akil put in eagerly.

"What does coffee have to do with anything?" I asked.

"My body runs on it. I drink three cups before noon."

"Oh, so that's where you get all your energy from," snickered Krystal. "Maybe you should cut back. You're always trembling."

The whole room seemed to take a breath. Soft laughter, coming from Akil, coming from within these walls. I stared at Akil, but he avoided everyone's eyes.

Krystal wasn't wrong. Akil was often trembling. But not for the reason she thought.

"How're you sure the newspaper club will agree to this?" Krystal asked.

I shrugged. "Every writer is looking for a juicy story." And then, dodging further questions, I said, "So—Krystal and I will lead the charge on investigating Jamie's death with the newspaper club. Akil and Alexander, you're our tech guys. You think you can trace the Proctor's IP address from those Tip Tap posts?"

"You're looking at the youngest two-time champion of NYU's Hack-a-Thon," Akil said, puffing out his chest. "If I can't track that sucker's IP address, I'll eat my own computer."

"Please don't do that." I glanced at Alexander, who was studying me with a small smile on his lips. "Alexander?"

He nodded. "You can count on us."

We had a plan. We would be fine.

As the others trickled out of the study room, one person remained behind. I'd expected this confrontation. Knew who it was, even before he spoke.

"Nancy, you—" started Akil. Then he cast a glance around the room, around these walls. Nobody here, and yet the sense that someone, or something, was listening in. "You didn't tell anyone about my . . . my *thing*. Did you?"

I shook my head. "No. I swear I didn't."

"But nobody else knew besides—besides you and Jamie."

"Jamie knew?" But it wasn't a surprise. Jamie seemed to always know everything.

Akil's face drained of color. "I don't know who you told my secret to—"

"Akil, I *swear* I never told a soul—"

"This'll ruin my life if it gets out. I'll lose everything." The word came out raspy and hoarse, like the hiss of death. "You know that, right?"

That wild gleam in Akil's eyes, the harsh lines of his set

jaw. I'd only seen him make such an expression once before. "I know."

For a year now, I'd known.

For a year now, Akil's secret, burning a hole in my chest.

APRIL, SOPHOMORE YEAR

In inceptum finis est.

Richard Sinclair's motto was fixed on a plaque that was mounted on a wall high above my head. I was sitting way in the back of the library—my usual seat, because it was closer to the stacks of books. Tall, dusty, endless shelves of books.

Back here, I could get lost among the books and never find my way out. Avoid everyone for as long as I wanted. There was only one other student sitting here, at the next table over—Kiara William, a girl with short black hair and brown skin, who I recognized from a few of my classes. We hadn't talked much, but we both frequented this spot in the library so often, I liked to think we'd developed a kinship.

I was working on a speech about climate change for the upcoming debate tournament. As the team's newly appointed secretary, I had to make a good showing. Being secretary of the school's debate team wouldn't mean much if I didn't bring home trophies.

I was so engrossed in my writing that I was surprised when someone sat across from me, and I was even more surprised to see it was Akil. He lowered himself into the armchair across from me and put his athletic bag onto the table.

"You're studying?" I blurted out.

"Why the tone of surprise?"

"Oh, I, um . . . I meant—"

"I'm kidding, Nancy. Relax." Akil cracked a grin. "I know I should study harder. That's why I'm here. Ready to study." He crossed his arms over his chest.

"Aren't you forgetting something?" I said, staring pointedly at my open textbook.

"What?"

"Your books, genius."

Akil sighed and then leaned in, casting a look around as if he were afraid to be overheard, even though we were the only ones, minus Kiara. "Okay, fine. If you have to know, I'm . . . I'm hiding from my parents. I can't go home. They're *suffocating* me. Telling me to be extra careful, that horrible accidents can happen to students. They've always been super strict, but now they've activated, like, Extreme Helicopter Parenting mode. It's been that way since . . ."

His voice trailed off, but I could fill in the blanks. Since the funeral. Since the Incident.

"Anyway, there was something else I wanted to do here," Akil admitted. "I, uh . . . wanted to see something."

I followed his gaze. He looked away quickly, but not before I realized what—or, rather, who—he was looking at.

"Is that 'something' sitting over there, studying?" I snickered. "Named 'Kiara William'?"

Akil's cheeks turned bright pink. "Don't—Don't know what you're talking about," he blustered. He shot out of his seat, causing the old chair to clatter. A few heads turned our way, including Kiara's. "A-Anyway, I gotta get going. Track practice in fifteen."

Akil was always rushing to track practice. He had aspirations to become a recruited athlete, and with his talent, he was well on his way. I knew that even though his parents could afford to send him to college, Akil was determined to get there on his own, without paying a cent. Desperate to use his talent to run all the way to the top.

He turned to leave—without his track bag. "You forgot something kinda important." I picked up the bag, but it was open, and the contents spilled all over the table.

Akil's neon green running shoes, a travel-size tube of sunscreen, a deodorant stick, and—a tiny transparent baggie, filled with white-and-orange Adderall pills.

I froze. I knew some students used them illegally, but they were the last thing I expected to see in my friend's bag, right here, right now.

"I got it," Akil said hastily when I moved to help him pick up. After he'd finished putting everything back in, he studied me with a strange, frantic expression I'd never seen before. "Did you see?"

I should lie. I couldn't. "Yeah . . . Akil—"

"You can't tell anyone."

"Of course not."

"Swear it, Nancy."

I raised my right hand because that was what I'd seen people do in movies. "I swear."

He gave me a long, hard look. Then, finally, a nod. "Good. Nothing happened here."

"Nothing happened," I agreed.

"And—Nancy. You know, if you ever need . . . anything . . . extra"—he paused, choosing his words carefully—"you can come to me."

Akil's offer, laid out on the table between us. I'd seen drugs and what they did to people in movies. But maybe. Maybe, by our senior year.

I smiled. "Thanks, Akil."

This was how Akil Patel did it all, I discovered that day. Maintaining a near-perfect GPA. Being the star of the varsity track team. Staying at the top of Sinclair Prep, year after year. Finding out his secret—his hidden flaw—was almost relieving, in a twisted way.

Now I knew Akil wasn't perfect. Now I knew he wasn't unbeatable.

I kept my word. Another secret to add into the mix. Another secret to bury in the darkest corner of my mind.

But there were always eyes watching at Sinclair Prep. Ghosts hovering unseen, whispering to each other, to the students, passing on our secrets.

Waiting for us to shatter. Waiting for us to join them.

CONFESSION SEVEN

A kid at our school died, and my parents' biggest
concern is my calc grade. Smh —Anon

★ ★ ★ ★ ★

Every writer is looking for a juicy story.

That was the explanation I'd given Krystal earlier. But there
was one more reason that I knew we'd have the newspaper
club under our thumb.

Akil left the study room, looking queasy but less suspicious of me. I hung behind and shot off a quick text.

Nancy: *Hey, when's the next newspaper club meeting?*
I've got a story ur students will def wanna cover.
Peter: *4:30 PM on Thursday. We're meeting on the school*
field to cover the track meet
Nancy: *Cool, Krystal and I will come by then*

Peter: 👍 *When am I gonna see you alone tho?*

Nancy: *Omg, I came over the other day. I've got too much going on with exams atm. And aren't u worried about us getting caught?*

Peter: *Have I ever gotten in trouble for anything, Nancy?*

Nancy: *You got kicked out of Stanford for dealing drugs . . .*

Peter: *No, I'm taking a gap year*

Nancy: *"Taking a gap year"*

Peter: *You're obnoxious. I'll be back at Stanford next year, don't worry*

Nancy: *If we get found out, ur parents will donate a bajillion dollars to the school to cover everything up. It's different for me tho. If I get caught, it's all over for me*

Peter: *. . . and when has that ever stopped you before?*

Nancy: *I hate you*

Peter: *No you don't* 🖤

Nancy: 🙄

Peter: *Come by the chem room tomorrow at 4. I've got something I wanna talk to you about too, about Jamie*

Nancy: *Ok*

At the beginning of freshman year, I'd made a promise. To be a good girl. To be the best. But, I'd soon learned, here at Sinclair Prep, the rules were different. Here, being a good girl and being the best were often mutually exclusive.

And between the two, I chose being the best.

I chose Peter, twisting him around my pinkie, breaking all the rules.

———————

It was hours later, after studying in the library and trying to brainstorm leads on the Proctor's identity, when I stumbled through the doorway of my apartment, exhausted and famished. Mama was cooking, on a rare evening off from the restaurant. The air smelled like comfort and a cheap, easy-to-make dish that we hadn't eaten in a while. Not since Baba had left.

"Is that—tomato and egg soup?"

"Yes. Are you hungry?" Mama called from the kitchen.

Tomato and egg soup, the dish my father used to make all the time. This dish, simmering with memories.

Ghosts at my school, and also ghosts at home.

My family couldn't have been more different from all those families at Junior Honors Night. My parents and I, we lived in a different world. A world where Baba had, for years, worked as a manager at New China Supermarket. Where Mama cleaned the Ruans' house, scrubbing away at the walls and floors until they gleamed, and worked at the Lucky Jade Kitchen too. A world where they both struggled to make ends meet to send me to the best school possible, sometimes fighting so loudly that their voices shook the flimsy floor beneath my feet.

And my already tiny family, my world, had broken when Baba packed up his bags and left us to return to China almost five years ago.

As I sat at the table, Mama slid a bowl in front of me.

I picked up my spoon, dipped it inside the steaming soup. Countless times I'd sat at this table. Countless times I'd gone through these motions. In the past, there would be a third person sitting at this table.

Baba, smiling. Baba, drinking his coffee. Baba, digging into a warm bowl of soup. Now, only the shade of his memory remained, and even that was fast vanishing.

My appetite disappeared, though I'd been ravenous moments ago. My stomach heavy, not with food. With loss.

I laid the spoon down. "When's Baba going to come back from China?"

Mama's expression closed off like a door slamming shut. "Eat your food," she said tiredly.

"You know, if there's one thing the past few days have taught me, it's that life is short." These words, locked away for too long. Spilling out of me. "Too short to not talk to your own family."

"Where is this coming from?" Mama's eyes narrowed. "Is this about . . . ?"

I knew what she couldn't bring herself to say. *Is this about Jamie?*

Guess we couldn't talk about Jamie in this household anymore, either. "Forget it." I stood up and headed toward my room.

"Le-Le," Mama shouted after me, "if you don't eat now, don't think there will be food for you later!"

Shutting my bedroom door, I collapsed onto my desk. I was exhausted enough to turn in for the night. But I had a killer to catch. And I hadn't even finished studying. Sighing, I hauled my folders out of my full-to-bursting backpack.

My phone lit up with a string of unread texts.

Akil: *Um . . . bad news guys. I checked Tip Tap.*
 The Proctor strikes again.

As I squinted at Akil's screenshot, my stomach plunged to
the floor.

Police said J.R. died of overdose, but she was rly
stabbed in the back . . . by A.L., A.P., N.L., or K.C.
Wonder how they'll react when Jamie stabs them back
from her grave? There's one way to stop it . . . and
that's to confess to the school what you did two years
ago, before you all pay a steep price. Jamie already did.
—The Proctor

Akil: *Yo, who the hell is "The Proctor" and what is their*
 goddamn problem?
Alexander: *A.L., A.P., N.L., K.C. . . . those are OUR*
 initials, right?
Akil: *Yeah and I'm pissed. This person won't leave*
 us alone
Krystal: *Wait . . ."two years ago" . . . is this about Em?*
Nancy: *Nobody knows what happened two years ago tho.*
 Nobody except us knows about the Incident. It was all
 covered up

Two years ago. "The Incident"—named by Jamie—that had
happened during our freshman year. The Incident that cemented

the five of us into a tight-knit group. The Incident, the beginning.

The number one rule of our group was that we didn't talk about the Incident. More than grades, more than extracurriculars, more than similar classes or ambitions or anything else, the Incident was what bound us together. We were friends, and sometimes we could forget why, really, but after something like *that* happens, there's no getting away. Ever.

Even when I attempted to reach that far back into my memory, my mind shut me out. The past was in the past. It didn't matter what dirt the Proctor had on us. We were going to figure out their identity, track them down, and bury them. Figuratively, of course.

> Nancy: *If this person rly knows this much about us, it's probably someone we spend a lot of time around. Be wary of who's hanging out around you these days.*
> Alexander: *But the most important question is . . . how does everyone have time for this shit? Is NO ONE studying for exams? I know they didn't all take the SAT back in March like we did*
> Akil: *Nah, everyone's talking about junior-senior prom in 2 weeks*
> Nancy: *I totally forgot prom was coming up*
> Alexander: *You mean you don't have a hot date, Nancy?*

Peter's face swam in my head, but I didn't even let myself go there. That was completely out of the question.

Nancy: *Do YOU have a hot date?*
Alexander: *Of course*
Krystal: *UM, SPILL?*
Alexander: *. . . with my textbook* 😭
Akil: *Gtfo. Unlike u losers, I do happen to have a date*
Alexander: *Your physics book doesn't count*
Akil: *Ok nvm, I don't have a date*
Nancy: *We shouldn't be worried about prom dates, we
should be worried about finding the killer. And
chem . . .*
Akil: *Ahhh yes, good ol AP Chem, the real murderer at
our school*

The thought of the looming AP Chem exam caused a pounding headache to develop at the back of my head, but I was determined to push through.

This was nothing. Nothing compared to what my parents had endured to rise to the top of China's exponentially tougher educational system, only to come to the States and have to work in manual labor anyway. Nothing compared to what they'd sacrificed to bring me here, to this day, to this moment.

Everyone wanted to hear success stories about those who came from nothing, working hard to become something extraordinary.

Nobody would want to know the gritty, unpleasant details about what it took—what it *really* took—to get there.

DECEMBER, SOPHOMORE YEAR

Everyone thought Jamie Ruan was perfect.

Nobody knew what she was willing to do, how far she was willing to go, to maintain the flawless image she'd crafted.

When our choir teacher, Ms. Rudzel, announced auditions for a solo in our Winter Showcase, nobody wanted the part as desperately as Jamie.

I was the only one who knew that Jamie came in an hour before school started, every morning, to practice singing the solo part. The only one who knew that she stayed an hour after school ended, every afternoon, to continue singing in empty classrooms.

The day of solo auditions, Jamie sang like her life depended on it. She sang the part almost perfectly.

"Our soloist for 'Carol of the Bells' is . . . Pam Jensen!" announced Ms. Rudzel. "Our backup soloist is Jamie Ruan. Congratulations, girls!"

Everyone clapped. The redheaded, freckled Pam Jensen beamed, basking in the applause, looking as though she could hardly believe the position she'd found herself in. Nobody beat Jamie at anything, ever. Nobody. Pam's expression took on the slightest trace of smugness, as though she knew this, as if she reveled in the knowledge.

Jamie attempted a smile, but it came out looking like she'd gotten a root canal.

I was torn between feeling happy for Pam, who sang like an angel, and feeling awful for Jamie, who'd practiced harder than anyone. I settled for putting my hands together two times, and then shooting Jamie a sympathetic look that she didn't return.

"I need you to do something for me," Jamie whispered when the bell rang, signaling the end of class. "You're headed to lunch now, right?"

"Yeah, aren't we all?" I gave her a strange look.

"I'm skipping. Come with me." The corners of Jamie's lips turned up into a familiar grin. A cruel grin. Jamie was up to something, and it would end in disaster for some poor, unsuspecting student. "Pam Jensen leaves the school grounds every day during lunch."

I didn't ask how she knew this. Jamie knew everything about everyone.

"You and I are going to trail her and find out where she's going, what she's doing. I would've left her alone, but . . ." Jamie shrugged. "She's in the way, now."

And people who got in Jamie's way tended to disappear.

My stomach growled, but I nodded. Turning down a request from Jamie was never a good idea. And even though I didn't want to admit it, my pulse quickened with the thrill of being part of another of Jamie's schemes. Jamie had come to *me*, after all. Chosen *me*.

Jamie led us to a yellow cab parked outside the front entrance. We piled into the car in time to see a sleek black Volvo pull up a few feet in front of us. Pam got in, sitting shotgun.

"Where to?" asked our taxi driver, a middle-aged man.

"Follow that black Volvo," Jamie commanded.

We followed Pam's ride down West Ninety-Third Street, until the car stopped at the intersection of Ninety-Third and Amsterdam. Pam got out at an Italian restaurant called Carmine's Pizzeria. An older man got out of the car with her. His hair was graying, but I could tell he had once been very handsome, and he still carried himself with an air of arrogance. The man wore a white dress shirt and black slacks and looked like he'd come out of an important business meeting.

Jamie started snapping away with her phone camera. "Get pictures!" she hissed at me. "Make sure you get Pam's face!"

Startled, I obeyed without thinking, taking a few photos with my phone.

The man put his arm around Pam, too low to be fatherly or friendly. Held her to his side, like a lover. As I watched, heart pounding, mesmerized, he bent down to kiss her on the lips, a long, deep kiss.

Snap. Snap. Snap.

Tip Tap, of course, was the surefire way to spread the

incriminating pictures. I AirDropped my photos to Jamie, and she composed the post on the ride back to the school, fingers typing madly away.

I stared at Jamie, at the dark bags under her eyes that seemed to grow more prominent. Looked almost like bruises. I stared at my phone, in awestruck horror of what it had done to poor Pam Jensen. Though Pam's fate was sealed the moment our choir teacher awarded her the solo over Jamie.

The gossip spread through school like wildfire. Everywhere I turned, Pam Jensen and her much older lover was the topic of conversation. A Tip Tap photo showed Pam and her tearful parents going into Principal Bates's office. The next, and final, showed them leaving the halls of Sinclair Prep forever.

Regret, bubbling up in the pit of my stomach. I forced it down. After all, the rules at Sinclair Prep were different. Like I said—people who got in Jamie's way tended to disappear.

"You didn't have to go so far," I said to Jamie. "Why did you?"

Jamie turned to me. Those eyes, freezing. Those eyes, burning. "Daddy said he's coming to see me sing. He promised. Daddy expects me to be the best singer there."

Three weeks later, on the night of the Winter Showcase, proud families and friends crowded the school's ancient auditorium to listen to all the choirs perform. Mama didn't come early enough and ended up sitting toward the back.

And Mr. Ruan sat in the very first row, front and center. Eyes freezing. Eyes burning.

When it was the girls' choir's turn to perform, Jamie sang the solo for "Carol of the Bells." She hit every note. She brought a few audience members to tears.

She was perfect.

CONFESSION EIGHT

Spotted: L.W. making out with N.W. behind the Richard
Sinclair statue. That statue's seen more action than our
dear Richie saw in his whole lifetime lmaooo —Anon

★ ★ ★ ★ ★

A mournful melody drifted from inside the chemistry classroom.
With one hand on the door, I paused and closed my eyes, taking
in the music. It sounded like the violin strings were crying.
Reaching up, I wiped away a tear that had trickled down my
cheek.

Peter Shui's music was magical, had always been. His senior
year at Sinclair Prep, he'd captured plenty of hearts with that
violin. Broken them, too.

The science hallway was empty. School had been over for a
while now, and most people were studying in the library or
headed to their extracurriculars. I should've been in the library
too, if it weren't for the text I'd received earlier today.

Peter: *Remember to come to the chem classroom after school. 4 PM. I have to talk to you about something important*

When the song ended, I knocked on the door.

"Come in, Nancy," came that soft, familiar voice.

I entered the empty chemistry classroom and shut the door behind me. The lab in the back was cluttered with the instruments from an experiment. Posters of the periodic table of elements and bad science jokes plastered the walls. As with most of the classrooms in this school, there was a white banner at the front of the room with Richard Sinclair's motto: *In inceptum finis est.*

And there was Peter, sitting on the teacher's desk, holding his violin. Closing his eyes, as though listening to an ongoing tune only he could hear.

"That was beautiful," I said. "What's that piece called?"

"Nothing, yet." Peter opened his eyes, and the spell was broken. He set his violin beside a huge stack of paper and hopped down from his desk. "Why don't you help me come up with a title? You're the one who's good with words."

A memory stirred. "I'll compose the song, and you'll write the lyrics," I said. Words Peter had spoken to me during my freshman year, and his senior.

Peter's eyes lit up. "Glad you remember our promise."

Self-conscious of how alone we were, and the fact that I was supposed to be studying, I said, "What did you want to talk to me about?"

"Prom is coming up soon, isn't it?"

I started at the unexpected topic. "Oh yeah, I guess it is. I don't really pay attention to that stuff."

"No? You don't have a date?"

First Alexander, now Peter. Why was everyone so curious about my date-less prom status? I narrowed my eyes, wondering if Peter was testing me. His serene expression revealed nothing. He may as well have been asking me about the weather. Infuriating. That was the only word for Peter Shui. "What if I said yes? Would you be jealous?"

Peter slid his hands into the pockets of his dress pants. He leaned forward, his lips passing so close to my ear that I could smell the fresh mint on his breath. "Why would I be jealous, Nancy?"

He was baiting me. I wouldn't fall into his trap. We hadn't actually talked about this—put a label on this thing we were doing together. Talking about it would mean admitting it was happening, that we were breaking rules on every level, from school to social class.

But what I knew was that I could never show Peter any weakness. And emotions were a weakness. Whoever showed emotion first would lose this game.

I cast Peter a sidelong glance. It was obvious why half the girls in the class had a crush on him. The half who didn't probably weren't into Asian guys, which, frankly, was their loss. Boyishly handsome, well-dressed, intelligent, and charming, Peter was only twenty. A Stanford would-be sophomore who'd nearly been kicked out of the school after a drug scandal last year. The Shui family pulled a few strings and donated a new building to the school. After that, "getting kicked out of Stanford" turned into "taking a gap year to teach."

Peter and I were from different worlds. We would never work. Yet an invisible, magnetic force drew us together. I couldn't stay away, no matter how hard I tried to resist.

I'll compose the song, and you'll write the lyrics. A promise I couldn't forget. A promise carved into my soul.

"What did you want to talk to me about? Was it only prom?" My voice came out husky. My cheeks heated, and I cleared my throat.

"No, I wanted to talk to you about Jamie. My aunt and uncle have totally melted down over her death, of course. As their nephew and Jamie's cousin, and as your—friend—"

I coughed.

"—and devoted . . . teacher," Peter amended, his smile crinkling the edge of his eyes, "I had to find out the truth for myself, as well as give you a warning, given the . . . Tip Tap stuff."

It took a moment for Peter's words to sink in. Then, anger flared through me. "I didn't kill Jamie. None of my friends did."

"I didn't say you did—"

"You were getting there."

"Well, can you blame me for being curious, given the rumors flying around?"

"You of all people should know how baseless rumors can be at this school," I said flatly, glaring at Peter. His eyes narrowed. Finally, I'd broken through Peter Shui's emotionless exterior. "When you, Richard Li, and David Kim were the Golden Trio here, there were all kinds of rumors flying around you guys. Sneaking into clubs and warehouse raves. Having sex in your parents' beach houses." They'd been the ones who caught Eric Lin red-handed with the answer key to the AP World History final exam, too. Scandal trailed the three boys like their dark, twisted shadow. Yet thanks to their families' wealth and influence, they always seemed to get off with a slap on the wrist, if not scot-free. "Are all those rumors true?"

"Funny you should mention Richard and David," Peter said.

"You didn't answer my question."

He continued as though I hadn't spoken. "That's the real reason I wanted to talk to you. They're both coming back to town for Jamie's funeral. Thought I'd give you a heads-up."

"Well." Peter's words had caught me off guard, but I refused to show my surprise and apprehension at this piece of information. "That's good, isn't it? The Golden Trio will be reunited."

Peter studied my expression. I kept it carefully arranged into an emotionless mask. "Only briefly. David has to fly back to L.A. the day after for his shoot. Richard has finals at Columbia. Nancy, I'm telling you because I—well, the way things left off two years ago . . . after . . ."

The Incident, I filled in silently.

"Richard and David hate my friends and me. I know." The Golden Trio had gotten involved the night the Incident happened. And I knew Richard and David blamed the Incident on my friends and me.

"'Hate' is a strong word, but . . . well. My friends aren't good at letting old grudges go. Be careful, okay?"

I stifled a gasp when Peter reached up and tucked a strand of my hair behind my ear and gently brushed my cheek. As he lowered his hand, I caught it in mine. Our eyes met for an eternity that lasted only seconds.

"Mr. Delaney!"

The door flung open, and Peter and I sprang apart. I recognized the flustered junior at the door as Nathaniel Goldman, the heir to Natasha Goldman's fashion label. Luckily, he didn't seem to notice how close Peter and I had been standing. He was too busy searching for the teacher who wasn't here. "Oh. Where's Mr. Delaney?"

"Thanks for your help on the homework, Mr. Shui." I said quickly. My heart was beating rapidly. That had been far too close.

An amused glint entered Peter's eye. "You're welcome, Miss Luo."

Without looking at Peter, I left the room, brushing past a clueless Nathaniel. The skin on my cheek and hand, tingling where Peter touched it. The beautiful melody he'd arranged, still spinning through my head.

FEBRUARY, FRESHMAN YEAR

Peter Shui had an effect on me that I couldn't explain. There were plenty of girls who liked him, and for good reason. Popular, handsome, rich, smart, talented—he checked all the boxes as a perfect Sinclair student, not to mention the perfect Asian son.

Sinclair Prep swam with handsome, rich boys. But it was Peter I liked best.

A few weeks ago, an anonymous user on Tip Tap ran a poll ranking the Golden Trio boys from most to least desirable. It was widely agreed that Richard Li, the tallest and most muscular of the three, came in first. David Kim, who told jokes that could make even strict Principal Bates laugh, polled at second. And Peter Shui, quiet, bookish Peter, who played the violin, came in third, trailing David by a few votes.

Peter seems really mysterious, someone commented below the poll. *I bet he's keeping a lot of secrets.*

Probably keeping them in that violin case he's always carry-ing around, replied another commenter.

Peter was keeping many, many secrets. And I was one of them. The knowledge filled me with glee. With exhilaration.

The downside to being Peter's secret was the fact that in public, there were always other girls with him. Prettier girls. Older girls. Richer girls. Girls with whom I couldn't compete. Girls who didn't even *know* I was part of the competition.

"Nancy, stop scrunching up your face like that," Krystal said, snapping me back to the present. We were at her pent-house in the Upper East Side on Fifth Avenue. It was a luxuri-ous space with wood-paneled rooms that were spotlessly neat, decorated with gleaming white and black furniture that made it the perfect spot for taking aesthetic Instagram photos. And it was empty, with Krystal's parents away on their vacation in Bora Bora.

But then again, Krystal's place was always empty.

Krystal tackled my face using a thick, round brush, and spread a bunch of white powder on it.

I coughed when some of the powder went up my nose and into my mouth. "I—I think that's enough, Krystal."

Krystal made a *tsk*-ing noise. Then she shook her head and let out a long-suffering sigh. "Yeah, that's about the best I can do. Tell me if you like it." She held up a hand mirror, and I took it from her.

At first, I didn't recognize the girl in the mirror. Mascara gave the illusion that my eyelashes were longer, and eyeliner made my eyes appear rounder. Krystal's expertly applied natural eyeshadow had a hint of gold glitter. My cheeks, rosy with blush. My long black hair, tumbling down my back in big, elegant curls. I wore a light purple Kate Spade clover eyelet dress, borrowed from Krystal's closet.

I looked prettier, older, richer. I looked like one of the girls Peter would be seen with in public.

"Wow, Krystal, I . . . you're amazing. You could be a beautician, for real. Like, this is *magic*."

Krystal beamed at me and dusted off the sleeves of her maroon Calvin Klein blouse. She kept up with the latest trends in beauty and fashion, and it was thanks to her, really, that I knew anything about fashion at all. Krystal's secret dream was to study fashion, but she wouldn't be able to, her strict Korean parents having their own ideas for their daughter's future—becoming either a doctor, lawyer, or engineer.

Still, it didn't hurt to keep this secret dream. As long as it remained secret, tucked into the corner of her heart.

"Don't you think this is going overboard, though?" I asked. "I know we're going to a fancy birthday dinner and all, but still . . ." It was way more makeup than I usually wore—which, admittedly, was some eyeliner and a simple coat of lip gloss, and that was if I bothered at all.

"Whoa, Nancy," came Akil's gasp from behind. I turned around and found him gaping at me, a Dorito raised to his mouth from the bag of chips he held in his arms. He was dressed in a navy blue Vince blazer. "You look . . ."

"Stunning, right?" Krystal supplied, with a proud glance at me.

"I was gonna say, you look . . . old. Also pretty, though," Akil added hastily when Krystal pinned him with her glare. "Anyway, when're the others coming? I'm starving already." He flopped down on the floor, stuffing another Dorito into his mouth.

"Our reservation at Sushi Maido isn't for another three hours." Krystal's face crinkled with disapproval as she glanced at Akil, who was going to town on the chips. "Alexander hasn't replied to my text yet, but Jamie said she'd be here any second." Her cheeks turned rosy.

Jamie and Krystal had begun dating—in secret—over Thanksgiving break. The two were practically inseparable in private. Everything was still so new to them.

I was happy for my best friends. But sometimes it did get a bit lonely third-wheeling around them. Good thing Akil and Alexander were here today, too.

"Where's Alexander? It's his birthday dinner, and the dude's not even here," Akil grumbled.

The doorbell rang moments later.

"Coming, Jamie!" Krystal rushed to open the door.

But it was Alexander who'd arrived first, not Jamie. He wore a dark brown sports jacket, and he'd managed to tame his messy black hair so it stayed flat for once. "'Sup?" He nodded at Krystal.

"Happy birthday!" Krystal shouted, throwing her arms around Alexander, who seemed caught off guard. He returned the gesture by patting her awkwardly on the back.

Next it was Akil's turn to wish Alexander happy birthday, but instead of hugging Alexander he bumped his fist.

Then, my turn. I was more conscious than ever of how different I looked. "Happy birthday," I said.

Alexander turned his gaze to me. His eyes widened. His mouth parted, and he stared for a few beats too long. Krystal looked between us, a small smile on her lips.

The heat of a blush flooded my cheeks. In an attempt to dispel the awkwardness, I joked, "I know I look different, but I'm Nancy. You might remember me. We've talked once or twice."

"You—you look—"

"She looks beautiful, right?" Krystal gave me an appraising glance. "I mean, more than usual, thanks to me. But of course our Nancy is *always* beautiful."

"Good catch," I said.

Alexander cleared his throat, and now he was looking anywhere but me. Feeling uncomfortably warm, I looked away too, staring at my hands as though they were the most interesting sight in the world.

Then the doorbell rang again, shattering the awkward atmosphere. Jamie swept in, wearing a cashmere Burberry coat. She wished Alexander a happy birthday and gave Krystal a quick kiss. All the attention turned to Jamie, as usual.

Krystal clapped her hands. "Great. Now that the party's all here, let's take a picture! It's not every day that Alexander turns fifteen, and that Nancy looks this great."

"Hey," I said.

We squeezed together to take a group selfie, with Krystal commenting on our angles, and Jamie complaining that the lighting was exaggerating all the pores on her face. But eventually, with everyone's approval, Alexander snapped a photo.

My phone pinged with a text notification. When I looked at the name on the screen, I quickly excused myself, pretending to need to get some water in the kitchen.

Peter: *Hey, wyd rn*
Nancy: *Hanging w/Jamie and them. Why?*
Peter: *Come chill at my place for a bit. I'm working on a
     new piece, and I want you to be the first to hear it*
Nancy: *Are you sure it's ok if I come over . . . ? Won't
     your parents ask questions*
Peter: *They're not home.*

". . . Nancy? You in?"

Startled, I tore my gaze from my phone screen and glanced up to find my friends all staring at me expectantly. "In for what?"

"Since we've got time to kill before the rez, Alexander wants to go see the new Marvel movie," said Jamie.

I thought fast. I wished I could say the decision was harder to make, considering that it was Alexander's birthday, but I didn't really like superhero movies. Plus, Peter's summons couldn't have come at a better time, right when Krystal had given me a makeover.

"Oh, I . . . I just remembered. I forgot to help my mom with something. I gotta go back home for a sec, but I'll meet you guys at the dinner later." I avoided everyone's eyes, especially Alexander's, so they couldn't sense my lie.

"What? Can't that wait until after the dinner?" Jaime pouted.

"It's Alexander's birthday," said Krystal.

Guilt shot through me. Now I really, really couldn't look in Alexander's direction. I was being a bad friend. This wasn't what a good friend would do. Peter and his song could wait. Should wait.

But it was exhausting making the right choices, never sticking a toe out of line, all the time. Couldn't I have this one thing? This one secret?

"Sorry. I'll be quick," I said.

As I threw on my thick winter coat and headed for the door, I thought I could feel their eyes lingering on me, Alexander's especially. I forced myself to think of Peter, only Peter.

And when I arrived outside his family's apartment on Madison Avenue, it was clear Peter was pleased to see me, too. His black bangs were flyaway, and the first couple of buttons on his denim button-up were undone. He looked frazzled, like he'd been in the middle of something all-consuming.

"Hey, Peter," I said, my voice pitched higher than usual.

Peter's dark eyes drank in the sight of me, then flickered up to meet mine. The approval I craved was in his smile. "Nancy. You're . . . wow. You're beautiful. Come in, I want you to hear this song."

Leaving all my doubts at the door, I followed Peter and slipped inside.

CONFESSION NINE

Does our school do drug testing for student athletes?
Asking for half the track team —Anon

★★★★★

In the gloomy late afternoon, the boys on the short distance team took turns sprinting down our school track. At the opposite end, co-captains Kimmie Tran and Georgia Banks led the girls' team in a warm-up. It was an unseasonably cold spring day with no wind, and had been raining on and off all day.

This was the last—and most important—meet of the nearly finished season. Our runners wore the blue-and-white Sinclair Prep track uniforms, while our biggest rivals, Anderson Collegiate, sported green and yellow. Crowds of students and parents gathered in the stands, a much larger number than the usual turnout. Anderson had thrashed us last year, and everyone was pumped to see Sinclair Prep return the favor this year. There were college scouts in the stands, too, eager to scope out the promising potential recruits, like Akil.

I couldn't shake the feeling the Proctor was among us. If I were them, I'd use this chance to do *something* at a school-wide event, especially if the targets—Akil, Krystal, and me—would be right under my nose on the field.

The thought forced me to quicken my pace as I walked up to the end of the field, toward half the newspaper staff, Peter, and Krystal. Peter and I casually greeted each other, like we hadn't met up and talked like old more-than-friends in the AP Chem classroom yesterday. Like we were nothing more than student and teacher.

Krystal had been standing slightly apart from the huddle, and drifted closer to me as I approached, her expression full of relief to see me. It wasn't hard to understand why. The five newspaper club staff members regarded us with haughty expressions. The editor in chief, Louisa Wu. Staff photographer Kiara William. Then there were three other students I only knew by name: sophomore Mark Gowain, junior Isabel Lim, and senior Nishant Kakar.

"I highly suggest we collaborate with the accused students. This will give *Sinclair Unveiled* some desperately needed visibility, no matter the outcome of the investigation," Peter was saying to his club.

"What's *Sinclair Unveiled*?" Krystal blurted out.

"Our newspaper," Kiara said through gritted teeth.

Krystal blushed. "Oh. Oops."

"See?" Peter said.

Nishant folded his arms across his chest. Mark narrowed his eyes and hugged his camera closer to his chest, as though afraid we'd run at him and snatch it out of his hands.

"A murder investigation involving high-profile minors." Louisa studied us not with distaste, but curiosity. With hunger. Clearly, the chance to get the inside scoop on a death that had shaken the school was too tempting for her to pass up.

Mark sighed. "Everyone's so busy using that dumb app Tip Tap, they've forgotten about us. This might be our only shot at fame."

"If this article gets big, it'd be a good resume-booster," Nishant mused.

"We're in!" declared Isabel.

"Great," I said. Even if the newspaper club was planning to use our reputations to boost their readership, it was nice to know that some people were sort of on our side.

"Meet us at the newspaper room tomorrow right after school," Mark ordered. Then he waved his hands. "Now, shoo. We have a track meet to cover."

Krystal grumbled, shooting a disgruntled look behind us as we headed toward Akil. "Those newspaper dorks are lucky we're giving them the news coverage they need for people to actually notice them. *Sinclair Unveiled*. Seriously. Who's even heard of that?"

"Hey, Nancy, Krystal—wait up."

I turned around to see Louisa and Kiara jogging toward us. Their high ponytails swung in near-perfect unison. Krystal stared openly at Louisa's leggings with unmistakable envy, and Louisa, following Krystal's gaze, gave her a lofty smile.

"Like them? I *just* got these limited-edition Fendi leggings."
Louisa patted her legs. "These cost four hundred bucks. They're
not technically on sale for another two months, but, well, my
father's got connections, so he can get me anything I want
early."

"Look," Kiara interjected, a solemn expression on her
face, "we wanted to say . . . you know, it's been rough on Louisa and me, since Jamie . . . you know." She gulped, and Louisa
squeezed her friend's hand. "I know it's probably been tough
on you guys, too, especially with people suspecting you and
everything. But Louisa and I are on your side, and we'll get the
newspaper to get to the bottom of this."

"So, wait. You don't think one of us hurt Jamie?" Relief
flooded through me.

"Oh, sweetie, no," Louisa laughed. "You can't even pull off
that outfit, much less a murder."

"I . . . thanks?"

After an awkward pause, Kiara said, "Um, so that's what
we came over to say."

"Thanks, guys. It means a lot," Krystal said. "Really."

Nodding, Louisa grabbed Kiara's hand, and then they
jogged back.

"That was weird," I said as we watched them go. "And . . .
nice?"

"Yeah. Not sure those leggings are the best look on Louisa,
though. They're kinda tacky." Krystal frowned.

"Huh," I said, which was about the only fashion input I
ever had.

"I heard Louisa's family is one of those new money families.

Those leggings scream 'Daddy got rich in China pretty recently.' You can always tell new money from old money."

"Right." New money, old money. The only kind I knew was no money. Suddenly, I wanted nothing more than to change the subject. "Let's go grab seats in the stands before they're all full."

We snagged a spot close to the track at the bottom of the stands. Before the competition shifted into full swing, we waved at Akil, who was warming up with his teammates in the middle of the track. It didn't escape my attention that when Kiara drew close to him, he tripped and fell on his face.

During the meet, my attention was divided between watching the runners and trying to spot any suspicious activity in the bleachers. Krystal and I were both on full alert, ready to head toward our friend if the Proctor tried anything.

My phone buzzed, and I jumped. But it wasn't a new post from the Proctor.

Mama: *Did you see Alexander today? He didn't show up for his shift at the restaurant or call in sick, and he didn't pick up his phone either. I'm worried*

Nancy: *Yeah, he was in school*

Mama: *Ok when you see him tell him he'll be working extra hard next time*

Nancy: 👍

Aside from being vice president of our class and keeping top grades, Alexander worked a handful of shifts every week at the Lucky Jade Kitchen as well. Maybe Alexander had forgotten about this shift. Couldn't blame him, given how many things he was juggling. But then why wouldn't he answer the phone when my mother called?

The sky darkened, and the lights along the track turned on, glowing like strange, otherworldly orbs in the misty early evening.

The excitement of the crowd crescendoed. One after another, each race was too close for comfort. Akil came in third and fifth for the boys' four-hundred- and two-hundred-meter dash events respectively. I couldn't see his expression in the dark, but I knew him well enough to know he'd be disappointed with himself. Representatives from top universities like Dartmouth, Columbia, and Duke had been scouting Akil for their track teams.

By the time the final race rolled around—the girls' hundred-meter dash—I'd gotten so wrapped up in cheering that I'd pretty much forgotten about the Proctor. Sinclair Prep trailed Anderson by two points, and Samantha Erwin saved the day by pulling off a first-place finish.

It had gotten cold, but I hadn't thought to bring a sweater. I shivered through my uniform, through the chill of the evening.

Freezing fingers landed on my shoulders.

"Agh!" I whirled around, heart hammering. Black eyes. Alexander's eyes. "You scared me! Don't *do* that."

"Sorry. I didn't mean to sneak up on you," Alexander said as Krystal suppressed a snort. "I would've texted, but my phone died." He gave a sheepish smile. His hair was mussed from something—maybe the misty weather—and his cheeks were flushed, as though he'd run all the way here.

"Why're you late?" Krystal asked.

"I had to wrap up a shift at the Lucky Jade Kitchen. Ran a bit over." Alexander's eyes, flitting away from mine.

Alexander Lin had never been a good liar. And now, though he didn't know it, I'd caught him in the act. He hadn't been working his shift. Mama hadn't been able to reach his phone. Where exactly had he gone? I wanted to ask, but not with Krystal here.

"You missed all the good stuff." Krystal sighed. "We had the most epic comeback win."

"Yeah? That's great. How'd Akil do?"

"Not that great," I said.

Then, a scream cut through the cheers. "Help! Somebody get help!"

The crowd quieted, and my gaze was drawn toward the source of the noise.

There, out of the mist, out of the dark, a figure rose from the ground. A student, wearing the blue-and-white Sinclair jersey. Collapsing onto the field in convulsions.

"Oh my god," gasped Krystal. "That's Akil."

Shoving past confused students and parents, we raced from the bleachers toward Akil's prone figure. But the track coaches and teammates formed a wall around him.

"Hey!" cried one of his teammates as I elbowed my way in, Krystal and Alexander on my heels. Akil lay on the grass, his whole body trembling. The school medic was checking his pulse, and a teacher was on the phone.

"What's wrong with him?" Krystal hissed at me.

The tremors, sweating, gasping. I was no medical expert,

but I knew enough from books and TV shows to recognize the signs of a panic attack.

Akil gasped. His breathing came out in ragged, uneven bursts. Sweat glinted on his brow. His eyes, wild. "I . . . don't know what . . ."

"You're having a panic attack," said the medic. "Everyone— back away and give him air!" she barked, and we all took a collective step back. "Do you need an ambulance?"

"Ambulance? N-No," Akil wheezed, trying and failing to wiggle out of the medic's grasp. "You can let go of me. I'm fine now." He broke free and then stood up, almost losing his balance. "See?"

"You're coming with me to the nurse's office, mister," said the medic, grabbing him firmly by the hand. "*Alone,*" she added when she spotted us taking steps toward Akil.

"We're his friends," I protested.

"He needs space from *everybody,*" she insisted.

Helpless, we watched Akil and the nurse walk off the field toward the school. Disappearing into a mist. Out of the mist, whispers, whispers everywhere. And then, a new notification on my phone screen, from Tip Tap.

Jamie has four former friends. Each friend has a secret. One day, Jamie goes missing. Which friend is guilty and deserves punishment?

Correct answer: a) the one who sunk the lowest to get highest

Explanation: J.R. definitely had a hand in dealing A.P. his stash. How far would A.P. go to protect his secret, his GPA, and his chances of becoming a recruited athlete? Far enough to take a little too much . . . from yours truly . . . and maybe even far enough to silence J.R.

That's one secret revealed. Three more to go. Unless someone wants to fess up to what they did two years ago. What's it gonna be?
—The Proctor

CONFESSION TEN

Confirmed: A.P.'s drug abuse finally catching up to
him at the track meet. Say goodbye to Dartmouth,
dude. —Anon

*****

The teachers searched Akil's belongings and, of course, they
found exactly what they were looking for. Then he was suspended from school for the next two days. He was lucky he
didn't get a harsher punishment for getting caught with drugs,
and I heard a rumor that it was because the Patels poured money
into Bates's pocket.

But I knew Akil, knew the pressure he was under, always
under, from his family. Whatever punishment Bates doled out
wouldn't compare to the punishment he'd face at home.

Nancy: *Hey Akil, you doing ok?*
Akil: *Not rly . . . I mean yeah I'm physically fine, but let's*

say I'd rather be anywhere but home rn. Plus the scouts
from Dartmouth and Columbia emailed me to let me
know they're no longer considering recruiting me . . .
pretty sure the others are gonna follow

Alexander: *sorry to hear that bro* 😫

Nancy: *I'm sorry Akil*

Akil: *It's ok guys, no one to blame but myself*

Krystal: *Can't your parents make a huge donation to*
Dartmouth or something so you can still get in?

Akil: *LMAO no way. I pissed off my folks so much that*
they're threatening not to pay for my college tuition at
all. So prob not . . . idk we'll see

Krystal: 💔

Nancy: *Akil, who gave u the drugs that u used last night?*
The Proctor said it came from "yours truly" which
means that whoever gave them to u has to be the person
behind all the posts

Akil: *That can't be it*

Nancy: *Why not?*

Akil: *The person who gave me those drugs was Jamie, a*
few weeks ago

Akil's response made no sense. And it made perfect sense.
Jamie knew his secret all along. Jamie had been the one sup-
plying Akil with drugs.

Jamie was dead, of course. But the echoes of everything
she'd done, the reverberations of everything *we'd* done, lingered here. Making sure this school remembered her. Making

sure we remembered all the secrets, and the people, we'd tried to bury.

> Alexander: *Yo, I'm sure you'll be fine, Akil. You'll prob be able to perform better at track meets now cuz I'm pretty sure the drugs were holding you back*
> Akil: *I wasn't doing them to perform better at track meets tho. I wanted to help myself forget*
> Krystal: *Forget what?*
> Akil: *What we did 2 years ago . . . The Incident.*

Akil's words, all the whispers within these walls, haunted my thoughts. But I couldn't let my mind dig up the past, now. Not when there were so many other issues to deal with in the present.

Peter's warning about Richard and David. Akil's panic attack, his secret coming out. The Proctor's next move.

And the worst part, the part I couldn't even confide in my friends: my Diss Diary. After revealing our secrets, the Proctor would turn my own words against me to pin the blame on me.

Why were they doing this? Maybe it was all to avenge Jamie's death. Or maybe the Proctor really thought we were the ones who'd killed her.

Or—were *they* the one behind Jamie's death? If so, my friends and I were in over our heads. And there was no way out.

I stared down at the AP Chem exam paper in front of me. I was sitting in the school auditorium with fifty juniors and seniors spread out in alphabetical order over hundreds of seats. The whole place was silent except for the test proctor's footsteps moving up and down the rows, and the scratching, the whispering, of number two pencils on paper.

Whenever I took a break from staring at the problems, I couldn't help but notice how the banner above, everything around me carried the school's motto. *In inceptum finis est,* labeled on the pencil shaft. *In inceptum finis est,* stamped on all the scratch papers.

When the exam was finally over, I let out a sigh of relief. I'd barely been able to concentrate, but it was done, leaving my brain fried.

The first thing I did was check my phone. A notification flashed, showing several missed group chat messages within the last hour.

Akil: *Yooo you guys are still at school right?*
Krystal: *Yeah ofc, why?*
Akil: *So I've been putting my suspension to use, and I figured out the Proctor's IP address*
Krystal: *DUDEEE WTF YOU'RE AMAZING*
Akil: *I'm coming to school so we can talk in person. Where will you guys be in like an hour*
Krystal: *Nancy and Alexander are taking the AP Chem exam rn, but that ends in an hour . . . and I'll be coming out of AP Chinese. We're going to the newspaper club after tho, so meet us there?*

Akil: *Dope, see y'all soon. Idk how to prepare to catch a*
psychopath but pls do that before we meet lol

Reading through the texts, I let out a whoop that caused a couple of seniors to stare at me. Finally, a piece of good news. I couldn't wait to get to the newspaper room.

Nancy: *Akil, you're amazing!! I take back any mean thing*
I've ever said about you 😊
Alexander: *Dude, that chem exam destroyed me but this*
news brought me to life again

But first, I had to focus on the issue seated two rows in front of me: Alexander. I had to figure out why Alexander had lied yesterday.

Alexander was rubbing the back of his hair, stretching his arms as everyone around us filed out of the auditorium. I rose, but rather than following the crowd out, I went over to Alexander and tapped him on the shoulder.

He jolted, then turned around and smiled. "Yo. Looks like Akil didn't even need my help cracking that IP address, eh?"

Wordlessly, I showed him my phone screen. Showed him the text from Mama last night.

Alexander's expression collapsed as he registered the words. Registered what it meant for him. He groaned, closing his eyes. "Nancy, I—"

"Alexander, why did you lie to us yesterday? What are you hiding?" I interrupted. "I'm not mad. I'm worried. The Proctor already came after Akil. I can't—" My voice caught. "I can't watch them come after you, too."

Couldn't sit back and let the whispers win. Couldn't watch the ghosts rise out of these dusty hallways to take us down.

"I'm sorry. I can't tell you," Alexander said quietly. "Please don't ask me."

I stared at him. At his guilty eyes, at his hunched form. "All right," I finally said. "All right."

My phone dinged between us, and Alexander glanced toward it. A shocked look, a horrible look, crossed over his face. "Are you—is that text from—"

With a sinking feeling, I snatched my phone out of his line of vision. As I'd feared, there was a new text waiting for me, from *him*.

Peter: *On ur way to newspaper?*
Nancy: *Yeah, give us 5*

"Let's go. We have to get to the newspaper room, remember?" I shoved my phone into my pockets. Heart hammering, face flushing hot. Alexander must have seen. Alexander couldn't have seen. He couldn't know.

Alexander's eyes, piercing me. Sharp and calculating.

I held his gaze, a silent challenge. *You don't ask about my secret, and I don't ask about yours.*

After a moment, a century, Alexander nodded. "Let's go."

I opened the door to the newspaper room, and from the walls, a dark shadow lunged at me.

"Whoa!" I cried, jerking back and nearly colliding with Alexander. "What the—?"

"Akil," Alexander gasped.

Akil grinned. He looked almost back to his normal goofy self. Back to the way he was before the track meet, before he lost his prospects of going to college as a recruited athlete. Almost, but not quite. Dark bags hung below his eyes. He'd lost a lot of sleep, like the rest of us.

"You're sure you shouldn't be at home resting?" I said.

"I'm fine, Mother," Akil said sarcastically. "I feel fine. Good enough to catch the Proctor, anyway."

That was what he said, but I had the sneaking suspicion that he was barely holding it together. I could see the cracks forming in his image. I saw those same cracks every time I glanced in a mirror. And it was the same way Jamie had looked before the end.

"It's true I'm not supposed to be here, though, so lower your voices, okay?" Akil added.

"You've got a lot of nerve sneaking into school." Alexander grinned.

"Well, this investigation can't wait. I've been working on this all night, and I've finally tracked down the Proctor's IP address. Here—come in. I'll show you."

When we entered the classroom, Isabel, Kiara, Mark, and Nishant sat at a round table holding a camera and notebook in the middle of the room. In the back, Louisa sat in front of computer monitors, absorbed in her typing.

My eyes were drawn toward Peter, who sat on the teacher's desk. Dressed in a black T-shirt and jeans, swinging his legs, he looked more like a student than a teacher. "Welcome." Peter smiled, his gaze lingering on me for a beat longer than the others. I turned away, my cheeks warming. "Make yourselves comfortable. I've actually got to leave for a staff meeting, but I'll trust you all to handle yourselves, especially since Akil here"—Peter nodded at Akil—"seems to know what he's doing with this investigation." With that, he departed. I watched Peter leave, trying to ignore the twinge of disappointment in my stomach.

I glanced back to find Alexander's eyes boring into mine. I quickly dropped my gaze. Couldn't drop the sense, though, that he knew, or at least guessed. I hoped I was wrong.

Akil pulled out his laptop from his backpack and booted it up, chattering a mile a minute at Kiara, who appeared fascinated by his every word. I joined the others crowding to look over Akil's shoulders. He'd pulled up Google Maps onto his screen, and his mouse hovered over a dot that he was enlarging. "So here's the place. It looks like a coffee shop."

"The Green Bottle Coffee a few blocks down from our school," I said. I passed by it every day. "No way. The Proctor's been posting from there?"

"Looks like it." Akil let out a low, long whistle. "We're so close to catching them, I can *feel* it."

"So . . . what exactly do you need our help for again?" Nishant asked.

"Okay, here's the plan. Obviously, we've tracked down the Proctor's IP address," Akil said. Eyes alight, livelier than I'd seen him in days—months, even. "The four of us are going to need your help, your camera equipment and stuff, to find the Proctor and get evidence of who they are." He nodded at the club members.

"You want us to come *with* you?" Kiara squeaked, looking both intrigued and horrified by the prospect. "What if the Proctor is, like, super dangerous?"

"We're not even sure if they'll be there. The odds are pretty slim," Akil admitted. "We could wait until the next post drops, but I figured since we're all here anyway, we might as well scope out the place now. And since I'm suspended, I don't mind staking out Green Bottle Coffee on Monday if we need it, in case the Proctor comes by."

Kiara gaped at him with reverence shining in her eyes. "Wow. That's really brave of you."

Akil sat up straighter. "And eventually, of course, you'll write an article about the investigation, and—" He frowned and cast a glance around the room. "Hey, where's Krystal?"

Somehow, in the excitement of Akil's big breakthrough, I hadn't noticed that Krystal hadn't shown up.

"Uh," said Louisa, and her jaw dropped as she stared at her phone. "I wouldn't count on Krystal coming through today."

Even before I grabbed for my phone and checked Tip Tap, I knew what had happened.

The first post on the app showed a picture of a young girl. A younger Krystal with a choppy pixie cut even shorter than the one she had now. Her eyes were lined with thick black eyeliner that made her look like a raccoon, and she wore black lipstick. She was dressed in all black. The girls in the picture with her dressed in black too, and wore matching angry expressions on their faces.

Jamie has four former friends. Each friend has a secret. One day, Jamie goes missing. Which friend is guilty and deserves punishment?

Correct answer: b) the one who ruined a girl three years ago

Explanation: We know K.C. as the queen of volunteering, the most selfless and fashion-forward soul in all of Manhattan. But who was K.C. *before* coming to Sinclair Prep? Definitely NOT Miss Volunteer Princess. Rumor has it K.C. was such a delinquent that she got shipped off to boot camp the summer before high school 'cause she almost killed someone in eighth grade . . . *tsk, tsk.* Not so goody-two-shoes after all, huh, K.C.? Don't tell us that old habits die hard, and you killed a certain someone for real . . .

Two secrets down, two to go. Fess up or get messed up.
—The Proctor

CONFESSION ELEVEN

Aight I'm holding my funeral next week after the AP
Calc exam destroys me, you're all invited —Anon

＊＊＊＊＊

Louisa and Kiara immediately put their heads together, gossiping about Krystal's troubled past. The others, though less invested, still gawked at their phones.

"Did you guys know about this?" Alexander asked, breaking the strained silence.

Akil shook his head. "Who did Krystal almost ki—?"

"It doesn't matter," I interrupted. "We've got to find her."

But just as I rose, the door banged open. Krystal stood there, panting at the doorway, an apologetic smile on her face. "Sorry I'm late. My mom called me and I got held up."

We all stared at each other.

Krystal wrinkled her nose. "What? I said sorry."

"Um, Krystal," I said tentatively, "have you checked Tip Tap?"

"No . . . should I?"

"No," I said at the same time Louisa put in, "Probably."

Realization dawned on Krystal's face. She yanked her phone out of her purse. I cringed, not wanting to see the look on her face when she saw, when she knew what had happened.

"Oh," came Krystal's small, quiet voice. She shoved her phone back into her bag and, without looking up, mumbled, "I . . . I have to—bathroom." With that, she turned on her heels and raced out of the room.

"Krystal!" Dimly, I was aware of my chair clattering to the floor in my haste to run after her, but I didn't care.

I sprinted through the halls, the halls with eyes and ears. Students who'd stayed for after-school activities stared unabashedly at the sight of Krystal and me running down the hallway. And they whispered, whispered the secrets we'd wanted to carry to the grave, the secrets we'd buried deep within ourselves. Secrets being dug up one by one.

I finally caught up to Krystal in the girls' bathroom. She stood in front of one of the sinks. The place was empty, silent except for the sound of Krystal splashing water onto her face.

"Krystal."

Splash. She raised her head, and mascara ran down her cheeks in black streaks. And her pale face twisted, twisted in the mirror. No longer Krystal.

There, a ghost of a girl. There, waiting in the cold, in the dark. Waiting for me.

I blinked and shook my head, and it was Krystal, I reminded myself—*Krystal*—in front of the mirror.

"Go away, Nancy," Krystal sobbed. "I—I want to be alone." She wiped the mixture of tears and water from her face, causing the mascara to smudge even more. "You saw what the Proctor said about me. Well, it's all true, all right? All of it. I'm not . . . I'm not who I say I am."

"Of course you're who you say you are," I said. "You're Krystal Choi, aren't you?"

"You know what I mean. I haven't been truthful about who I used to be before starting school at Sinclair Prep. The person I am now is basically the *opposite* of who I used to be. I—I pretend to be good, but really I've done some *awful* things."

Hadn't we all? Done awful things to stay at the top. Horrible, twisted misdeeds, for the chance to have everything, everything this school had promised us.

"You're not pretending to be good," I said. Because I needed this to be true, needed to know that some of it was real. "You *are* good. It's called character growth."

Krystal released a laugh-sob, and turned around, finally, to look at me. Krystal, fashionista Krystal, makeup expert Krystal, like this. Broken. Unmade. It was unnatural.

"Back in eighth grade, I joined a gang." Her voice was raspy, hoarse, as though she hadn't spoken these words aloud in years, in centuries. "I wanted to prove that I was tough. I wanted to do something that would force my parents to pay attention to me. They were too busy at work, or networking, or out with their friends."

Krystal, alone in that gleaming, picture-perfect penthouse. Alone, always alone.

She sniffed. "Sometimes I felt like my parents forgot they even had a daughter. So I decided I was going to do whatever I wanted. And one night toward the end of eighth grade, my girls and I got into a street fight. It was bad. Really bad. One of my closest friends . . . *died*." And she whispered the words as though afraid someone else was hearing, someone lurking unseen. Someone who could punish her. But there was nobody here.

"I hurt someone from the other gang so badly that I put her in a coma, and she . . . she still hasn't woken up. That got my parents' attention, all right. They sent me to boot camp. After that summer, I realized I didn't like who I was before. I wanted to change, and Sinclair Prep was the fresh start I needed. I wanted—I wanted to prove that I could be good." Krystal inhaled, a long, shaky breath.

"Oh, Krystal." I reached out to hold her hand. She squeezed it.

"My parents did a good job clearing most of my tracks. I don't know how the Proctor found out, but I guess they looked up the enrollment for St. Jude's Reformatory School," mumbled Krystal, more to herself than to me. "I wanted a fresh start here. I wanted the past to stay in the past. Like with . . . with the Incident."

I wanted the past to stay in the past.

But if there was one thing I'd realized, it was that the past never stayed buried for long. The messiest parts of our pasts, coming back to haunt us now, one by one.

And now Krystal grabbed both my hands and squeezed them, a desperate gleam in her eyes. "Be careful, Nancy. Whoever this person is, they've done their homework. They mean serious business."

"We won't let them get away with it." I wouldn't let them get away with it. With shattering my friends, one after the other. "Do you want to go back to the newspaper club?"

Krystal hung her head. "I can't face anyone. I think I have to go home today. Don't worry about me." She dropped my hands. Picked up her black leather backpack. Looked at me once more. "Good luck. And *be careful.*" Then she pushed open the bathroom door and left.

Krystal's secret violent past now out there, out in the open. I should've been more surprised to learn about it. To learn that she'd put someone in a coma.

But then, in the Incident, we'd all done something much worse.

———

When I entered the newspaper room, everyone's eyes swiveled to me.

"Krystal went home," I said. "She's . . . she'll be fine." I hoped. I caught Alexander's and Akil's worried gazes and nodded. "Let's go catch the Proctor."

We had to make this person pay for splitting Krystal open like that. For ruining Akil's chances at a track scholarship. Had to stop them before the situation got even worse, before *I* took the fall for Jamie's death.

Louisa and Isabel stayed behind to finish up some work for the newspaper. With Akil, Kiara, and Nishant in the lead, the rest of us shoved through the crowd of Manhattanites on the sidewalk. A yellow cab honked its way through an intersection. A pair of women in their midthirties power walked past us. Even in the middle of the afternoon, this city was always bustling with people in a rush to get to wherever they were going.

"Akil," I yelled above the noise, "do you even know who we're looking for? How are we supposed to identify the Proctor?"

"We're *probably* looking for a student wearing a Sinclair Prep uniform. Somebody suspicious-looking."

Mark, who was huffing and puffing to keep up with us while holding his camera, groaned. "Well, that narrows it down to . . . everyone who goes to Green Bottle Coffee."

Mark was spot-on. As we reached the coffee shop, I peered through the glass at the crowd of customers. A trio of Sinclair Prep students sat at the table in the window. There were a few more Sinclair Prep students among the cluster of people waiting impatiently at the pickup counter.

Our group stopped at the entrance, parting to let people past. Akil turned to face us, biting his lip. "Okay, so . . . here's the plan. Kiara and I will go ask the baristas if they've seen anyone shady come within the last half hour or so. The rest of you, scope out the shop. Look for any Sinclair Prep student who's alone. That's most likely our person. Everyone got it?"

Carefully sidestepping the people leaving the coffee shop, I craned my neck to try to see around the whole place. There was an unhelpful number of Sinclair Prep students present.

But there, at the very back of the shop, was a scrawny blond boy wearing the Sinclair Prep uniform, sitting alone with his laptop. I started toward him, but then my gaze fell upon a lone girl with long red hair, also in our school uniform.

Mark came up behind me. "You think it's one of those two?"

"I . . . don't have a clue," I confessed.

"Well, it can't hurt to get a little closer to them," Alexander said, and the three of us headed their way. Mark was taking pictures already, though I didn't know of what.

Then, Akil's shouts rose above the din of the coffee shop. "Guys! Up here!" He waved at us from the counter, where he stood in front of a young male barista.

When we hurried over, Mark snapping away with his camera, the confused-looking barista slid a piece of white paper in front of us. "This is what you guys came here for, right?" he asked.

I squinted at the words printed in Times New Roman font. Alexander stood close so he could read over my shoulder.

Decepit te!
—The Proctor

"I don't know what 'decepit te' means," Akil confessed.

Nishant sighed and rubbed his forehead. "It means 'tricked you' in Latin."

"Why would the Proctor write . . . oh." Akil's triumphant expression crumpled as the realization dawned on him.

"We've been had," I groaned.

The barista followed this exchange with great interest, watching us, wide-eyed.

"Who gave you this paper?" Kiara asked.

The guy shrugged, brown eyes reflecting puzzlement. "Some guy handed me this paper. Paid me a hundred bucks to hang onto it. He told me to give it to a group of Sinclair Prep students who'd come in asking about any suspicious customers. Said you guys would recognize the name 'The Proctor.'" His forehead scrunched up. "Are you kids caught up in a scavenger hunt? Some kind of game, maybe?"

A mirthless laugh escaped my lips. Well, technically this was a game, though nobody was having fun except the Proctor.

Another dead end. Or maybe not. "What did this guy—the Proctor—look like?" I asked.

The barista frowned. "He wore a black suit—he had brown hair and sunglasses—looked like a security guard, or a doorman, maybe."

Black suit. Brown hair. Sunglasses. That described almost every rich Sinclair Prep student's butler or bodyguard. That gave us next to nothing to go on. I halfheartedly glanced toward the street, but unsurprisingly didn't see anyone who might fit that description. Whoever it was had disappeared a long time ago.

I reached for the piece of paper, pinching it between my thumb and forefinger, and picked it up carefully. "We can take this as evidence," I said.

"Good thinking." Alexander gave me a lopsided grin as we ducked out of the coffee shop.

"This whole thing was a bust. What a waste of time." Akil kicked the ground, and Kiara patted him on the back in sympathy.

"No, it was pretty thrilling. I think that's the most excitement *Sinclair Unveiled* has seen since . . . ever," said Mark.

"And I've got the paper, too," I pointed out. "We can give it to Bates and have him get the police to look into it for fingerprints."

"Wait, Nancy—put it in this." Akil took something out of his backpack—a boxful of ziplock bags—and, when I handed over the Proctor's note, carefully placed it into one of the bags. Then he handed it back to me.

"You keep ziplock bags on you?" Nishant gaped at Akil.

"Watching *CSI* taught me to be prepared for anything," Akil said seriously. "That show's more useful than all of our classes combined, to be honest."

We headed back to school. The plastic baggie with our evidence, clenched in my fists. Scorching me, white-hot.

NOVEMBER, FRESHMAN YEAR

I was burning up inside, burning up with this secret.

After bumping into each other a few times at lunch and in the halls, Peter asked for my number. We texted here and there, and then, before I knew what was happening, we texted all the time. Peter, sending me recordings of his music. Me, showing him snippets of my poetry.

Peter, one of the Golden Trio, the elite at Sinclair Prep. Me, a no-name freshman. It was like a dream. It was a secret I longed to shout from the highest rooftop in the Upper West Side.

But no one, *no one* could know, Peter emphasized.

And so no one knew except that statue of Richard Sinclair, which had overseen everything from the beginning. But it was only a statue, of course.

Jamie, I could tell, sensed something was up. I'd saved Peter's number into my phone as "P." Luckily, she hadn't figured out that "P" was her cousin Peter.

"Oooooh. Who's the lucky guy?" Jamie asked one day.

Startled, I twisted around to stare at her and nearly dropped my phone. I hadn't noticed her reading my texts over my shoulder. "N-Nobody."

That only made Jamie smile. An innocent schoolgirl smile, but too calculated to be quite authentic. "You can tell me who he is, you know. I won't tell."

"I said, he's nobody," I mumbled.

"Mm-hmmmm." Jamie slung her arm around my shoulder. "As long as he's making you happy, that's all I care about."

I wanted desperately to believe her, and so I did. Wanted Jamie to care about my happiness above everything, to be a good friend, a true friend.

Happy, though—I didn't know about that. Peter was a bright spot in my life. His attention made me special, made me the best. He'd chosen me. He'd made me.

Peter made it easier to forget that my father was communicating less and less from overseas, until he pretty much vanished from my life.

Peter made it easier to forget the way my mother and I couldn't stop lashing out at each other instead of talking about it—about Baba leaving, tearing this gaping hole into our already-tiny family.

Peter invited me to the movies, and I snuck out behind Mama's back. It was a night filled with a bad rom-com, too much popcorn, and stolen kisses. It was a night of exhilaration. A night where nobody—not Mama, not the students of Sinclair Prep—could tell me who I was supposed to be.

When I got home, my giddy mood slipped away like sand

through my fingers. Mama was home much earlier than she said she would be. And she was furious. Red splotches rose to her cheeks, and her hands were fists on her hips.

I was in huge trouble.

"Where were you?" my mother demanded. "You were supposed to be studying at home."

"I . . ." I thought quickly. "I-I was with Jamie. W-Working on a project. At her place."

"Jamie?" Mama squinted at me. I could tell she didn't quite believe me. "So if I call Jamie right now, she can tell me you were there?"

"Y . . . Yep." Trying not to panic, I reached for my phone and wondered how well I could text with my hands behind my back.

But Mama must have read my mind. She held out her hand for my cell phone. Her face was steeled.

The jig was up. I handed my phone over, winced, and turned away, doing my best to tune out the conversation. I could already hear Mama doling out a harsh punishment for me once she found out I'd snuck out behind her back *and* lied to her face about it.

". . . oh—she *was* there tonight? Really? Math project? Okay. Thank you, Jamie."

I lifted my head. Mama was holding my phone out toward me, the anger in her face replaced by exhaustion.

"Next time you have a project, tell me," she scolded. "Don't make me worry."

"Of course," I said quickly, hardly daring to believe my luck. Jamie had covered for me. I owed her big-time.

My phone pinged with a text.

Jamie: *Let me guess—you were out with your secret guy?*
😊 *Don't worry. I've always got your back. But you do owe me a chocolate chip cookie from the cafeteria tomorrow.*
Nancy: *Thx. You're the best* 🖤

I loved when Jamie and I could be like this—when grades and money and status and family didn't get in the way of everything. I loved simply being friends.

"Le-Le . . ." Mama pursed her lips, and then she did something unexpected. She raised her hand, hesitating, as if unsure herself about what she was going to do. She patted my hair with her hand.

"Mama?" I said, surprised.

"Don't lose sight of your goal, okay?" Mama urged me softly. "I push you hard because I know you are strong. Strong enough to be my good girl. Letting anything get in your way would be a mistake. The opportunity you have is very precious. I would give anything to be in your shoes. Do you understand that?"

I looked at Mama. Her eyes glittered with tears. She looked at me as though I were the only thing in the world still of value. As if I were the most precious thing.

Baba might have left me, but Mama was still here. Still fighting. Still believing in me.

I had never wanted anything in my life as much as I wanted to prove myself worthy of that look.

"I understand," I said, my throat tight and burning.

Mama's message was this: friends like Mrs. Ruan came and went. Same went for men, like Baba.

Mama's message was this: I shouldn't let anyone else get too close. The only person I could depend on was myself.

I dug my sharp nails into my skin, gritting my teeth, welcoming the pain. The sharpness, the focus.

Jamie was my friend. A good friend who'd pulled through for me. Yet I couldn't help but wonder what my life would be like if I could bring home a test score that was higher than hers. Or if she would simply disappear, taking her impossibly high scores with her, making it so much easier for me to be the top student.

Maybe then Mama would finally be proud of me.

For that, I would do anything. Anything at all.

I dug my nails deeper and deeper. I didn't stop. I didn't stop until they drew blood, the droplets welling from where nails pierced skin. Later, those open wounds would turn into scars. Into a promise. Into a blood oath.

CONFESSION TWELVE

I'm going to Stanford to study engineering in the fall. I
don't like Stanford or engineering. I'm only doing it to
make my parents happy . . . —Anon

*****

While Akil returned to the newspaper room with the club
members, Alexander and I headed down to Principal Bates's
office to turn in the Proctor's note. The empty halls were quiet
but for the sound of our footsteps and the creaking of the pipes
in the walls.

Principal Bates welcomed us with a tired smile and blood-
shot eyes. He looked like he'd been running this school for a
century already. He sprouted a prominent five-o'clock shadow,
and dark circles lined his eyes.

"So let me get this straight." Bates paced back and forth in
front of his desk. "You pinpointed the location where those

Tip Tap posts originated—Green Bottle Coffee. A barista said he'd been paid to throw you off this culprit's tail, and the evidence is this piece of paper?" He raised the ziplock bag, his expression full of skepticism.

"The culprit's fingerprints are probably on that paper," Alexander said. "We're hoping you can hand it over to the cops and have them investigate it."

Principal Bates gave Alexander a long, hard look, sizing him up. It was obvious that, to some degree, he still suspected we were involved in this somehow. "I'll be honest. The story sounds a bit far-fetched. But, as we don't have other leads, I'll ask the police to look into the paper," he said finally.

"You were the one who told us to come here if we heard any information. We wouldn't come here with some 'far-fetched' stories," I insisted. I didn't care if I was being rude to our principal. I wanted to get the message across loud and clear. "We are—" My voice caught. "—were Jamie's friends. We want the truth."

"I want the truth as much as you do," Bates said, his eyes burning. He glanced at the ziplock bag and then sat down behind his desk. He gave us a strained smile, which I understood to be a dismissal. "Thank you."

Even though I'd made myself sound certain in front of Bates, the truth was I was less certain about my friends than ever. Of course, I didn't *really* think any of them could have done anything to Jamie. But from the public perspective, there were many reasons that the four of us would look suspicious. And that was what the Proctor wanted, wasn't it? To pull these secrets out from their graves. To make us appear the most suspicious, the most *capable* of killing Jamie.

"Nancy, you good?"

I jerked. I hadn't realized I'd spaced out, and had been staring at Alexander, who was peering at me with concern. "Yeah, I'm fine. We should go home. It's getting late."

At my words, Alexander glanced down at his phone and swore. "I'm late for—for my shift." There, a slight pause in Alexander's words. Eyes, now avoiding mine. I didn't miss it. He really wasn't a good liar. "I'll see you tomorrow."

After letting Alexander get several paces ahead of me, I made up my mind. I was going to follow him and get to the bottom of his secrets. His lies.

———

Tailing anyone in this crowded city was almost impossible. The only way I kept Alexander from leaving my sight was by ruthlessly shoving past pedestrians. It seemed like he really was headed into Chinatown. I followed him onto the 1 train all the way to Canal Street, careful to keep a small crowd of people between us.

The smells of Chinatown—fried foods, fish, Chinese medicine—grew stronger as we walked down Canal. I trailed Alexander down the sidewalk. My suspicions were confirmed: we were going the opposite direction of the Lucky Jade Kitchen. Alexander rounded the corner onto the Bowery, deeper into Chinatown.

My mind raced faster than my feet as I tailed Alexander. I'd spent enough time hiding my own secrets that I could spot when someone else was hiding skeletons in their closet.

Here were the facts I knew about Alexander Lin:

He was a scholarship student, like me.

He worked at the Lucky Jade Kitchen.

He shared an apartment on the Lower East Side with two college students.

He never liked going into details about his parents, but I knew they were traveling abroad somewhere.

His brother, Eric Lin, had been a star scholarship pupil at Sinclair Prep before he was caught cheating and thrown out of the school, all prospects of college gone.

He was hiding something. Probably.

We veered away from the bustling Bowery toward a run-down section of Chinatown. There were empty, abandoned shops, their storefronts decorated with half-lit neon signs and scrolling messages that flashed Chinese characters, promising cheap massages and haircuts. A couple of smashed cans and pieces of paper rattled across the sidewalk. We passed by grocery stores spilling wares onto the sidewalk, souvenir shops, and a mahjong parlor. Still Alexander didn't stop—not until he reached the end of the road, where Chinatown led out into the rest of the city.

If Alexander turned his head a little bit, he'd see me. I ducked behind a clothing rack full of qí páo, traditional high-necked, form-fitting Chinese dresses. From here, I watched Alexander at a safe distance.

A few moments later, the answer rolled up in the form of an Asian guy a little shorter but about the same build as Alexander. Couldn't have been older than maybe twenty. I squinted. He had shoulder-length black hair, and wore a black tank top with ripped blue jeans. Krystal would have called the sight of him a fashion disaster.

The young man struck me as familiar, but I couldn't quite place where I'd seen him before.

Alexander gestured with his hands, and the other guy folded his arms across his chest. It looked like they were arguing. From this distance, I could hear that they were speaking in Mandarin, but their speech was a little too fast for me to follow.

Alexander reached into his pocket and dug out his wallet. He flipped it open and pulled out a wad of cash, which he stuffed into the guy's hands.

The stranger flipped through the bills. Apparently satisfied, he bopped Alexander over the head with the wad of cash, then shoved it into his pocket and left.

Alexander stood there for a moment longer, watching the guy as he departed. I wished I knew what kind of expression his face was making. As if he'd read my mind, he turned around. Heart thumping, I ducked back behind the qí páo, nearly toppling over the rack.

Had Alexander seen me? I held my breath for what felt like far too long, listening to the sound of his footsteps as they approached the rack, and then growing fainter as he moved farther down the alleyway.

I straightened my trembling knees and stood, struggling to process the exchange I'd witnessed.

Was Alexander in money trouble? Had he been paying off that guy for some kind of job? Or—maybe he'd done something he needed to cover up, something awful.

I didn't notice until it was too late that the footsteps had come back—then the rack of clothing parted, and a face appeared between the dresses. "Gah!"

Alexander crouched. There was no trace of his usual smile, his usual laid-back manner. "Nancy, what do you think you're doing?"

"Dress . . . shopping . . . ?" I tried weakly. Okay, so it wasn't one of my better on-the-spot lies.

"You were following me. Did you see?"

I didn't play dumb this time. Ducking out of the dress rack, I straightened and looked Alexander square in the eyes. I tilted my head up defiantly. So he'd caught me tailing him. So what? I'd caught him in the act of doing . . . well, I didn't know what, exactly, but something not great.

"What are you involved in, Alexander? That guy—did you pay him off for some job, or was that hush money, or—?"

"Have you been watching too many crime dramas?" Alexander groaned. "I promise it's nothing like that. And lower your voice, would you?" He cast a nervous look around the alley, but nobody was stopping to eavesdrop on a pair of teenagers. He sighed. "I guess I'll have to explain everything to you. Come back to my apartment with me."

———

Luckily, Alexander lived a few streets away. A turn onto Chrystie Street and we were there, gazing up at a four-story brick apartment building.

When I stepped into the cramped, three-bedroom apartment

Alexander shared with two roommates, I wasn't sure what to expect. It was a simple place. The walls were bare except for a few *Fortnite* gaming posters. It was mostly tidy, but there were small messes here and there: an empty water bottle on the floor, a half-eaten PowerBar on the kitchen counter, an open bag of chips on the coffee table.

"My roommates are in class, so they won't be back for a while. Make yourself comfortable," Alexander said, gesturing toward the black couch in the middle of the living room. I sat slowly, still taking in the apartment around me. "What's so interesting about this place?"

"I . . ." It felt like a home, I realized. Alexander's apartment, bare and simple though it was, was filled with signs that people actually lived here, interacted here. This place was more welcoming to me than Jamie's, Krystal's, and Akil's fancy homes had ever been. My wandering eye caught something. "Wait. Is that photo . . . ? Is that the phone selfie we took that one time at Krystal's, before your birthday dinner? During freshman year?" I pointed up at the one framed photo that sat on top of the bookshelf sitting across from me.

"Oh, yeah. It's a great photo."

"I remember that day." The day Krystal had given me a makeover. The day I'd skipped out on going to the movies to hang out with Peter instead. And when I left Peter's place, the train had been delayed, so I got to Alexander's birthday dinner at Sushi Maido half an hour late.

In the photo, I wasn't even smiling—just staring straight-faced into the camera. It was probably the worst picture of everyone else, with Krystal mid-blink, Jamie frowning, and

Alexander giving a straight smile. Meanwhile, the light hit my cheekbones at the perfect angle.

I looked sultry, like a model. Like a girl who belonged among the elite at Sinclair Prep.

"You look good in that photo," Alexander said.

A warm blush rose to my cheeks. "Thanks." I wondered if he'd framed that particular picture because *I* looked good in it. But that was egotistical thinking. Wasn't it?

Alexander nodded, looking a bit flustered. A moment passed as we averted our eyes from each other. Then, Alexander said, "Okay, so, back there—what you saw—" He dropped his head into his hands, sighing. "You remember my older brother, Eric?"

"Of course I do. I—wait."

The young Asian guy. His hair had grown out a lot since I'd last seen him, but now there was no mistaking who he was.

"Back there . . . that was *Eric?*"

Alexander nodded. "Eric is . . . he . . . he's not well." His voice cracked. His shoulders slumped, as though he'd been carrying the weight of the world on top of them and could no longer do so. "After he got caught cheating and was kicked out of Sinclair, he went . . . well, things are kind of bad. He's out on his own, in trouble for some petty theft. I figured it's better for me to . . . to hide him. Keep a close watch on him, give him what he needs to live. Eric's always insisted that he didn't cheat on that AP World exam, and I believe him. But, you know— some powerful people—that stupid *Golden Trio*"—Alexander's eyes flashed as he spat out the name, and it was then, only then, that I put together the pieces, truly understood why he seemed to dislike Peter—"they accused him of cheating, and there was proof against him. I told Eric we should clear his name anyway, but he begged me not to do anything. He was scared of what the Golden Trio might do to retaliate against us. People like them—they're not like us. They don't face the same consequences we do.

"After that . . . I mean, everything was over for Eric. His scholarship, his high school diploma, his dreams of the Ivy League. Everything . . . gone. People like us—we don't—we don't get second chances, you know?" Alexander's chest heaved, and he balled his hands into fists as he blinked back tears.

"I know we don't," I said quietly. The world never let me forget that. One misstep and it was over, all over. "Alexander . . . I'm so sorry."

"Eric says he never cheated, and I trust him."

"Of course he didn't." Alexander's hand was lying there on the coffee table between us. Instinctively, I reached over and held it.

A single tear trickled down Alexander's cheek. "I'm not ashamed of him. I'm not. My . . . my only brother. He's the only one I've got."

I swallowed. Questions swirled around in my head, but now wasn't the time to badger Alexander with them. I squeezed his hand, and he squeezed back.

"You'll keep this a secret, right?" Alexander whispered. He raised his head, locking gazes with me.

"Of course. Your secret's safe with me."

If there was one thing I could do well, it was keeping secrets.

CONFESSION THIRTEEN

Thoughts and prayers with Jamie's family and friends
💔 —Anon

* * * * *

The funeral for Jamie was held on Saturday.

I woke up to Mama knocking on my door. "Get up, Le-Le. Jamie's funeral starts in one hour."

The outfit I'd chosen for the funeral was a simple lace dress. White, the color of death for Chinese funerals. I stared at my face, at the faint, little brown spots that dotted my upper cheeks, which stood out prominently against my pale skin. Freckles— from standing in the sun too long, Mama claimed—that my family had always seen as imperfections.

I practiced smiling in the mirror. First my own smile, tentative and shy. Then Jamie's, confident and sly.

It was a cloudy day, a perfect match for the gloomy mood.

Mama and I rode the train in silence. When we arrived at the First Congregational Church on the Upper East Side, I was on full alert. There was a strong possibility the Proctor could be here. They knew so much about Jamie and her friends, after all. I couldn't let my guard down.

My gaze swept the crowd of mourners. As with everything they ever did, the Ruans had gone all out; several of their family members who lived in China had flown in, and they were all dressed in lavish, but respectful, white clothing. My eyes sought out one figure in particular—and there. I found him.

Peter's sharp brown eyes met mine, and we exchanged a quick smile. In that trim white suit, he cleaned up well. He always did. Then my gaze slid toward the two guys sitting right next to Peter, and my heart sank into my stomach.

Peter had warned me, but it still wasn't enough to stop the dread that filled me. It had been almost two years since they'd graduated and left Sinclair. Two years since I'd seen them, been confronted with their anger toward me. But I'd recognize those profiles anywhere.

Richard Li and David Kim. The Golden Trio, reunited for Jamie's funeral. The last I'd seen them all together like this, it had been for a different funeral two years ago, and the irony of that wasn't lost on me. Painful memories surfaced, but I forced them back. Not here. Not now. Today was about Jamie, and only Jamie.

Luckily, Richard and David had their backs turned and hadn't noticed me. I ducked my head down before that changed.

A text notification popped up on my phone.

Peter: *Good to see you and ur mom made it*
Nancy: *It's Jamie's funeral, we wouldn't miss it*

"Nancy, stop texting. It's rude. Dǒng guī ju," Mama hissed. She craned her neck and peered over my shoulder, but I shoved my phone out of sight. If my mother knew I was texting a guy— even worse, a guy who was currently my student teacher—she'd faint dead away. That was definitely not dǒng guī ju, or practicing my manners.

We snagged a spot at the end of the front row. Everyone, and I mean *everyone*, had turned out to pay their respects to Jamie and her family. Even people who'd been talking shit about the Ruans for weeks. After all, if the wealthiest, most influential Asian families didn't turn up, people would have talked. And then those families would lose face, or miàn zi. That was the worst thing of all, a fate worse than death.

I wondered what it'd be like to have so many relatives and friends fly in from all across the country and globe to mourn your death. I'd be lucky if my father showed up to my funeral; forget the aunts and uncles and cousins I'd never gotten the chance to meet. I wondered how many funerals of relatives and friends Mama had missed because we couldn't afford tickets to visit China. How many lives she'd left behind, the goodbyes she'd never gotten to say.

Jamie had so many people to shed tears for her. Friends. Peers pretending to be friends. Extended family. I had only a handful of friends and my mother. A familiar jealousy rose within me, but I shook it off quickly.

Remember: today wasn't about me. It was about Jamie.

It was always about Jamie.

A group of girls I recognized as Jamie's volleyball teammates gathered in a group, dabbing at their tears with their sleeves. Alexander, Akil, Krystal, and their parents sat near me and Mama. They waved at me, and I waved back.

"So sad," Mama mumbled, patting my hand. "We're attending a funeral for Jamie, only two years after attending a funeral for another student . . ." She heaved a sigh, like the weight of the whole world sat upon her shoulders. "Zhēn kě xī. What a shame."

I squeezed my mother's hand. "Yeah."

Jamie Ruan's smiling face stared down at us from the portrait above her closed casket. She posed with a volleyball tucked under her arm.

The golden inscription along the side of her casket read, *In inceptum finis est.* Even in death, this school was claiming her.

The pastor walked up to the altar, taking slow, careful steps, his expression solemn. "We are here today to pay our love and tributes to Jamie Ruan, an outstanding student at Sinclair . . ."

His words didn't matter, I realized. He was merely reciting what we already knew. Everyone knew Jamie as the top student, the class president, the captain of the girls' volleyball team. Then they knew her as the daughter of a corrupt businessman. She'd lived and died by that image.

But the pastor and the others didn't know Jamie like I did.

They wouldn't remember Jamie as I did. As the girl with the toothy grin and fancy, frilly red dress, who'd been one of the first to welcome me when I was new to town. I remembered her as the girl I'd ridden bikes with in Central Park or through Chinatown during so many hot summer afternoons.

Jamie Ruan was the girl I'd fought with, the girl I could never surpass. The girl who'd drifted away from me with each passing year of school, who could be as selfish and imperfect as the rest of us. Memory after memory of our complicated friendship tumbled through my mind, from Shuang Wen Chinese School and Sinclair Prep—*the Incident*—and everything in between.

A young Jamie passing me her last White Rabbit candy during Chinese class.

A slightly older Jamie handing me a lemonade popsicle as we biked through Central Park, leaves crunching under our tires.

A Jamie who appeared weary of everything, standing beside me, as we lowered our heads, mourning the dead. Mourning Em.

Maybe Jamie would have wanted us to remember her only as the perfect 4.0 student, as the girl who could do no wrong. But she'd been so much more than that. So much more than a number in our ranking system. She'd been someone I'd shared some of my darkest secrets with, and who in turn had shared hers.

Jamie Ruan had been a daughter. A friend. A rival.

A *person*.

I hoped everyone could remember that. Flaws and all, Jamie Ruan had been much more than a Sinclair Prep statistic or the daughter of a corrupt businessman.

When the funeral service ended, we stuck around for a little bit. I desperately wanted to leave. Richard and David were mingling, and every time they drew close to me, I ducked down and let my curtain of hair hide my face.

"We have to speak with Jamie's family," Mama said softly, dabbing at her tears with her handkerchief.

No. Anything but that. Richard and David stood with Peter, right next to Jamie's immediate family. "I don't think Jamie's family would even want to talk to us," I blurted out in my panic. "You said we aren't supposed to talk to the Ruans anymore, remember? Because of the scandal."

Mama stared at me like I'd uttered something disgusting, and I dropped my gaze to my feet. "They lost their daughter, Le-Le. How could we ignore them right now?"

I opened my mouth, but no words came out. I had no response to that.

Mrs. Ruan was sobbing into a handkerchief, her voice so loud that her words carried over the crowd. "I don't understand . . . who would do such a thing . . . Jamie was so happy."

Jamie was so happy. I narrowed my eyes as a memory flashed to the surface of my mind. I'd almost forgotten the words Jamie had told me months ago.

I'm not happy, she'd said. Her eyes had been so serious and sad, filled with some internal storm that had frightened me with its intensity. *I'm not happy, Nancy.*

I hadn't known what to say, so I didn't say anything. I'd figured Mr. Ruan would be released soon enough, that Jamie would go back to being the rich, popular, untouchable, perfect girl again. And I was done talking with her, couldn't bring myself to be her friend after our blow-up at her birthday party. Done letting Jamie run our friendship, run my life.

But now, I wished I'd pressed Jamie. I wished I'd demanded to know why the girl who had it all looked deeply sorrowful and pained. Why she looked like she actually had nothing.

Now it was too late. Jamie had gone somewhere I couldn't follow, where my words would never reach her.

Jamie was so happy, Mrs. Ruan had said. If she believed that, then she knew less about her daughter than I'd thought. Maybe if Mrs. Ruan had spent less time with her girlfriends and more time at home with Jamie, she'd have at least known that much. Known that Jamie Ruan, the girl who had every-thing, had never had the one thing she wanted above all. Jamie's parents hadn't even known that Jamie was bi, that she'd dated Krystal for a while during freshman and sophomore year. They couldn't have possibly known if she was happy or not.

They'd never really known their own daughter beyond her accomplishments, beneath her seemingly perfect surface. And now it was too late.

It was going to take us a while to reach Jamie's family, given how many people wanted to speak with them. Richard and David still had their backs turned to Mama and me. Maybe I could escape to the bathroom and never come back. Before I could think of an excuse to get away, a low voice shouted: "You!"

My heart leapt into my throat. It was Richard. Taller than almost everyone here, he glared at me over the heads of the crowd like he wanted nothing more than for *my* funeral to be next. I backed away and almost tripped over someone's foot.

"You must've done this to Jamie. It was you!" Richard began shoving his way toward me, but Peter swooped in and grabbed his arm.

"What are you doing?" cried Mrs. Ruan, who gazed at Richard like he was a wild creature set loose. "This is a funeral. A funeral for *my* daughter!"

"You should be asking *her* the questions." Red-faced, Richard pointed through the crowd—straight at me. Gasps and murmurs of confusions followed. I buried my face in my hands, but not before catching sight of everyone's heads turning toward me. "She's more than capable of doing something like this. Y-You guys have no idea. Ask her about the truth about Em, what happened two years ago. Ask!"

"Richard, that's enough," I heard Peter yell.

Richard fired back, "No, *I've* had enough of all this—this pretending and lying and hiding the truth."

"Le-Le, what's going on?" Mama whispered. She wrapped a warm arm around my shoulder. "You're shaking! What is that boy talking about?"

"I . . ." I took a deep breath and braced myself for what was to come. Richard, who knew about the Incident and had been sworn to secrecy, had finally cracked. He was going to spill our greatest, darkest secret to everyone present.

"Get out!" a female voice bellowed. Tiny Mrs. Ruan strode toward Mama and me, the hem of her white dress billowing around her feet. I couldn't tell if her eyes were red-rimmed from tears, or anger. "Both of you. *Out.* How dare you show your faces around here and cause a disruption at Jamie's funeral. I want you out of my sight!"

Mama drew herself to her full height, her body trembling in rage. I hadn't seen her like this since Baba had left us. "How dare *you* and this boy harass my daughter. We came to pay our respects. Now we'll go. No need to see us out," she snapped. "Our pity was wasted on you."

"The Ruans have no use for your pity," spat Jamie's mother. She was so furious that her jade earrings shook. "*We* pity *you.* Get out. We won't see you again."

Shaking, I allowed my mother to drag me out of the church. I knew that at least five people would have already posted about the blowup on Tip Tap. It was probably going to take me the rest of my time at Sinclair to live down a scene like that.

And yet, part of me was happy that Mama had gone to bat for me. Mama never raised her voice against anyone, ever.

It wasn't until we were home that my mother dropped my arm, turned around, and pinned me with a stare that could've pierced right through me. "Le-Le, you can tell me the truth. What were they talking about? Did you do something to offend the Ruans?"

"No." It was the truth. I hadn't done anything—not to them, at least. "They must—they must still have a grudge against us, since we stopped talking to them after Mr. Ruan's scandal."

After a long moment, my mother softened her gaze. It seemed like she believed me. "The Ruans' world is very different from ours. I was right to ask you to stay away from their daughter." She shook her head sadly, and then glanced at the clock. "I have to leave for work. There are leftovers in the fridge. Study hard today."

"I know," I mumbled.

I'd known all along that my world was different from Jamie's. Knew I had to be careful. Knew I had to contort my body, do whatever it took to fit in. Bad things happened to those who didn't play by the rules.

Just ask Em.

JANUARY, JUNIOR YEAR

"Sometimes I wonder what it'd be like to die," Jamie said with a wistful sigh. Whispered it to the textbook in front of her, to the library walls that surrounded us.

I started, my SAT flashcards falling through my fingers, clattering to the table. "What?" Sure that I'd heard Jamie wrong. These words, uttered like a confession, so unlike her.

"I feel . . . not myself lately. Weak." Jamie turned her eyes up to me, now. Pleading eyes. Sunken eyes. "Haven't you ever wondered what it'd be like to—to disappear?" Jamie gripped my arm like a drowning man to a lifeboat. "Am I—Am I weak for having those thoughts, sometimes?"

Jamie, like this, scared me. Jamie, and these words that said more than I was willing to hear. Jamie, and her eyes begging for help I didn't know how to give.

I forced myself to look away from the sight of Jamie, Jamie unwinding. Less than twenty-four hours before our next SAT practice test, only six weeks until the real thing in March, and here she was distracting me from my studies. Mama might even say Jamie was being pathetic for not being able to handle this school and all its demands.

And I didn't have time for this. Didn't have time to entertain the whimsies of rich kids who had more than me, always had more than me, even if they didn't graduate at the top of the class.

"Yes," I said, and it was like I wasn't me, like the harsh words coming out of my mouth weren't my own. "Yes, Jamie. You are weak."

Jamie, who'd always been above me, now a tiny ant at my feet. And I crushed it and left without looking back at the ruined remains.

CONFESSION FOURTEEN

Is it normal to daydream about flinging yourself off the
balcony and never worrying about Orgo again? —Anon

*****

By Monday, the rumors about Krystal had died down somewhat. Everyone was more preoccupied with the upcoming
exams. Finals week was both a blessing and a curse in that
sense.

Krystal put on a brave face and came for classes, despite all
the pointing and the staring. Despite the jeers she got from
some of our more meatheaded classmates, like Parker Xiao
and Jack Kimball.

"Bet *she's* the one who did it," Parker said to Jack in an
exaggerated whisper-shout as they passed Krystal and me in
the hall before third period. "Probably beat Jamie to death . . ."

Krystal flounced past in her Azzedine Alaïa black leather

booties, dignity intact, as though she couldn't hear them, even though her tightly clenched jaw told me otherwise. But I shot Parker and Jack the middle finger behind her back. Krystal had enough dignity for the both of us, I think.

Unfortunately, the true consequences of Krystal's secret being exposed went beyond the whisperings of the school. We'd made it to our third period class—AP Lang—when Krystal let out a choked gasp, staring at her phone.

"What is it?" My stomach lurched. Already, I was preparing for the worst. "Is it another post from the Proctor?"

"N-No . . . I—the director of the James Hale Law Summer Internship Program just . . . rescinded their offer," Krystal said. "Saying they don't think I'd be the right fit for the job, due to recent information that's come to light about my background."

"Oh, Krystal . . . I'm so sorry." I knew Krystal had been looking forward to the internship, even though it wasn't a fashion internship, like she'd wanted. It was one her parents had approved for her.

"They—they can't do this," she spluttered. Then, in a tremulous voice: "Can they?"

I shrugged helplessly. Wishing I knew what to say. Wishing I knew what to do to make this right.

"My parents are going to kill me when they find out," Krystal moaned. And she hardly said another word for the rest of the class.

The knowledge that we'd be regrouping with the newspaper club this afternoon kept me going through the school day. But when I headed down there after classes, I found a crowd of students and faculty standing outside the door, Principal Bates and Peter among them. Murmuring, whispering.

My heart sank. "What's happened?"

The nearest club member, Isabel, turned to me with tears in her eyes. "S . . . Someone wrecked our room."

I forced my way to the front to peer through the window.

Papers that had been neatly stacked on the center table were strewn about the floor. Books pulled from their places on the shelves were scattered carelessly on the carpet. The chairs had been knocked onto their sides. Mark's camera had been smashed to bits. It looked like the intruder had torn through all our possessions in search of something.

Louisa and Kiara stood beside me, staring in, looking shocked and horrified.

"What happened here?" Principal Bates asked them.

"W-We got here for today's meeting, and the room . . . it . . . it was like this," Louisa squeaked. She gestured toward the room, then drew back and wrapped her arms around her body, shivering.

"Did you see who it was?" demanded the principal. They both shook their heads.

"Why would someone attack the newspaper club?" Peter asked, pounding a fist against the window in frustration.

Mark stepped forward. "Um . . . Mr. Shui . . . you should check Tip Tap."

His words caused a flurry of movement as everyone pulled out their phones. And there it was, the first post on Tip Tap.

This is what happens when curious student journalists and nosy teachers snoop around where they aren't wanted. Let this be a lesson.

Stay out of this. In this game, you can't win.
—The Proctor

Guilt twisted in my gut like a knife. It was my fault the newspaper club had been trashed. My fault for coming up with the idea to ask them for help with the investigation.

The message here was clear. Nobody was to help us. And we were not to uncover the Proctor's identity.

In the crowd, Peter's eyes met mine, his face arranged in an unreadable mask. I knew what that look meant. He'd given it to me at the end of my freshman year. He wanted nothing more to do with this investigation. With us.

"We're done here," Peter said in a quiet voice.

Bates scrunched up his nose. "We haven't even gotten started, Mr. Shui. I'm going to check the footage on the security camera. Everybody else, stay outside this classroom."

Peter wasn't talking to the principal, though. He was talking to us. The newspaper club, our only allies, were deserting us. We were going to have to face the Proctor alone.

In the room, Bates stood on a stool to check the camera next to the American flag. After a few moments, he stormed back out, looking frustrated. "Camera got turned off. Looks like our culprit covered their tracks well. I'll have to head down to the security office. Peter—get these students away from this room." Muttering into a walkie-talkie, Bates hurried past us and down the hall.

Alexander and Krystal turned up a few minutes later, and by then Peter had dispersed the crowd. I relayed what had happened to them, saw my own shock and horror reflected in their faces as they registered what this meant for us. Extracurriculars were cancelled for that afternoon.

Now that our work with the newspaper club had been destroyed, and our plans to go after the Proctor had gone up in flames, I went home. I texted Peter from the subway.

Nancy: *Hey, I'm rly sorry about what happened to the club room earlier today.*

Peter: *It's ok. Not ur fault. I'm glad u texted tho, cuz I do wanna talk to you about something kinda serious*

Nancy: *What's up?*

Peter: *I don't think we should be too friendly with each other anymore. At least, not for now while this all blows over . . . It's too risky. Treat me like any other teacher, and I'll treat you like any other student*

Nancy: *Are you saying this cuz ur worried about the Proctor coming after you if you help me?*

Peter: *Even if I'm only a student teacher, I'm still a teacher, and you're my student. My job is on the line and so is your enrollment*

Nancy: *Didn't stop you from being friendly before*

Peter: *That was then, now is now*

Nancy: *k whatever*

Peter: *"k" . . . sounds bad*

Nancy: *k*
Peter: *It's only for now. Wait a little bit, ok?*

Even though the logical decision was to shut this down—not only for now, but forever—still a part of my mind whispered, whispered that Peter was leaving me for a second time, because I wasn't good enough for him.

Because wasn't that the truth? I had never been good enough. Not for him, and not for them.

My mother had once told me to become strong. Once, I had promised her I would become the best. Once, I believed I could give my family everything—everything they'd given up, given to me. Everything they needed me to be.

But the truth was, I wasn't strong enough.

The truth was, I had never been good enough for my parents' impossible dreams, and never would be. The proof was that Baba didn't stick around to watch me grow up.

———

I was six years old, standing in front of the intimidating, sleek, tall building. The black gates rose sky-high above me, impossibly high. Mama and Baba stood at my side, holding my hands.

"Richard Sinclair Preparatory School. The best private high school in America. You will get into this school one day," Baba said with confidence. He gave me a rare smile. "You are going to prove that you're the best. You are not weak."

I nodded because I knew it would give me Baba's

approval. And nothing was more important to me than his approval.

———

I was nine years old, sitting at the tiny, cramped dining table across from Baba. Mama bustled around the kitchen making dinner. She ignored Baba; they'd had a fight over something earlier.

Baba grunted as he marked up my math worksheet with his red pen. I bit my fingernail nervously. My father was in a foul mood, which meant he'd be extra strict.

"Nine out of ten," Baba reported, sliding the piece of paper back toward me. He frowned. "This isn't good enough. Do it again."

Nothing was ever good enough for my father. "But, Baba," I pleaded. "Jamie invited me to go hang out at the pool. You promised I could go."

"I'm taking back that promise."

"You can't do that! Take-backs aren't fair."

A cold, ugly look cut across my father's face. I knew enough to shut up before he got really angry.

"Nothing in life is fair. But that's why you have to work your hardest when the other kids are playing. You have less than them, which means you must be better than them. You must work ten times as hard as your classmates to have what they have. Remember that, Nancy. You are not weak."

I bit my lip. I picked up my pencil and then brought the lead down on the paper so hard it snapped and went flying.

I made a pact with myself. If Baba wanted me to, I would prove that I wasn't weak. That I was his good girl, good enough to be his daughter. I was the best.

———

I was twelve years old, holding Mama's hand at the airport. My mother wept. I didn't really understand why. Baba was only supposed to go back to China for a brief work stint. Besides, Mama had screamed at him to leave the night before—so why was she upset now that he was doing that?

Baba was upset, too. I could tell because he'd ignored Mama the whole time we drove to the airport.

Before he left to board his plane, my father turned back to look at Mama and me. The years we'd spent in the States, barely scraping by, hadn't been kind to him. Wrinkles lined his forehead and cheeks.

My father raised a hand in farewell. He didn't cry. Baba never cried. But his eyes were slightly redder and brighter than usual.

"Work hard, Nancy. Harder than anyone else. You're the smartest girl there is. And remember—you are not weak."

———

I was fourteen years old, holding my acceptance letter to Richard Sinclair Preparatory School, complete with a scholarship that covered full tuition. The official-looking letter, embossed with the prestigious school's stamp, with its motto.

In inceptum finis est.

Those school gates that had always risen too high for me to climb, I'd broken them down with nothing but sheer willpower. I was in. I'd made it.

I was bursting with excitement to tell Mama—and Baba. Until I remembered that Baba had been gone for two years now. That he'd broken his promise and hadn't returned to the States.

But Baba had believed in me. *You are not weak,* he'd insisted.

I hadn't been good enough for him before. But now, I would work hard—harder than anyone. I had to show my father how strong I was. If I could do that, he would return to Mama and me.

Yes. The only reason Baba had left us was because I hadn't been good enough. Strong enough. It was my fault. Mine. At Sinclair Prep, I would prove that I was every bit as strong and capable as my parents needed me to be.

Then, even if we'd forever be wanderers in this country, never able to find a place to truly call home, we could at least be a family again.

CONFESSION FIFTEEN

I get beat if I bring home anything less than an
A-minus. —Anon

*****

A day went by without much incident, besides Akil's return to school. Our morale for catching the Proctor had hit an all-time low. This person knew our secrets, was always a step ahead of us, and had thwarted us at every turn. How could we defeat someone who could predict our every move?

The only hope we had was in tracking the fingerprints on that note the Proctor had left behind at Green Bottle Coffee. When the four of us went down to his office after school, Bates informed us that the police had only been able to identify the fingerprints of a fresh Fordham University graduate, Andy Markham, the barista from Green Bottle Coffee.

Another dead end.

But at least the Proctor hadn't made any new threats. At least nobody knew my secret—yet.

The whole school was buzzing with one hot topic. And it wasn't, amazingly enough, the Proctor. No, it was prom. Everywhere I turned, I saw posters advertising junior-senior prom along the walls. Every day, there was new gossip about who'd asked whom to prom.

Nothing like prom season to remind me that my sorta-fling with Peter was totally over, and I was alone. True to our agreement, we were cordial in the classroom and didn't speak to each other outside it. There was no lonelier feeling in the world than going from sharing a special bond with someone to being a step above strangers. It was lonelier than never having that bond in the first place.

"I can't believe everyone's so caught up with prom. Our classmate is *dead*, and the Proctor is still at large," I grumbled at lunch, shoving my green beans around in my Tupperware. "What's so great about prom, anyway?"

"You're not going to prom?" Krystal asked.

I'd never been in a less prom-y mood. "No. Are you?"

She shrugged. "Yeah, why not?"

"Who're you going with?" I asked.

"Akil," she said immediately.

Akil spat his pizza back onto his tray. "What? Since when?"

"Since now," said Krystal, rolling her eyes. "You don't have a date, so take me."

"You can't assume I don't have a date! Wh-What if I do?"

"But you don't."

"Yes I . . . well, I at least was *thinking* about . . ."

"Thinking about what?" Krystal asked. But I had a feeling I might know what—or, rather, *who*—Akil was thinking about: Kiara. Though, I didn't see Akil and Kiara hang out much, so I couldn't say for sure.

"Never mind. No, I don't have a date." Akil slunk lower into his seat.

"Do you really think we should be going to prom when the Proctor is out here ruining our lives?" I asked.

Krystal put down her salad fork and sighed. "Nancy, chill. It's *because* the Proctor is ruining our lives that we have to make *sure* we show up to prom."

"I'm not following."

"We have to show the whole school that we're not letting the Proctor affect us."

I mulled over Krystal's words, slowly warming to the idea of showing up to prom. She was right. If I were the Proctor, taking some kind of sick pleasure in watching my friends and me squirm—us having the time of our lives at prom would really rub me the wrong way. "If this person is going to ruin our lives anyway, we might as well have fun, right?"

Krystal grinned. "That's what I'm talking about, Nancy. Now you need a date."

"A date . . ." Peter's face popped up into my mind, but I shook my head. Peter and I were finished. Plus, he was my teacher, so it was outside the realm of possibility. I wouldn't even let myself go there.

It took me a beat to realize that the table had gone silent.

Akil and Krystal were staring expectantly at Alexander, whose face had turned bright red. Krystal coughed, and then kicked Alexander not so subtly in the shins.

"Ow!" he yelped.

"You need a date. Nancy needs a date." When Alexander stayed silent, Krystal sighed loudly. "C'mon, put it together. Aren't you supposed to be a genius, Lin?" she teased.

"I . . ."

Great. Krystal had made her meaning so obvious that even I was blushing. Alexander? And me? Going to prom together? No way. Yeah, he was handsome, and smart, and a good friend . . . but that was it. We'd been *friends* for so long now. I didn't—couldn't—see him that way. Especially not when I was still hiding this secret, this burning secret.

I was going to kill Krystal after this.

"Nancywillyougotopromwithme?" Alexander dropped his gaze to the table, and his neck was fire-engine red.

"Oh. You mean as . . . as friends?" I blurted out, feeling heat creep up my own neck.

"Yeah, of course as friends," Alexander said quickly.

"I feel like I'm back in elementary school." Krystal rolled her eyes. "Nancy, I'll see you at Meryl's Boutique after school, 'kay? We have dresses to buy."

I returned her smile, feeling better than I had since Peter's texts yesterday. Then, as though my thoughts alone had summoned him, Peter emerged out of the lunch line carrying a tray of food. Our eyes met for a second, and he looked away and quickened his pace. I couldn't stop my stomach from dropping in disappointment.

Prom. Peter's senior prom. The memories surfaced. He hadn't taken me to prom, though we'd been secretly seeing each other at the time. Instead, he'd taken Amy Lee, captain of the girls' tennis team, who went on to attend MIT. At the time, I'd been green with envy. Two years later, I was still pining after the same guy. Nothing had changed. Pathetic.

"Something the matter?" Alexander asked.

There was an edge to his voice that made me look at him. I saw his gaze following Peter's movements as he disappeared into the teacher's lounge. "No," I said quietly. "It's nothing."

"You and Peter . . ." Alexander's voice was controlled, and suddenly I got the sense that this was something he'd wanted to bring up for a while.

My face heated. Peter and I must not have been careful enough if Alexander had picked up on the vibe between us.

Luckily, I was saved by a distraction in the form of Jack Kimball, one of the rich, cool jock types—and Akil's former track teammate. He came up to Akil and slapped him playfully on the back.

"Ow!" Akil rubbed the spot where he was hurt and glared at him, nonplussed, before he registered who it was. Jack was the son of a wealthy investment banker, and yet at Sinclair Prep, he was one of the least remarkable attendees. According to rumors, Jack could bench press two times his own body weight, which was already pretty heavy. "Uh, you need something, bro?"

"So that's how you managed it, Akil," Jack said brightly. "You could've let my buddies in on the secret, you know. We need the grade boost more than you." He gestured at the table behind him, where half the football team was gathered, staring at us and laughing. "You got any more on you?"

Akil blinked rapidly. "I don't—uh—"

Jack leaned in. A shadow fell over his face, darkening his blond hair and brown eyes. "Now that you've been kicked off the track team, Dartmouth has no choice but to recruit me instead of you." He leered. "Enjoy Hunter College."

Akil's face reddened, but his usual witty retort didn't come.

"Don't listen to that idiot," Krystal said, shooting Jack a glare. "You can still get into plenty of schools, Akil. You've gotta rely on your actual grades now."

"Yeah," Akil murmured, but he didn't seem to believe it himself.

"Ooooh, we've got a tough one over here," Jack said mockingly. "Are you gonna almost kill me for that, Choi?"

Krystal stood, her hands curling into fists. Her chair screeched across the floor behind her. "Listen here, you punk—"

"Krystal." I yanked on her shirt, trying to get her to sit down before she attracted too much attention. Too late. The eyes of everyone sitting around us were glued to our lunch table now, eagerly awaiting the showdown.

"I guess the stories are true," I heard someone whisper not so quietly. "Krystal Choi *is* a former delinquent. I mean, look at her."

"I bet she really did do something to Jamie," another added.

"Shut up," I growled, but that only made Jack's crooked smile grow wider.

"For someone who's naturally smarter, you should've been smart enough to know not to butt in," he said.

"Naturally smarter?" I snapped. "What the hell does that mean?"

"You're Asian, which means you're naturally smarter," sneered Jack. "That's the only reason you're able to get top grades."

My vision turned red. I thought of Mama, her hands raw and split and bleeding. Baba, an ocean away, his face aged with failure and shame. I thought of hours upon hours upon hours, days blurring into weeks blurring into months, of silent sacrifice, silent screams.

Me, studying and pushing and clawing along the path my parents bled for me. My body, raw and split and bleeding.

I wanted to tell Jack that he had no idea what he was talking about. I wanted to tell Jack that the reason I got top grades was because I couldn't not get them. Could not let my parents' sacrifices and dreams go to waste.

Me, putting on this same school uniform every day, this same flimsy costume of immigrant success. My mother, wasting. My father, leaving. And through it all, me smiling, me pretending, but nobody seeing me, nobody listening to me.

No lonelier feeling in the world than having people stare at you all the time, but nobody truly *seeing* you.

I wanted to tell Jack that I had to pretend for my parents, for our family back in China, for myself, that we had succeeded. That we had grasped the American dream. That we hadn't come all the way to a strange and foreign country, left behind everything we knew, for a false promise—a sham built upon lies and broken bodies.

I said all of these things to Jack. But the words never left my lips.

I said none of these things.

I said, "Go to hell, Jack."

Krystal, next to me, was barely keeping her fury in check. For a moment, I really did think she was going to swing at Jack. I wanted nothing more than to let her.

But the moment passed, and I realized I had to step in before Krystal or I did something we'd regret. And then an idea struck: we had everyone's attention, and it was likely the Proctor was in this very room, or at least that whatever we said here would get relayed to them via Tip Tap.

Raising my voice, I announced to the whole lunchroom, "We're going to Meryl's Boutique after school today. Tell the Proctor they can meet us there—if they dare. We've got information they want, and money."

Then, leaving the tables around us speechless, I grabbed Krystal's hand and fled the cafeteria.

"Nancy, you *want* the Proctor to come after us? Are you nuts?" Krystal hissed at me.

"Maybe." I hoped I hadn't made a giant mistake. But I didn't think I had.

The Proctor might have outsmarted us, might have trampled our morale, but we would only lose against them if we quit fighting. And, after all, hadn't the Proctor taught us this lesson themselves? That anything, any*body*, we tried to bury, could resurface, alive and kicking, when we least expected it.

As I'd calculated, within minutes, my Tip Tap feed was full of posts relaying my challenge to the Proctor. Whoever it was had to have gotten the message now. All Krystal and I had to do was stay true to our word and see if the culprit would come hear us out.

After school, I headed over to Meryl's Boutique. It was conveniently close to the school, on the corner of West Ninety-Fifth and Broadway, across from a luxury apartment building. It had been Jamie's go-to after-school shopping spot. The boys would never be caught dead shopping with us, but Krystal, Jamie, and I—it had been our favorite hangout area.

Now, there was only Krystal and me. Krystal was easy to spot even on the crowded sidewalk. She waved her arms wildly at the entrance. When I reached her, her nervous expression gave way to a small smile. "This place brings back memories, huh?" Then, her face darkened again. "You really think the Proctor's going to show up here?"

"I don't know," I confessed. "I think they'll give us *some* kind of response, though. People like that really like attention. The more we give them, the more they'll respond." I'd observed this pattern in a lot of my classmates, who'd thrived on being showered with attention all their lives.

"Good thinking." Krystal nodded thoughtfully and ran her hands along the fabric of a black lace dress on display. "I hope whoever it is *does* show up. I'm prepared to settle this once and for all, with money or . . . another way." She cracked her knuckles. That steely glint in her eye. A hunter's glint. It wasn't hard to imagine what she meant by "another way."

My senses were on alert as we browsed the store. Meryl's Boutique was a popular after-school shopping spot, so the store was filled with students sporting the Sinclair Prep uniform. Any one of them could be the Proctor.

"I think this thing is a bust," I told Krystal after a little while had passed.

"Mmmm. Maybe not." She nudged me, and I looked toward where her finger was pointing. A middle-aged woman with a blond pixie cut was approaching us. I recognized her as the store manager.

"You're Jamie's friends, aren't you? Krystal and Nancy?" she said, a small, sad smile on her lips. We nodded. "You used to come in here all the time a couple of years ago, along with those other girls."

Krystal and I waited for the woman to get to the point. She pasted a bright, practiced smile on her face and stretched out her hand, which held a folded slip of paper. "A gentleman came in here, asking me to pass this note along to you. Is this part of some kind of game?" she asked, looking mystified.

"You could say that," I muttered. A game that we'd never wanted to play.

"What did the man look like?" Krystal demanded.

"Tall, brown hair—he wore sunglasses, so I couldn't really see his face very well." The woman gasped, and her hand flew up to cover her mouth. "You two aren't in trouble, are you?"

"No," I said quickly. I didn't think I'd ever been in so much trouble in my life, but I didn't want to scare or worry the poor lady.

Krystal flashed her a tight smile. "Thank you!" It was a dismissal. The store manager looked like she wanted to stay and talk some more, but a nearby girl tapped her on the shoulder and asked her a question about a dress.

Krystal whirled on me. "Nancy, that means—"

"Yeah. It's the same person the barista mentioned back at Green Bottle Coffee."

Out on the street, Krystal unfolded the note. It trembled ever so slightly in her hands. I peered at it over her shoulder and read the printed Times New Roman text.

> I admire the effort, N.L., but you'll never be able to stop me from ruining your lives. Not for all of K.C.'s daddy's money.
>
> In the meantime, enjoy the rest of the show I have for you! Next installment should be here in 3 . . . 2 . . . :)
>
> —The Proctor

Krystal and I gazed at each other in horror. In unison, we pulled out our phones to check Tip Tap. There, at the top of the feed, was a picture of the empty alleyway in Chinatown. A black-haired teenager stooped over what looked like a homeless man. The identity of the teenager wouldn't be obvious to just anyone from that angle, but I would recognize that profile anywhere.

> Jamie has four former friends. Each friend has a secret. One day, Jamie goes missing. Which friend is guilty and deserves punishment?
>
> Correct answer: c) the one hiding a criminal

Explanation: Our VP A.L. is always busy, but apparently not with school and work, like we all thought. C'mon, A.L.—I know blood is thicker than water, but hiding a wanted man? Not sure Harvard's going to like the sound of that!

What's more important? Protecting your criminal scum of a brother, or protecting your precious record? Choose quickly. I hear the police got an anonymous tip-off of big bro's whereabouts . . .
—The Proctor

"Alexander," I gasped. "We have to get to him before he does anything he'll regret."

Krystal already had her phone to her ear. I waited; we waited. After about a minute, she lowered it. "Went straight to voicemail." As she tried again, I sent Alexander a few texts. They showed that they'd gone through, but there was no reply.

Krystal glared at her phone in frustration. "Idiot. Where could he be?"

My gut told me there was only one place Alexander would go to at this moment. "Follow me. I know where to find him."

CONFESSION SIXTEEN

Anyone know if P.S. is single? Lol asking for a friend
hahaha —Anon

*****

We took an Uber from Meryl's Boutique to Chinatown. We got out of the car when it stopped in traffic on Canal, and took off running—or as close to running as was possible on the crowded sidewalks.

"Nancy, where are we going?" Krystal panted. "Alexander doesn't live that way!"

"We're not going to his apartment. It's—it's this place where he's been going, and—well, you'll see." I grabbed hold of Krystal's hand to keep us from being separated by all the people and skirted a large jewelry cart. I rounded the corner and then stopped right in front of the alleyway, causing Krystal to bump into me.

"Ow!"

We were too late. There were two NYPD officers on the scene, a tall Latina and a burly Asian man, speaking into walkie-talkies. Alexander and an older Asian man and woman stood in the alleyway. It looked like they were being questioned.

Krystal grabbed me and yanked me around the corner, out of sight of the police.

"What're you doing?" I hissed.

"Uh, keeping your best interests at heart. You're welcome," she sniffed.

"But Alexander—"

"Needs our help? Uh-uh. The last thing he needs right now is for us to get involved when we don't even know what's going on. He's a big boy. He'll be able to get himself out of this mess."

I wanted to shake Krystal. Didn't she realize? "Getting out of a mess" wasn't something that most people could *afford* to do. Alexander had said it himself the other day. People like him, people like us, didn't get chances like that.

"Unlike you, Alexander doesn't have rich parents who can bribe law enforcement to clear his criminal record." The harsh words left my mouth before I could stop them. Krystal's jaw dropped, but for once, she didn't have a retort. "Sorry. I went too far."

"No." Her voice was stiff. "You're right. Maybe Alexander can't buy his way out of this. But money isn't everything. He's still got his charm and brains."

I said nothing.

"What? What's wrong, Nancy?" Krystal's words came out like a challenge, as though she were daring me to tell her what was wrong.

"You wouldn't get it."

"No, I *do* get it. You think I haven't noticed that every time the topic of money comes up, you get a thorn in your side?"

"Why *wouldn't* I 'get a thorn in my side'?" I put the words in air quotes. "You think I don't know what people say behind my back?" Those whispers, I heard them all the time, knew what they were saying even out of sight. "That I'm a charity case scholarship student who—"

"Most of us *aren't* saying that behind your back, Nancy. And the ones who are, aren't worth a second of your time. I thought you knew I was better than that, at least."

I was stunned to see hurt tears swimming in her eyes. Instantly, regret filled me. "I *do* know that."

"You've gotta hold your head up high. Trust me, a lot of students are impressed by you, by how ambitious and capable you are. This is the top private school in the country. And you won a scholarship. You don't ever have to feel inferior to anyone. If anything, they should feel inferior to you."

"Inferior to me? As if."

"I know for a fact that Jamie at least was worried you'd surpass her."

It didn't seem possible that Jamie could have been worried. That Jamie could have felt even an ounce of the inferiority I'd always felt toward her. "*What?* No way. There's no way."

Krystal shrugged. "And I mean, you surpassed Alexander too. And Akil. And me."

My eyes widened. For the first time, I considered the possibility that Krystal and my friends might have been envious—of *me*. Come-from-nothing, scholarship kid Nancy.

Maybe I'd been too harsh. "I . . . sorry. I didn't mean . . ."

Krystal slumped against the wall. "No, I'm sorry too. I think we're all kind of stressed with everything that's been happening."

For a moment, both of us were silent. Thousands of unspoken words hung suspended in the air between us.

"Did I ever tell you the reason I broke up with Jamie?" Krystal asked quietly.

I thought back to the winter. "You said you couldn't see a future with her . . . right?"

A long, sad sigh. "Yes, but that was only part of the reason. The main reason was because . . . I could tell Jamie wasn't in love. Not with me. Not with anyone. Jamie was in love with power. She was in love with this . . . this imaginary version of herself, perfect in every way. I realized that Jamie could never love me, not the way I deserved to be." She pinned me with a long, hard look. "I'm telling you this because you remind me so much of Jamie sometimes. You and Jamie are more alike than you think."

I swallowed. Krystal's piercing gaze, her sharp words, made me uncomfortable. Made me uncomfortable because some part of me knew they were true. Sometimes when I looked in the mirror, it was like Jamie had come back to life. Jamie in my smile. Jamie under my skin.

"And Alexander—well, I hope you're not going to break his heart one day. Like Jamie broke mine."

"I . . ." I wouldn't. Wouldn't repeat Jamie's mistakes. Alexander and I weren't even together.

Before I could say that, though, Krystal's eyes widened as they gazed at something—or someone—above my shoulder. She straightened. "Alexander! There you are."

I whirled around. Looking disheveled, but alive and with no NYPD officers on his tail, was Alexander. The blank, white shock on his face told me he hadn't expected us to be waiting for him. "What're you guys doing here?"

Krystal ran up to Alexander, threw her arms around him, and then pulled back and punched him on the shoulder. "We're here to make sure you didn't get arrested, punk!"

"Where did the police go?" I asked.

"Told them it was a false tip-off. Eric isn't there."

"You *lied* to the police?" Krystal gasped. She stepped back and regarded Alexander with new respect in her eyes. "Broooooo. Didn't know you had it in you."

"It's not . . . not a lie," Alexander said in a hoarse voice. "My brother isn't there."

"But the picture on Tip Tap showed him—" I started.

"He's not there anymore," Alexander clarified. "Eric *was* staying with that man and woman up until last night. He—he left." Alexander's voice broke.

"What do you mean, *left*?" Krystal whispered.

"I mean he's gone. Vanished. The man and woman who live there said he left a message for me. 'I'm sorry I couldn't be strong. Take care of yourself.' That's . . . that's it."

Alexander's expression crumpled. Without thinking, I moved forward and enveloped him in a hug. He leaned his head against my shoulder, as if he'd been carrying a weight that had grown far too heavy for one boy to bear on his own.

"I told him about the Proctor. I shouldn't have. Eric must've realized that—that he was my biggest secret, and the Proctor would come after us. I'm such an *idiot*."

"No, you're not, Alexander," Krystal said, voice tight with emotion. "It's not like you could've predicted Eric running away. And—at least this way, you didn't get in trouble for hiding him. Your record is still totally clean. You're still a shoo-in for Harvard."

"I don't even know if I'll see my brother ever again." Each word came out of Alexander's mouth like he was sentencing himself. "And did you know—today's Eric's birthday? Today my brother turned twenty. And he's spending the day completely alone." The tears burst forward, streaming down Alexander's cheeks. He cupped his hands around his face and screamed up into the sky, "Who gives a *damn* about Harvard or my stupid record?"

Krystal stayed silent, and so did I. There was nothing any of us could say or do to make up for what Alexander had lost. Nothing was worth it. Not even Harvard.

———

Even though the rumors and speculations about Eric followed him everywhere, Alexander held his head up high the next day. By lunchtime, the news of Eric Lin's reappearance, then disappearance, was in full swing. The students loved that they got to revisit old gossip. Loved to dig up these skeletons, crush them to dust.

Three secrets had been revealed. There was only one left. Mine. And I couldn't let that secret come out. I couldn't. It would ruin me.

Worse, once that secret was out—well, the Proctor had warned me nice and early, during honors night. My vengeful note to Jamie was going to come out to the whole school. I would be blamed for a crime I didn't commit.

I had to stop the Proctor before that happened. But we'd exhausted all our options. We'd tried to track down the Proctor, only to discover they were one step ahead. We'd tried getting the Proctor to come to us, but whoever it was wasn't interested in money or making any kind of deal with us. No— this person had one goal, and one goal only: to *ruin* the four of us.

During AP Chem, while pretending to work on our problem set, I dug through my memory for anyone who might have a grudge against my friends and me. Well, aside from students who wanted to knock us out of our top rankings . . . which included pretty much everyone. There was Richard Li, too, who'd been furious to see me at Jamie's funeral. Was it a stretch to think he and David Kim could have a hand in this—maybe even the whole Golden Trio, including Peter?

"Miss Luo."

It was almost as though by thinking of Peter, I'd conjured him from the front of the room toward me. I glanced up at the sound of his soft voice. Ignored the way my heart rate sped up at the sight of him. "Yes?"

Peter gestured toward the door. "Can I speak with you in private?"

"Okay." I didn't let my surprise show on my face. Peter and I had barely exchanged three words since he'd cut things off abruptly. What did he want now?

Alexander was giving Peter a death look, which it seemed Peter was choosing to ignore. I flashed Alexander a soft smile, reassuring him it was okay. He didn't return it.

I followed Peter into the empty hall. When the classroom door swung shut behind me, Peter turned and pinned me with a smoldering stare. "How have you been?"

"Um, good." No way had Peter pulled me into the hall to ask about my day. Maybe he'd changed his mind about us keeping our distance. The thought allowed hope to bloom briefly in my chest, even though I didn't want it to. "You?"

"I've been better." Another pause.

"You pulled me out of class for this? Couldn't you have texted?"

Peter shook his head. "It's not just that. I wanted to speak to you in person to make sure that—that you've never told anyone about—about, uh . . ." Casting a nervous look around the empty hall, Peter pointed at me and then himself.

The balloon of hope in my chest deflated. Peter didn't want things to go back to the way they'd been before. He wanted to know his own cowardly skin was safe. "I never told anyone, no."

"Not a single soul? Never?"

"Of course not. I'm not an idiot," I said firmly. "Is that all?"

"I—I'm worried. The Proctor is going around exposing all these secrets about your friends. I don't want to be . . ."

"You don't want to be implicated," I finished dully.

Peter nodded, his eyes wide with relief. "It's that . . . well, I have a job and a . . . a reputation to keep. You get it. Don't you?"

I did get it now. Peter's message was loud and clear. It struck me hard enough to make me lose my breath for a moment. To Peter Shui, I could never be more than the girl he was secretly seeing. Even though, once upon a time, he'd made me believe otherwise.

That was what they'd all done to me, wasn't it? Peter, Jamie, my parents. Everyone, everyone making me believe I could escape this soul-crushing system, could fly as high as I wanted.

None of them were around when the truth sent me crashing down.

SEPTEMBER, FRESHMAN YEAR

It was the second week of school at Sinclair Prep. I'd made a few friends, mostly thanks to Jamie, who had all the connections and had become the most popular girl in the class by the end of the first day. Jamie was good at that, making friends. Talking to people. Getting them to like her—or if she couldn't, getting them to fear her.

I wasn't Jamie. I wasn't a people person. Hanging back and observing, absorbing and learning—that was more my speed.

Here were the things I'd learned from my first official week as a freshman at the Richard Sinclair Preparatory School:

- Coursework was as intense as the brochures had promised, and even some freshmen were put into advanced placement courses. (I was in AP Chinese, which was harder than I'd thought it would be.)

- Freshmen were at the bottom of the social ladder, but most of the upperclassmen were too exhausted from schoolwork to bully us, like what happened in movies. (I wasn't sure if I should be relieved about this, or apprehensive for my future. Probably both.)
- There was some group of senior boys called the Golden Trio, who were the hottest, richest, smartest guys, and pretty much ruled the school. (I'd glimpsed them from afar, and they looked like they'd walked off the set of an Asian drama. Major *Boys Over Flowers* vibes.)

Instead of spending my lunch breaks in the cafeteria with everyone else, which felt too overwhelming, I took my lunches to different places in the school. To the library. To the small courtyard behind the school, a rare spot of greenery in Manhattan.

September in the air. Not too warm, not too cold. Brilliant colors painting the autumn leaves. Many fewer people out here to distract me. Perfect conditions for writing.

I was here to get good grades, as I'd promised Mama, but I was determined to write even better poetry. Maybe win a few writing contests.

The flat marble surface in front of the Richard Sinclair statue was empty. Apparently, there was some story behind the statue that students had made up a long time ago. That at midnight, anyone who touched the statue of Richard Sinclair would see the ghosts that haunted this school.

I didn't believe in a tale like that, and I sure wasn't ever coming to the school grounds at midnight to find out if it was true. What was important was there were few students around.

Sitting down on the bench in front of the statue, I took out my notebook to keep working on my poem. I crossed out a few words and added a few words. Then, I was interrupted by a rustling noise, followed by the sound of music. A sweet, gentle melody. A violin, nearby.

As though in a trance, I turned around toward the source of the music. It was coming from the other side of the statue. Quietly as I could, trying not to disturb whoever was playing the music, I crept closer and found myself looking at a moving painting.

There was an Asian boy who had to be a few years older than me. Loose black hair fell into his eyes. Hands, sweeping a bow across violin strings. Long, slim fingers, caressing the instrument.

I didn't realize the melody had stopped until a voice said, "Can I help you?"

The boy was staring right at me, setting his violin down.

My cheeks burned. I couldn't help but feel as though I'd intruded on something very private. "Oh, sorry—I didn't mean to—"

"Is that poetry?" He was peeking at my new pink notebook, his head tilted sideways.

"Um . . . yeah, I guess."

"Are you a poet?"

"No," I said quickly. Then, with a sheepish smile, "Well, hopefully one day."

"I've been wanting to team up with a poet. I'll compose the song, and you'll write the lyrics."

"Excuse me?" He'd spoken with such familiarity that I thought maybe I'd met him last week and forgot. No, I definitely didn't think I would've forgotten meeting a guy this handsome. "Do I . . . Do I know you?"

The boy blinked, long eyelashes fluttering, as though I'd spoken in a foreign language. As though no one hadn't not known him before.

Then it registered. I'd only seen him from afar last week, when he'd had two other tall, imposing senior boys flanking either side of him, but now I was almost certain who he was.

"David . . . Kim?"

He snorted. "Close. David Kim's my friend. I'm Peter Shui." He held out his hand for me to shake.

My cheeks burned again. Well, I'd had a one in three shot of getting the name right. "I'm Nancy. Nancy Luo." I reached for his hand, and a shock jolted between our skin.

Peter's smile, glimmering. Peter's eyes, hungry, like Jamie's. Like mine.

"Nice to meet you, Nancy Luo."

CONFESSION SEVENTEEN

Asian don't raisin. That's it. That's the whole post.
—Anon

★ ★ ★ ★ ★

Peter's eyes, empty. He suddenly didn't look as handsome to me as before. Had that mole always been under his lip? It looked like he'd shrunk maybe an inch or two as well. I did my best to ignore the burning feeling in my throat, and the stinging of tears in my eyes.

"You're disappointing," I said.

Peter blinked, taken aback. He clearly hadn't expected that. Neither had I. Probably, no girl had ever found Peter Shui, golden boy extraordinaire, *disappointing*.

But as soon as I spoke the words aloud, I realized that was the only way to describe how I was feeling: disappointed.

What had happened to the boy with the violin behind the statue, the boy with those hungry eyes?

"Well, if that's all," I said, turning around on my heel and heading back into the classroom. Even though I was so tempted, I ignored the urge to turn back and catch sight of Peter's expression.

Alexander glanced up from our list of names as soon as I sat next to him again. His black hair fell across his eyes. I caught Isabel Lim giving him an admiring glance from across the room.

And when I looked at Alexander, really looked at him, it struck me, at that moment, that he really *was* handsome. I'd known it all along, but maybe with Peter in the way, I hadn't truly registered it until now.

"What did Peter want?" Alexander muttered, his eyes following Peter's movements as he sat back down at his desk. He glowered at our teacher. Now that I knew the full story behind Eric Lin and what had happened with the Golden Trio, I understood why Alexander had never seemed to like Peter.

"Something related to the homework. Nothing important."

"You and Peter are pretty close, huh?"

I kept my gaze fixed on my desk, but I could still feel Alexander's eyes boring into the back of my head. Forced my shoulders up and down in a casual shrug. "Not really. We talk about the class here and there. He's kind of a dick, though."

At my words, Alexander's lips curled up into a small smile. I returned it, though it was impossible to summon the energy to feel really happy.

Time was ticking down to catch the Proctor before I paid the ultimate price. And here I was, spinning my wheels, still with no clear leads on their identity. *Pathetic.* That was what

Jamie would have called me. Jamie would have known what to do to beat the Proctor at this twisted game.

What had happened to the boy with those hungry eyes? I had no right to criticize Peter. What had happened to the *girl* with those hungry eyes?

What would Jamie do, if she were in my shoes?

Jamie never backed down to anyone. She was the aggressor, if anything. Jamie would find a way to lure out the Proctor. Offer them something besides money, something they couldn't pass up. I didn't know anything about the Proctor besides that they knew everything about my friends and me, but one thing was obvious—the Proctor loved getting dirt on people in high places.

"You can't get your mind off it either, can you?" Alexander asked. I blinked. I hadn't realized that, lost in my thoughts, I'd been staring at him. "The Proctor."

"Yeah. I . . . I still think we have to draw them out of hiding somehow. Give them bigger fish to fry."

Alexander stared at his phone. He clenched and unclenched his hands into fists. Clenched and unclenched. Then, seeming to make up his mind about something difficult, he began typing on his phone. When he was finished, he dropped his phone onto the table between us. "Think they'll pay attention this time."

"What did you . . . ?" A notification popped up on my phone, and my voice trailed off as I read the latest Tip Tap message.

@The Proctor, you want us to fess up to what we did
2 years ago, right? You want to expose our worst

secrets? I'll give you an even better secret if you stop things here and show us who you are. Those secrets you know—they're small fish. I have dirt that could shake the foundation of Sinclair Prep. I'll tell you and the rest of the school.

Meet in the cafeteria @ 3PM sharp.
—A.L.

Seconds later, the reply:

Sounds delicious. See you there.
—The Proctor

Slowly, the buzz of voices grew louder as more and more of our classmates caught up on the latest exchange on Tip Tap. Their eyes locked onto Alexander's figure, unable to look away, as if he were a train wreck about to happen.

It worked. Alexander's plan had worked. I couldn't tell if that made me happy, or terrified.

"Are you *nuts*?" I demanded. "You're not seriously telling the whole school about the Incident?" Panic, clawing at my chest. None of us were ready to be exposed like that. To cut ourselves open, letting our bloody secrets hang out for all to see.

"No. Not that. Eric knew a big secret about the Golden Trio. He told me, but he made me swear I'd never tell anyone."

My eyes widened, then darted toward Peter. I couldn't

pretend that didn't pique my curiosity. "You're going to break that promise?"

"Yeah, well." Alexander swallowed, his Adam's apple bobbing up and down. Harsh lines formed on his face. "Eric's not exactly around to stop me, is he?"

If this secret got out and the Golden Trio's legendary reputation took a beating, that spelled bad news for us, especially Alexander. Peter, David, and Richard combined probably had enough power behind them to rally a whole army in their defense. We'd basically be poking a wasp nest. "Alexander, it's okay. You don't have to do this."

"I do. Otherwise, your secret gets exposed next. And who knows what else this sicko has planned?" Alexander's dark eyes, shining fiercely with protectiveness, flicked to mine. His jaw was set with the determination of a young man about to go to war. "It's obvious that this person—the Proctor—is the son or daughter of a businessman. You had the right idea yesterday when you called them out. The only way to win against someone like that is to strike a deal with them—a deal they can't pass up."

I glanced over at Peter, who studied Alexander with narrowed eyes and a slight smirk. I didn't deserve Alexander's protection. He'd regret giving it to me as soon as he found out what I'd been doing—and *who* I'd been doing it with. My stomach twisted with nausea.

"Don't you want to know my secret?" I mumbled.

"No. Whatever it is, it's your business."

I looked up at Alexander's determined expression. For the first time in a long time, I felt—I *knew*—that I was safe.

Strange, wasn't it, that never for a moment had I felt any sense of safety with Peter.

———————

As soon as class ended, we headed down to the cafeteria. The hallway seemed to stretch forever ahead of us. I barely noticed the stares and whispers of our peers. My mind spun with Alexander's words: *I have dirt that could shake the foundation of Sinclair Prep.* What dirt could he possibly have?

Krystal and Akil joined us as soon as we entered the cafeteria, confusion and concern written across their faces.

"Bro, you sure you know what you're doing?" Akil asked after giving Alexander a skeptical look.

"I'll beat the living daylights out of the Proctor as soon as they show their identity." Krystal cracked her knuckles.

Alexander gave them both a tight smile. He seemed different. Normally, Alexander was comfortable hanging back in the shadows. Now that he was in the spotlight, he stood taller. Seemed much surer of himself. Almost regal. As a crowd of students gathered around us, Alexander stood on a table and cupped his hands around his mouth. "Students of Sinclair Prep, may I have your attention, please!"

Almost instantly, the crowd quieted. The students were all mesmerized by him. Watching with bated breath. Alexander's gaze scanned over the crowd, searching for one figure. I didn't know how he knew what to look for, since we didn't even know what the Proctor looked like.

"Show yourself, the Proctor," Alexander bellowed. "I won't say anything unless you reveal your identity."

Nobody stepped forward. Behind Alexander's back, Akil, Krystal, and I exchanged nervous looks. The crowd grew restless.

"Tell us the big secret already, Lin, if you aren't making it up," someone hollered.

"As soon as the Proctor joins us—" Alexander was interrupted by phones buzzing across the cafeteria. In unison, everyone's hands dove for their phones.

"Uh . . . I don't think the Proctor is joining us," Akil said in a quiet voice.

With a sinking sensation in my stomach, I glanced at the latest post. I found myself staring at a caption, and below it, a dark photo. Two people, arms wrapped around each other, an Asian guy and girl kissing in a dimly lit room.

My heart, thudding. Palms, sweating.

On a night, six months ago.

Dread in my stomach. Dread, snaking its way up my lungs, choking me.

Jamie has four former friends. Each friend has a secret. One day, Jamie goes missing. Which friend is guilty and deserves punishment?

Correct answer: d) the one who traded conscience for grades

Explanation: So now we know why N.L. has been passing AP Chem exams with flying colors. Hey N.L., if you still need a date for prom, I hear P.S. doesn't have one . . . Oops, I forgot—it's cuz he's a teacher, right? And being with him like that wouldn't be legal. Not that that's stopped you before, you naughty, naughty girl.

P.S. Sorry, A.L. We'll chat about your secret another time. This show's just getting started . . .
—The Proctor

Once, on a night six months ago.

Jamie asked the four of us, "What would you be willing to do to stay at the top?"

My answer lay in a single choice.

NOVEMBER, JUNIOR YEAR

The AP Chem unit test was the last big exam before Thanksgiving break, and I really needed to ace it if I wanted to cling onto my A and stay afloat at the top of the ranks. Everyone was in lockdown mode. Jamie invited us over to her penthouse to study. "Us" meaning Alexander, Akil, Krystal, me, and Peter.

Peter was the last to arrive at Jamie's. After the butler greeted him, he took turns greeting us from a careful distance. It was clear that even though he was Jamie's cousin, he wanted to keep this study group strictly professional. When Peter's eyes met mine, that heart-stopping half smile rose to his lips.

My cheeks flamed. "Hi."

"Hi, Nancy," he said with distant politeness, as though greeting someone who had only been to him one of many students. After our brief, secret fling two years ago, Peter had gone off to Stanford for his freshman year. Though he was back at Sinclair Prep as my student teacher, we hadn't spoken much.

Nan-cy. I loved the way my name rolled off Peter's tongue, like it was a tasty sweet he was trying out. It gave me hope that the old feelings were still there. Our two-and-a-half-year age gap seemed smaller than ever.

"I want to clear up something before we all get started," said Peter once the five of us were assembled around him at Jamie's dining room table. Akil and Alexander gave Peter tight smiles. Peter had that effect on most of the guys in our class—I guess they thought his presence threatened their masculinity.

"I'm here as a resource to answer any questions you guys might have about the course material." Peter's eyes twinkled. I was pretty sure I didn't imagine the fact that they lingered on mine for a heartbeat longer than on the others. "That's all."

"C'mon, Peter." Jamie batted her eyelashes at our student teacher and made a pout with her perfect cherry lips. "Stop acting like my mother doesn't hand you your favorite snacks from the Asian market every time you come over. If you were a real good cousin, you'd give us the answers to the final exam."

"Ah, but then you wouldn't be learning, now, would you?" Peter flashed her a grin and then turned to the rest of us with a "well, get to it" look on his face.

"Ugh. Don't expect any sweets next time you're here," Jamie sniffed.

Pretty soon, the boys had gotten over their annoyance at Peter's presence and were hogging all his attention with questions. Jamie and Krystal were studying with their heads bent together, taking turns to peek at each other every so often, then pretending they hadn't been looking at each other. They were still adjusting to the friend zone post-breakup.

I had my head bent over my giant textbook, doing my best to concentrate on the text even though it was swimming before my eyes. I could barely focus with Peter in the room.

I knew what I felt couldn't be more than a silly schoolgirl crush—at least, not for this year. If anything happened, Peter would get fired, and I'd be in big trouble.

The scent of Peter's cologne filled my nostrils. I looked up as he slid into the empty seat next to me. My heart began pounding madly.

"You've been awfully quiet, Nancy," Peter said with that soft smile still on his lips. Nancy. There it was again. My name, except a million shades more beautiful. "Everything going okay over here?"

"Um, y-yeah." What was it about Peter that turned my brain to mush? "Yeah, everything's fine. I'm, um . . . going over some . . . some . . ." I glanced at the open page before me. ". . . phosphate backbones."

Peter's eyes danced with mirth. "You didn't sound too sure about that."

"Stop flirting with her, Peter," Jamie said loudly. "Nancy isn't like the other girls you fool around with."

That stung. Did Jamie mean that I wasn't like the others, because I was poor, and they were all rich?

"She's not one of your airheaded college chicks. She has

very high standards," Jamie clarified. "You won't win her over that easily."

My face heated. Great. Now everyone had stopped what they were doing to stare at Peter and me. My eyes met Alexander's across the table. His hands gripped his textbook so tightly it shook, and he glared openly at Peter.

"I didn't mean it like that. I'm her teacher." Peter's reply was smooth. A little too smooth, I thought. Maybe hoped. "I wanted everyone to get the most out of this study session before the final exam."

"I'm sure if Nancy needed your help, she'd ask," Alexander fired back.

The two boys—well, one man and one boy—stared at each other across the table. The tension was so thick in the air I could've cut it with Jamie's protractor, which lay only inches from my fingers.

"Does anyone want drinks?" Jamie asked, in a voice full of forced bubbly-ness. "Daddy left some aloe vera in the fridge. It'll help, uh . . ." Her eyes darted from Peter to Alexander, and she bit her lip. I couldn't tell if she was fighting back a smile or a cringe. ". . . cool us down a bit."

"Aloe vera sounds great," Alexander said, still glaring at Peter.

"Exactly what I needed." Peter enunciated each syllable as he returned Alexander's challenge.

"O . . . kay." Jamie darted out of the room into the kitchen. She returned with a giant jug of aloe vera and placed it in the middle of the table, along with five fancy wine glasses. The gesture might've been casual if it weren't for the sly little smirk on her face—a smirk that I'd grown to know all too well over the years. That smirk told me Jamie Ruan was up to no good.

My phone buzzed in my lap with an incoming text.

Krystal: *How does it feel to have two hot guys fighting over you?*

I blushed, not daring to look up in case Krystal was grinning at me. I was sure she was. I could feel those sharp eyes of hers practically drilling holes into my head.

Nancy: *They are not fighting over me. Have you been watching too many K-dramas lately?*
Krystal: *LET ME LIVE OK*
Nancy: *NOT AT THE PRICE OF MY REPUTATION*
Krystal: *Wait, so you admit they're both hot then*
Nancy: *I admit nothing*

"I'll help myself to the aloe vera first, then, if you guys are just going to stare at it," said Akil. He seemed to be oblivious to what was going on—either that, or he didn't care enough to let Peter and Alexander's staring match get to him. He lunged across the table and poured himself a glass full of aloe vera. "Well, doesn't anyone else want some?"

The two boys looked away from each other as we all took turns pouring the aloe vera into our glasses. Jamie was last, that sneaky smile still playing across her lips as she eyed Alexander and Peter over the rim of her cup.

"Back to studying," Peter said gruffly. He stacked his papers against the desk and seemed to deliberately avoid Alexander's gaze.

Akil took a huge swig of the aloe vera juice, and immediately made a face at Jamie. He swallowed the drink and then puckered his lips, staring down at the cup as though it had tried to bite him. "Did you put something in this?"

"A little something to make the evening more fun," said Jamie with an oh-so-innocent note to her voice that fooled no one.

"Something like . . . vodka?" Akil added.

Peter eyed his drink like it had grown fangs. "Are you serious, Jamie? You spiked our juice?"

"Oh, come on. Stop acting like a saint. You drink with me all the time, and plus, my parents won't be back in town until tomorrow. I don't know why you're being such a tight-ass today, but stop. You're seriously killing the mood."

"I'm being a 'tight-ass' "—Peter put the word in air quotes, a disgruntled expression on his face—"because you invited me over as a teacher today, to teach you guys. I can't teach a bunch of drunk students!"

Jamie's lip curled. "Alcohol improves memory," she said, her tone of voice soft but mocking.

Peter's face reddened. I got the feeling he'd told her that once to justify his own actions and was now regretting that intensely. "But going into my exam hungover is not going to help your chances."

I felt like I was watching a Ping-Pong tournament, my eyes darting from Peter to Jamie back to Peter, and occasionally sneaking a look at Alexander, who I caught staring at me.

Jamie leaned over and whispered something into Peter's ear. When she pulled away, his eyes were closed in resignation. Jamie smiled in triumph.

Before either of them could say anything, I watched as Alexander downed his glass of aloe vera in three huge gulps, and then wiped his mouth with the back of his hand. His eyes were back on Peter, as though challenging him.

"Now that's what I'm talking about!" Akil whooped and clapped Alexander on the back. Some of his spiked aloe vera sloshed out of his cup and onto the table. "Whoops. Sorry, Jamie."

Jamie crossed her arms over her chest and glared at Peter. "Tell them what you told me about your . . . experiments with alcohol and exams in college."

Peter sighed and rubbed his forehead. I could practically see the stiff and law-abiding teacher persona leave him, replaced with the young man who was barely older than us. Who, two years ago, had walked the same unforgiving halls of Sinclair Prep as we did. "I drank my way to an A-plus on the orgo final at Stanford," he admitted, as though convincing himself as much as us. "You know what? Screw it."

"That's more like it," Jamie said approvingly. Akil cheered. Alexander looked on coldly as Peter reached for his cup and downed it, which was all the encouragement the rest of us needed.

I knew what I was doing was stupid. I knew even if Peter and Jamie thought alcohol improved memory, which sounded like some bullshit college students told themselves as they drank their way through finals week, it was a dumb move for me—someone whose sole alcohol consumption consisted of occasionally getting a sip of her parents' Chinese white wine.

But I never did anything stupid. Since Peter and I broke things off two years ago, I never did anything except what Mama told me to do. Never put a toe out of line, never had any excitement.

And I was sick of it. Tired of day in, day out studying. Day in, day out perfect Nancy.

Plus, Peter would think I was some pathetic little high school girl if I didn't drink, too. It was stupid, but I cared what he thought.

I squeezed my eyes shut and gulped down the spiked aloe vera before I could have any second thoughts. The taste of something sharp and bitter overpowered the otherwise sweet juice. Despite how much I wanted to, I forced myself not to spit it back out.

"Now it's a study party," Jamie giggled. She poured more aloe vera in everyone's wine glasses.

"You're the worst," Krystal groaned.

"I hate vodka," mumbled Akil, who was somehow already bent over his textbook already. "This better get me a damn A-plus on the final."

At first I thought I was fine. Even after finishing my second glass, I felt perfectly normal. I even powered through three chapters of AP Chem review.

And then all the alcohol hit me at once.

My head belonged to me one moment, and then the next

thing I knew, it didn't. My brain floated away, no longer anchored inside my own body. I watched everything around me happen in a dream.

Akil lay fast asleep, openmouthed and drooling against the giant chem textbook. Jamie and Krystal had abandoned their textbooks and were making out instead. So much for trying to be just friends. Alexander's seat was empty, and I had no clue where he'd gone.

And Peter, charming Peter with his charming smile, sat right beside me. He gazed at me like he was a drowning man and I was the last life vest left on the planet. "You okay, Nancy?"

Nancy. Even in my floaty state, the sound of my name passing through his lips was enough to send shivers down my spine. I must have made a noncommittal noise in the back of my throat because Peter's voice, sounding distant but soothing, returned. "You're so pretty." He reached up and tucked a loose strand of hair behind my ear. His intense gaze made my cheeks warm.

Boys didn't call me pretty. Brainy, yes. Know-It-All Nancy. Nerdy Nancy. I'd heard myself nicknamed every variation of the word "smart."

But never pretty. Peter was the first one to call me pretty. It made me fall for him during my freshman year, and it made me fall for him again now.

"You think so?" I hated how breathy, how stupid and air-headed I sounded. But that didn't matter now. Nothing mattered now except the way Peter's stare was heating me up from the inside out.

"I've thought so since the day I met you. Even more so the first time you walked into my classroom earlier this year. Isn't that messed up of me?"

And before I could stop it, the alcohol spoke through me. "If that makes you messed up, then I'm messed up, too." Because I felt it as well. Felt this incredible, undeniable pull.

A pause. Peter and me, teetering on the edge of something dangerous, teetering on the edge of the world.

I pushed him back, and then I leaned in and kissed him. Emptied my head of every last rational thought, including the voice that would've told me that a teacher kissing a student was illegal. I pressed my mouth against his soft lips and chose to forget.

Peter pulled back and whispered into my ear, "Let's be together again. I can give you everything, Nancy. Grades. Money. Status. Would you like that?"

"Why me?" Peter could have any girl, any girl he wanted at all. But here he was, with me. Here he was, choosing me. And I needed to know why. Needed to hear it from his lips.

"Because you're special, and I like you."

The words were intoxicating, like hypnotizing music to my ears. *The* Peter Shui still liked me. Peter thought I was special. For once in my life, I *felt* special.

"Here." I was dimly aware of Peter slipping something—a rolled-up piece of paper—into my hands. His hands working their way down my neck and traveling the length of my spine, hovering along the waistband of my jeans. I grabbed the front of his shirt and pulled him closer, deepening the kiss.

"Oh my God, Peter. What're you doing to her? She's a minor,

you lech," I heard someone scream. It sounded like Jamie's voice. "And you're her teacher!"

It was Jamie's voice, I realized through the jumbled haze of my thoughts.

Peter's hands disappeared from my body. "S-Sorry," I heard him mumble.

"No. Don't be sorry," I managed to whisper. Then I blacked out.

When I woke up, it was still dark out. Jamie was shaking me. My head throbbed, and I opened my eyes to the sight of an empty dining room table across from the fancy couch where I'd been sleeping.

"It's okay now," Jamie had reassured me in a soothing voice while tilting some water into my mouth. "I sent Peter home. Jesus, Nancy, how much did you drink?"

"What . . . time is it?" I groaned. Somehow, even the darkness of the room made my eyes hurt, so I shut them.

"It's ten."

"What?" My eyes flew open, and my heart lurched. Mama was going to kill me.

Jamie spoke at rapid-fire speed, which always happened when she was nervous. "Don't worry. I told your mother you started feeling sick while we were studying, so I let you nap for a bit at my place. Now I'll get an Uber to take us to your home, and we'll never speak of this again, all right? You'll be okay. Nobody else knows what happened with you and . . . well. You know who." Jamie rubbed my back, tracing soothing circles with her hands. "You're okay. I'm here for you."

I nodded and immediately regretted it. My head hurt like someone had tried to cleave it in half. My stomach was churning, and I wanted nothing more than to be home in my warm bed.

Maybe I'd made bad choices tonight, but I was glad Jamie had been by my side. Moments like this were the reason why Jamie and I were still friends, though she could be awful and spoiled. Moments like this, I wished Jamie could let more of her true, genuine self shine through.

"The guy you were seeing during our freshman year," Jamie said suddenly. " 'P.' That was Peter."

It wasn't a question. I knew there was no point denying it, so I nodded. Didn't speak. Didn't ask how, or why, she'd remembered an initial, that P, for so long.

"I thought so. I'm glad I got to the bottom of it."

Jamie's wording seemed strange to me. Almost like she'd wanted this scene between Peter and me to happen. Planned the evening, from the guests to the drinks, and predicted the outcome.

But that couldn't be it. Right? Jamie was my friend. She wouldn't do that to me. Even she wouldn't sink so low.

Jamie was my friend, and she was the one helping me through this night of bad decisions. I shook my head. I'd had too much to drink.

"I won't tell anyone," Jamie whispered, reading the scared expression on my face accurately. "I wouldn't do that to my dear cousin, or to you. You can trust me."

When I finally got home, I slept badly, and woke up at five in the morning, three hours before my AP Chem exam.

I was sunk.

Or so I thought, until slowly, ever so slowly, I unfurled the slip of paper Peter had tucked into my hand. Written on it were two columns. The one on the left was filled with the numbers, and the one on the right with letters.

1) A
2) D
3) E
4) A

The list went on through number one hundred.

I aced the AP Chem exam with flying colors, shocking Mama, who'd no doubt thought I was doomed to fail. Maybe now, at long last, I could live up to the daughter she'd always wanted me to be. Maybe if I saw Baba again in the future, as a rich, successful lady, he'd regret abandoning his family. Better yet—maybe he'd hear about my success and come back to America to be with his wife and daughter.

Or maybe I was a hopeless, stupid girl who dreamed too much, after all. But if this was a dream, then I didn't want to wake up.

I texted Peter to thank him after the exam was over. Then he and I fell into a cycle of meeting up in secret once or twice a week, with one unspoken rule: nobody could ever find out about us, or we would both be ruined.

"Only for now," Peter would say. Softly, pleadingly. Cruelly. "Only while I'm still your teacher."

I wondered if what existed between the two of us, whatever it was—if any of it was real. Or if it was another silent negotiation to Peter. He gave me the grades; I gave him myself. We both gave each other the pure exhilaration of doing something we knew was wrong. Of throwing caution to the wind. Shattering all the rules.

Being with Peter, carrying this dirty secret around with me, made me feel so different from boring Nancy. It made me feel powerful. He made me feel powerful.

I loathed it. And I craved it.

I knew then that I was hopelessly, dangerously addicted. Peter was going to ruin me. Burn away the good girl I'd always been, destroy everything I'd ever worked to become.

I would gladly let him.

CONFESSION EIGHTEEN

Honestly, who needs to watch Asian dramas when you
go to Sinclair Prep? —Anon

*****

"Nancy, is this true?" Alexander's stunned voice called me back
to the present. It was as though a spotlight had been turned
on to me. Dozens—maybe even hundreds—of eyes were glued
to me, but I barely noticed them. The only thing I saw was
Alexander's expression, an ugly mixture of hurt and betrayal.

Oh, God, Alexander hated the Golden Trio. He hated
Peter. He'd been about to go against his brother to protect my
secret, protect *me*. Now he was going to hate me. And I deserved
it. Deserved all of it.

"Please tell me this isn't true." His voice, pleading, hardly
above a whisper.

"I . . ." Half-formed thoughts spun in my head, the panic

keeping me from thinking clearly. Peter and I had so painstakingly kept our relationship a secret. Who had found out? Nobody had known—except Jamie. And Jamie was dead. Wasn't she? My phone buzzed in my hand. I looked down.

Peter: *Can we meet ASAP?? Green Bottle Coffee?*

"I have to go." I shoved my phone into my pocket and ran out of the cafeteria, ignoring the cries of my friends behind me. Someone—Louisa, I dimly registered—tried to grab my arm, shouting something about a newspaper article, but I shook her off. My breath came up short. The logical part of my brain knew that meeting up with Peter was the worst thing I could do at this moment. But right now, while my whole world was burning down around me, the only person I wanted to talk to was him.

I can give you everything, Nancy. Grades. Money. Status.

Peter had promised me. Peter would make sure everything turned out okay. He'd promised.

I spotted Peter the instant I walked inside the coffee shop. He looked the same as he had half an hour ago, except his hair was slightly more disheveled, the one imperfection in an otherwise flawless image.

"Nancy. Sit." Peter gestured to the empty seat in front of him. No panic showed on his face, though our secret was out and his job was on the line. Peter had never been one to show emotion. But even for him, this demeanor was a little too calm.

"The Proctor. They found out about—about us. I don't know how," I blurted out. "I swear, I didn't tell anyone."

"I believe you," said Peter.

"Y-You do?"

"I know you. You're not stupid. And this person—whoever they are—is exceptionally good at finding out other peoples' secrets."

I exhaled, slumping back into my chair. "So, um . . . what do we do now?"

"There's going to be an investigation. Tomorrow, most likely first thing in the morning, Principal Bates will call you and me down to his office. I'm going to deny everything that happened," Peter said, as robotic as though he were stating the weather. "As long as I deny it and you play along, we'll both be fine. One photograph can't prove anything. Plus, my family made a massive donation to the school when I graduated. They'll listen to anything I say."

Peter's words made perfect sense. But part of me felt the tiniest bit disappointed by his plan to deny the truth—to deny *us*.

"Let's just get through this," Peter said, leaning in close. "After everything blows over, we can see each other again."

I nodded. This was temporary. One day, once we moved past this, Peter would be able to give me everything he'd promised. He'd show me off proudly to the world as *his*.

"Nancy . . . do you regret what we did?"

Surprised, I didn't know what to say for a moment. As soon as I returned to school, I would be the target of rumors and insults. What kind of person *wouldn't* regret all her destructive decisions that had led to this day?

I swallowed, my mouth dry. "No. I don't regret anything."

A small, satisfied smile traced Peter's lips. He'd known exactly what I would say. Some twisted part of me was reflected in him, and some equally twisted part of him was reflected in me. That was what had bound us together against all rules, against all odds. Peter reached over and patted my hand. "That's why I like you, Nancy."

Shivers, running down the back of my hand where he'd touched it.

Peter left Green Bottle Coffee first. I waited fifteen minutes, which he'd asked me to do so nobody saw us leaving together. Tomorrow. Tomorrow morning, we'd clear our names. Peter would be fine after this. Everything would go back to normal for him.

But me—I knew what the Proctor had in store for me next. The revenge note from my Diss Diary. The one in my handwriting that would be used to frame me for Jamie's murder.

No matter what, I would soon be sunk if I didn't silence the Proctor first. Time was running out in this game of cat and mouse.

But did I *regret* writing that letter, or being with Peter? Never.

CONFESSION NINETEEN

Final grades came out, so now I'll be the one to go
missing next, 'bye —Anon

*****

As Peter had predicted, the next morning Principal Bates called us to his office. The whispers and stares followed me down the halls all the way there.

I'd spent entirely too much time in this office.

Bates glowered over the top of his glasses. Peter and I sat two chairs apart in front of him, keeping an ocean of distance between us.

"Mr. Shui. Miss Luo. Since last night, I've received several allegations from staff and students alleging an extremely serious, illegal relationship that occurred between the two of you. I don't want to believe it, but there seems to be photographic evidence." The principal raised a sheet of paper showing the photograph of Peter and me, blown up.

"I can explain," Peter said quickly. "It's not what it looks like."

Rage twisted Principal Bates's expression. "Oh? You mean this *isn't* a picture of you and your student involved in an intimate situation? Peter, I know your parents have given generous donations to this school, but this matter is out of my hands. It's gone public now, and I can only do so much to hush up the details. I have to answer to the Board of Trustees, and to the alumni and families who donate to this school. There need to be consequences, visible consequences, or else I'll have furious parents banging down my door. Do you understand the position I'm in?"

Bates's voice shook with anger. Now, even now, he was more concerned about the reputation, the *prestige,* of Sinclair Prep. More concerned about image than what was going on in these walls—these walls that saw and hid everything.

Peter's jaw clenched. He'd probably never been in so much hot water before. I didn't see how he was going to deny his way out of this. The evidence was right there in front of everyone.

"The truth is . . . Miss Luo made advances on me. I rejected them, of course, since I've only ever seen her as my student. Unfortunately, the photo doesn't show that."

The world, stopping. The room, spinning. Peter, pushing me over, pushing me into the dark.

"Miss Luo, is this true?"

"I . . ." My mouth dried. "N-No, that's not—" I faltered when Peter cut me a warning look. A look that said if I didn't back up his explanation, I was going to regret it.

My family made a massive donation to the school when I graduated, Peter had told me. *They'll listen to anything I say.*

Only now, I saw the thinly veiled threat behind those words. This school would listen to anything Peter said—over me.

If I didn't play along now, not only would the school punish me, but Peter would hate me too. He needed me, needed me to lie. After, he'd get us out of this mess.

And the words, they came out of my mouth, a mouth that didn't even feel like mine. Ghosts, forcing them from my lips. "It . . . It's true."

There, the admittance Bates was waiting for. Open revulsion on the principal's face. There, I'd done it. No amount of wishing would turn back time, could let me take back my confession.

"You're suspended from school and all school activities for one week, effective immediately."

The words sent me tumbling over the edge.

"A—A *week?*"

"Yes, and be grateful that I don't expel you on the spot, or take away your scholarship. I'm only showing you lenience due to your outstanding academic record. I never expected this from you, Miss Luo." Principal Bates shook his head. "You can forget about valedictorian. Sinclair Prep will never bestow that honor upon someone who so grossly violated the school rules."

A distant ringing in my ears. Bates's walls, the school walls, closing in on me, tilting and squeezing.

I was suspended. I wasn't going to be valedictorian. I was now a student who'd inappropriately thrown herself at a teacher. Banned from student activities.

"Wait—" I started to protest.

"*All* school activities, Miss Luo."

"Mr. Bates, sir, perhaps you could make an exception," Peter intervened swiftly. Peter was going to use his influence to get us out of this mess, I knew he would. "Miss Luo's actions were inexcusable, but she already paid for prom, and students look forward to this event all year."

Even though there were still angry red splotches on Bates's face, he glanced between the two of us and sighed, seeming to deflate. "Well . . . this is Miss Luo's first violation. And, as long as you're fine with her attending prom, Mr. Shui, I don't see why I wouldn't be," said Bates. He threw me a sharp look. "Thank Mr. Shui for his generosity, Miss Luo."

"Th-Thank you." My fingers curled into fists in my lap. I'd taken the fall for both of us. Getting Bates to . . . let me go to prom. It was the *very least* Peter could do for me.

My plans, my achievements. Good girl Nancy Luo. The perfect image I'd built, everything I'd worked for, the title of valedictorian at my fingertips. It was all crumbling around me. Hadn't some part of me wanted this, though? Some twisted part that delighted in this. Knowing all along that this was the only way it could end. Everything, up in flames. Everything, to ashes.

We left the principal's office and Peter walked me in silence to the classroom wing. The walls, torching me from all sides. Whispers, fast as wildfire, louder and hotter—

"Nancy. Nancy. *Nancy!*"

Peter's voice brought me back. We'd stopped in front of the school doors, and after darting a glance around to make sure nobody was around, he spoke in a low voice, in a voice that was like the hiss of flames. "From now on, this is how things have to be. You don't talk to me, you don't look at me. I'll have my parents send along another donation to the school. Bates—back there, he had to be harsh, but he'll come around once everything has quieted down. This is all temporary. Soon it'll blow over, and everything will go back to the way it was before."

Everything between Peter and me was like this. Temporary. Fleeting. Secretive.

I can give you everything, Nancy. Grades. Money. Status.

"I don't want that anymore," I whispered. Wanting what didn't belong to me, what could never be mine, was what got me into this mess in the first place. I had to deny the part of me that delighted in ruin, smother it until it was gone.

"What? You don't want . . . this?" Peter gestured to the space, to the chasm, between him and me.

For Peter, I'd gotten myself suspended. Peter, who couldn't be mine, could never be mine. Peter, who couldn't understand that there were some things even money couldn't put right.

"Stay away from me," I said, enunciating each word loud and clear. "Please—whatever twisted games you're playing—leave me out of them."

"Nancy—"

But it was me this time, turning away from Peter. Me this time, slamming the door on him, on us. I stayed strong. I didn't look back.

I rode the train home, ignoring my phone blowing up with

texts from my friends. Once I reached my apartment, I headed straight for the answering machine, erasing the message from the school about my suspension. Mama wouldn't return from work until late, so the chances that I could hide this from her were good.

And I had to hide it from my mother, had to do whatever it took to make sure she never found out. If Mama ever knew, ever even *suspected* what I'd done, she'd know at long last that I'd been pretending to be a good girl. Pretending for her.

At home, I stopped pretending to be strong. At home, I let myself collapse onto my bed. Peter's words echoed in my head over and over until they were seared into my brain. Everything, *everything* between us had been a dream. This was the reality. Breathless and aching and broken.

Tears rolled down my cheeks, though deep down, I knew Peter Shui wasn't worth it. But still, a whisper in my ear. Maybe I hadn't been good enough for Peter to want to be with me, a girl whose father wouldn't stay. Not good enough for a boy like Peter, a boy who was destined for greatness and wealth.

Peter and me, we'd been teetering on the edge of something dangerous, teetering on the edge of the world.

Peter pushed me over, and alone, I plunged into the dark.

It was after 10:00 p.m. when Mama came home. I'd spent the whole evening ignoring my cell phone to cry, and I no longer had any tears left. I didn't feel sad, or hurt, or betrayed. All those emotions had been burned away from my heart.

"How was your day, Le-Le?" my mother called from the kitchen.

It was time to do what I did best: pretend. Mama didn't know about the suspension. Mama didn't know any of it, and I would do anything, anything, to protect her from knowing what I'd done.

I put on a false, cheery voice, a sense of calm nestling into my chest. "I've never been better, Mama."

My mother was right. I was strong. I would do anything—*anything*—to keep my scholarship. To prove myself to the other students, to their rich, snobby families. To my own family.

Nobody could take the top rank away from me. Remember: back then, I made a promise. Remember: we sacrificed everything.

Jamie was the only one who knew about Peter and me. The only one who, when alive, had the power to destroy me.

I wasn't glad that Jamie was dead. I would never be glad that she was dead. But I *was* glad that Jamie's death proved one thing: being filthy, stinking rich didn't make a person immune to meeting a terrible fate. Didn't make them immune to the fire.

When she died, Jamie was supposed to bury my secret with her.

Now, it was my turn to bury the person who'd let it out.

CONFESSION TWENTY

So instead of going to prom, who wants to cry with me
tonight over how badly finals week went? Haha jk . . .
unless . . . —Anon

*****

Being suspended wasn't as bad as I'd imagined. Nor did I have
to try too hard to keep the information from Mama. She rose
and left the apartment before me every day, and returned later
than me in the evenings. She wouldn't know I wasn't going to
school as long as I didn't tell her.

Plus, now that I had decided I wouldn't stress over homework or tests, I had so much free time on my hands. And Tip
Tap kept me updated on all the latest school gossip.

I waited with bated breath to see if they'd pulled out their
trump card on Tip Tap—pinning Jamie's death on me, with
my revenge letter as the "proof." The next day, it arrived: a new

post from the Proctor. But this one wasn't my condemnation. It was different from the other posts.

To an old friend: will you be my prom date?

If yes—meet me at the place where the beginning foreshadows the end. Prom night. 9 PM on the dot.

If no—enjoy the finale I have planned.

Hope I'll see you then. 🖤
—The Proctor

Immediately, my phone began blowing up with texts from Krystal and Akil.

Akil: *Top 10 Worst Promposals, yikes*
Krystal: *The Proctor is obviously giving us a hint. No idea what it means tho . . ."where the beginning foreshadows the end" where the hell is that? And what's this about an "old friend"? Any of you remember an old friend who happened to be a killer??*
Akil: *Maybe they're desperate for a prom date and shooting their shot last minute, it's hard out here yo*
Krystal: *Omg I can't with you . . . and what the hell is "the finale" they have planned? Sounds scary*
Akil: *Nancy hbu? What do you think?*
Krystal: *Nancy?*

I should respond to my friends. Should think about the Proctor's cryptic message.

But I couldn't muster the energy to care. With this suspension on my permanent record, I wasn't getting into any of my top choice schools. My reputation—trashed. Peter and I—finished. Alexander wasn't even speaking to me, judging by the string of texts I'd sent him that he ignored.

Krystal: *Nancy? You good??? We're really worried, you*
   haven't been picking up any calls or replying to texts
Akil: *Your thing with Peter isn't that bad, ppl are being*
   stupid. Idk why they're not more worried about exams.
   It'll all blow over soon
Krystal: *Nancy pls respond! We're here for you. We're your*
   friends, you have to talk to us
Akil: *Plus we still have to find out the identity of the*
   Proctor so I can beat the shit out of them, remember??
Krystal: *Yeah so we've been talking and we THINK the*
   Proctor might not even be a student. Like they seem too
   powerful . . . might be one of the faculty, tho I can't
   figure out what their motivation would be
Akil: *That's Krystal's theory . . . and it's got a lot of holes*
   in it if you ask me
Krystal: *I'm sorry, do YOU have any better ideas?*
Akil: *Yeah I do. Pretty sure it's the ghosts. Or like, maybe*
   that old statue of Richie comes to life when we're not
   looking and goes around threatening and killing
   innocent students
Krystal: *NOT FUNNY, AKIL*

I read all the texts, but I couldn't summon the energy to respond. Inside, I was drained. Inside, I was empty. It was better this way, facing the consequences alone.

Statues. Ghosts. We'd run clear out of better theories. We'd circled back to the beginning now.

Because that was what this was really about, wasn't it? The beginning.

From the start, there had been signs. Signs that Jamie's unhappiness had always been there, lingering beneath the surface of those carefully crafted smiles. I was sorry I hadn't seen those signs earlier. Before it was too late.

FEBRUARY, JUNIOR YEAR

"I'm not happy, Nancy."

I paused in the middle of my math homework and looked at Jamie. She was curled up in the beanbag by the pink writing desk in her bedroom. The sunlight slanted through the curtains, throwing her puffy eyes and miserable scowl into full light. "What do you mean?"

"I mean, I'm not happy."

I bit my lip. I had no idea where this confession was coming from. Or did I?

Jamie had everything that mattered—picture-perfect grades, picture-perfect extracurriculars, picture-perfect family. Bright and peppy, she exuded happiness. I mean, she lived like a princess out of a fairy tale. She had butlers to serve her every whim in the penthouse and her family's house in the Hamptons. Jamie's extravagant lifestyle was such a far cry from my existence in my family's tiny apartment, I could weep.

Sometimes, though, I got the sense that the Jamie we saw

on a regular basis wasn't the only Jamie. Sometimes, in rare vulnerable moments like this, I got a glimpse of a darker Jamie swimming beneath the surface of wide smiles and perfectly groomed features, struggling to break free.

"Do you want to talk about it?" I shut my notebook and set aside my pen to make it clear that Jamie had my full, undivided attention. "Is this about Krystal?" Although Jamie appeared unaffected and unchanged at school in the aftermath of their breakup, I'd definitely noticed she looked mopier when she thought she was alone.

"No."

"Your father?" According to her, Mr. Ruan had gone away on another business trip the day before.

"Never mind. It doesn't matter." Jamie jumped up from her seat and gave me a falsely cheery smile.

"Jamie, whatever it is, you can trust me."

"I just remembered Daddy left us some Chè Trôi Nước. Sweet rice dumplings." Jamie spoke in that fast, agitated way she sometimes did when she was worked up. I couldn't get a word in edgewise if I tried. "He brought them back from Vietnam after his last work trip." A shadow crossed Jamie's face, but she replaced it with that same, sunny smile a moment later. "Want some?"

I forced myself to grin. Between the two of us, we had enough insincerity to run a political campaign. "Sure."

"I'll go grab us some from the kitchen." Jamie took a step, and a slip of paper fell out of her jeans pocket and onto the floor.

I picked it up. "Hey, you dropped someth—" My words

faltered when I saw what was written on the yellow notebook paper in big, bold black letters.

DADDY SCREAMED AT ME UNTIL I CRIED TODAY, ALL BECAUSE I GOT ONE POINT OFF MY MATH TEST.
I SWEAR I WILL KILL HIM. IF I DON'T KILL MYSELF FIRST.

Jamie whirled around and snatched the paper from my fingers. She was no longer smiling. "What?" she snarled. "Don't snoop in my private business."

I gawked at Jamie, the poker-faced girl I'd known for so long. But I couldn't put up with it any longer. The insincerity, the pretending. Something about Jamie's home life was terribly wrong. "Why . . . why did you write that?"

It was the wrong thing to say. Jamie's eyes hardened. She flinched, but didn't answer me, although that was answer enough. Then she squared her jaw and straightened her back. I could almost see her walls go up, walls as high as the ones that surrounded us at Sinclair Prep.

"I was mad. I didn't mean any of it."

"Are you sure?"

"Are you accusing me of lying?"

"I'm not—"

"You'd better not. You're lucky someone like me is even friends with you," Jamie spat. "Maybe if Sinclair Prep doesn't work out, you and your mom can be maids here together."

Anger flared inside me at the insult. I knew Jamie was angry and hurting and trying to get a rise out of me. And this was how it was, wasn't it? This, the kind of friendship Jamie and I had. Normally I wouldn't let her provoke me into an argument, no matter how spoiled she was, how horrible she could be.

But today, I was stressed out over a B-plus I'd gotten on my history paper, which had widened the gap between Jamie's rank and mine. Today, I was fed up with everything—school, Jamie, Mama never being around, Baba never coming back.

"You've always thought of yourself as better than me," I hissed. I stood and drew myself to my full height. I was half an inch taller than Jamie, which was the one thing I'd ever consistently beat her at. Now, that half an inch felt like a mile as I faced down a shaken Jamie. Guess she hadn't expected me to fight back. "And yeah, I can't measure up to you in a lot of areas. I don't have much I can call my own in this world. I don't have butlers, rich parents who can send me to the best tutors, or even the best grades in school. But what I *do* have is thanks to my mother. So don't ever, *ever* insult her or call me 'maid girl.'"

I took a deep breath, my chest heaving. An invisible energy charged through my body. I was doing this, doing it at last. Standing up to Jamie. I couldn't remember the last time I'd felt so alive. And I wasn't finished. I had one last, dirty card to play.

"Besides, you and me, we aren't all that different," I whispered. My eyes drifted downward toward the slip of paper crumpled up in Jamie's fist. Her gaze followed mine. "Neither of our fathers want us."

I'd done it. Crossed that invisible, ever-present line. Jamie's eyes flashed. Her chin trembled. With a cry of anger, she slammed her fist on top of her desk.

"Don't compare our fathers." Jamie enunciated each word. Spit them at me. And she didn't look like the Jamie I knew anymore. The deadened look in her glittering black eyes reminded me of endless, winding tunnels of darkness. Of a place where I could get lost and never find my way back. "Daddy is the vice president of a Fortune 500 company. Your dad is some deadbeat who probably found a girl half his age to bang back in China."

A distant ringing noise entered my ears. I wouldn't let anyone speak ill of Baba—least of all some pampered, spoiled rich girl who'd never understand what it meant to claw her way toward an impossible American dream.

I was so pumped up on adrenaline that I hardly registered my body moving of its own accord. My fist flew upward—then stopped.

Jamie flinched and screamed so loudly that for a moment, I thought I'd punched her. But I hadn't. I hadn't even come close to touching her.

A whisper in the back of my mind told me that her reaction was odd. But I shut it out. Whatever. Jamie didn't want to tell me what was going on. And if she was going to insult me by calling me "maid girl," then I didn't care.

For too long I'd stayed in this friendship, excusing Jamie's horrible behavior toward me and other people. Guilted by what we'd both done in the past. Convinced that if I stayed by Jamie,

I could feel some of her power, some of that kindness buried deep inside her.

But it wasn't enough. And that was the problem, wasn't it? It would never be enough.

I turned to leave, but Jamie's hand wrapped around my wrist.

"Wait. Don't go. I'm . . ." Jamie sounded on the verge of tears, so different from the angry girl who'd stood before me mere moments ago.

I looked at her and immediately regretted it. The expression on Jamie's face would haunt me in my dreams, even when I closed my eyes. It was a look that begged for help that I didn't know if I could give. That I didn't even know if I *wanted* to give.

Jamie had helped me in tight spots before. My mind flashed back to when she'd covered for me the night I'd snuck out with Peter, without me even asking her to.

But this was bigger than boys. Much bigger. And I couldn't do what she was asking me, begging me, to do.

"I don't think I can help you, Jamie." I didn't think anyone could, except maybe a professional. Gently but firmly, I pried her fingers off my wrist. "I have to go now."

Jamie's mouth parted, as though she wanted to say something more. But then she shut it. "Of course," she said frostily. "Of course you have to go." Something in Jamie's expression shut down, and she resumed the look I was more familiar with— that of a girl who ruthlessly strove for the top grades, never settling for less than the best.

The girl who was never weak.

I should have pressed further. But I remembered those words: *maid girl*. I remembered the superior, defiant look in Jamie's eyes, the look that told me my strong, hardworking mother and I were lower than dirt. I remembered. The anger rose to a roar. I left.

When news of Mr. Ruan's embezzlement broke out, when Mama stopped working for the Ruans and told me not to talk to Jamie again, it was easy to follow her orders. Things between Jamie and me had been rocky, anyway.

Then Akil dropped Jamie. Then Alexander dropped Jamie. Then Krystal dropped Jamie.

Soon, Jamie's group of friends dwindled to Louisa and Kiara. Yet her grades never suffered. She continued holding her head up high.

And I swear, every time Louisa, Kiara, and Jamie whispered together, their whispers were directed at me.

"We're friends with Jamie now, and she doesn't need you anymore."

Jamie whispering, "Of course I don't need you. Why would I? I've beaten you again and again and again, proving that I am the stronger one. Even when my family's reputation's been soiled, I am *always* the stronger one."

We didn't speak again. Jamie didn't need me? More like *I* didn't need *Jamie*.

We didn't speak. And then Jamie was dead.

And it was too late for anything but regrets for the words we never said.

CONFESSION TWENTY-ONE

Any ladies who wanna be my prom date, drop ur IG in
the comments —Anon

*****

On Saturday night, at last, it was junior-senior prom. This
year's theme was "masquerade," which meant everyone would
be showing up in masks. I was relieved. For one night, I could
hide behind my mask. For one night, I could pretend I was
somebody else, anybody else but the scholarship student, the
girl who'd messed around with a teacher.

The most important thing was that according to the Tip
Tap message, the Proctor would be there tonight, the biggest
night of the year. And my gut told me they were planning their
greatest act. I'd either catch the Proctor in the act, or the Proctor would bury me.

My blood boiled with the desire to get to the bottom of it,

the bottom of it all. I had nothing to lose. I stared at my reflection in the mirror, the smattering of freckles across my cheeks standing out as starkly as the black of my pupils. "Game on," I whispered.

I headed into the living room, where Mama sat at the kitchen table, on her evening off from work. She clutched a book in her hands: my copy of *Wuthering Heights*. She'd been flipping through it slowly for the past year, teaching herself English.

We hadn't spoken much since I'd asked about Baba. I knew I'd crossed a line by bringing up the fact that we hardly ever talked about him, that he was forever a giant, unseen, suffocating force looming in the room.

I cleared my throat. "Mama?"

"Hmmm?" My mother didn't take her eyes off the book.

"I'm going to prom, and I need a dress. Like, today. Do you have anything I could wear?"

Mama lifted her gaze to meet mine. "I do have one dress." Her expression, thoughtful. Her voice quiet, wistful. She stood, her book forgotten on the table. "Follow me."

She headed into her bedroom toward the closet. I waited as she flipped past her sparse outfits. She pulled out something floral and red, holding it out in front of me.

"A qí páo." I was taken aback by the vibrancy of the dress. It looked like it'd never been worn. Like it belonged to someone with a whole lot more money than us. "Mama, you had this all along?"

"I brought it from China." She ran her fingers over the fine silk. "This is the nicest dress I've ever owned. I've only worn it once before."

"What for?"

Mama closed her eyes. A dreamy smile tugged her lips. "I once sang in a huge concert hall, back in China when I worked as a singer."

I suddenly got the feeling that I knew nothing at all about the woman who stood before me. "You . . . sang? You were a singer?" At first it seemed unimaginable, but then a fuzzy image sharpened into a scene that unraveled like something out of a movie in my head: a younger Mama, stepping under the stage lights with that fierce red dress on.

I'd never known Mama to be anyone but a weary, over-worked, and underpaid worker. But back in China, once, she'd been a girl with dreams, too. She'd given them up—for this. For a restaurant job that barely paid the bills. For a lonely life far away from family, a life that was so hard.

"That was many, many years ago," Mama said with a sigh and a shake of her head. "It's all in the past. I don't sing anymore."

"Why not?"

"For the same reason your baba gave up photography and came to America to work a steady job. So we could have you, and make a better life together."

"But . . . is this really a better life?"

Mama patted my hand. Didn't answer the question. "You can have this dress now." She handed the qí páo to me.

I took it gently, as though the dress were made of the most precious material in the world. A dress made of dreams.

There was so much I could have said in that moment.

I'm sorry you gave up everything.

I'm sorry I couldn't give you the world in return.

I said, "Thank you for this dress."

"Bú yòng xiè." *No need to thank me.*

It was one of those rare moments where Mama was really smiling, and I'd never felt prouder to be her daughter, and even if I could never live up to her expectations, and even if we were still poor, and even if Jamie were still gone, this fleeting moment could feel beautiful.

This fleeting moment was something I would fight to protect. Even if it meant fighting dirty. Even if it meant sacrificing everything.

CONFESSION TWENTY-TWO

Can't wait to see you losers at prom! Keep an eye out
for me. I'll be the one in the mask —Anon

★ ★ ★ ★ ★

Alexander: *Hey . . . checking in, are you still coming to
prom with me?*
Nancy: *I'm going alone. Sorry! Nothing against you.
I wanna be on my own for a bit*
Alexander: *It's cool, I get it. Why haven't you been
texting Akil and Krystal back tho? They told me they're
really worried*
Nancy: *I've got a lot going on atm*
Alexander: *I get it. We're meeting at Krystal's at
5 to head over together if you decide you wanna
come with*
Nancy: *I'll see you guys at the school*

Alexander: *Are you sure?*
Nancy: *Definitely*

I stared at the three little blue dots in iMessages that told me Alexander was composing a reply. But the response never came. I tucked my phone away, out of sight. It didn't matter. It was better this way. I didn't need anyone else. Like how my parents had come to the States on their own, I could find and stop the Proctor on my own. I had to. I'd die trying.

It was chilly, abnormally chilly for a May evening. Low sixties, and dropping into the fifties later in the night. I'd forgotten my jacket in my rush to head out the door, and sitting in Mama's qí páo on the train, I regretted it.

Luckily, the inside of the school was warm, and I followed the crowd of prom-goers as they headed all the way to the back of the school, to the Sinclair Prep ballroom. The ballroom was especially toasty, and I warmed up soon after arriving. The room was packed with masked juniors and seniors checking in for the event. Loud music blared from inside, and everywhere I looked, there were girls in high heels and dresses, boys in tuxes and dress shoes.

My dress, so unlike the Louis Vuitton or Jovani designer wear that dominated the event, drew some stares. But I wasn't the only girl wearing a qí páo. A couple of the Chinese international students donned multicolored qí páo. We smiled when our eyes met, as though we were sharing our own little secret.

Focus, Nancy. I was here to catch the Proctor once and for all. The culprit had left only that one cryptic message:

To an old friend: will you be my prom date?

If yes—meet me where the beginning foreshadows the end. Prom night. 9 PM on the dot.

If no—enjoy the finale I have planned.

Hope I'll see you then. 🖤
—The Proctor

The "old friend" referred to me. I was sure of it. Who else could it be but me, the one whose Diss Diary had been stolen, who was set up to take the fall for Jamie's death? And "the finale" was no doubt the Proctor's grand reveal of my name on the cover of my Diss Diary, making me out to be the culprit behind Jamie's death.

The rest of the note still stumped me, but there were a few clues I could go on to try to figure out who here was the Proctor.

This last game was between the Proctor and me. I wasn't going to get my friends involved, or put them in danger. I had to do this on my own.

According to the boy at Green Bottle Coffee and the store manager at Meryl's Boutique, the Proctor was associated with a tall, well-dressed brown-haired man with sunglasses.

My gaze swept over the attendees, searching for someone who matched that description. The odds were slim, but maybe, just maybe—

And then, there. A tall figure wearing designer sunglasses caught my eye. I pushed past Parker Xiao and Lindsey Kerrigan, who were posing for pictures and gave me disgruntled shouts. But before I could get any farther, a hand clapped down my shoulder, stopping me in my tracks.

"Nancy!"

It was then that I realized I'd made a mistake: I hadn't put on my mask yet. Sighing, I turned around and found myself facing a girl with shoulder-length black hair, wearing a black sparkly mask. She wore a long black coat that covered her dress. I couldn't tell who it was under that mask. "Um, who are you?"

"It's me. Louisa," the girl said. "You look *amazing*. I freaking love your dress." Louisa was with her date, a masked guy.

Beside Louisa, a girl who could only be Kiara wore a white mask, along with a white dress that popped against her brown skin. Her black hair had been done up in an elegant bun. She held hands with a masked boy. Even now, even while I was intent on tracking the Proctor, I couldn't help but feel a twinge of pain for Akil and his long-running crush.

"I love your hair, Nancy," Kiara said, her voice a little too sweet to be genuine.

"Thanks. You girls look great, too." I didn't know why Louisa and Kiara were being so friendly. We'd barely spoken a word since the Proctor trashed the newspaper room. Plus, they knew about my secret relationship with Peter. Like everyone else, they should've been avoiding me.

I looked over the girls' heads, but the person who might've

been the Proctor's right-hand man had already vanished from sight.

Louisa stepped in closer, as though confiding a secret. "Listen, I was hoping you'd be willing to talk to *Sinclair Unveiled* about you and Peter. I mean, um, Mr. Shui. We've heard his side of the story. Now we want to hear yours."

I really didn't want to talk about Peter right now. Especially because he was sitting at the sign-in table not twenty feet in front of me, helping students check in for prom. "Can we talk about this later?" I brushed past Louisa and secured my glittery black mask over my face.

"Nancy!" huffed Louisa.

"Whatever," I heard Kiara say. "She'll come crawling to us when she realizes she has literally no one else to talk to."

I turned in my ticket at the table, not sparing Peter so much as a glance. I headed into a huge room filled with round tables decorated with fancy scented candles and "champagne," which was really sparkling juice. Students stood in groups, talking and laughing with a carefree happiness that rarely graced the halls of Sinclair Prep.

I observed my classmates from a corner, grateful for my mask. Nobody came up to talk to me. Nobody could tell who I was. For the first time in weeks, I was out of the spotlight at Sinclair. Everyone else was too busy having fun to pay attention to Nancy Luo, cheater, seducer, terrible friend, target of the Proctor. I would cherish the feeling of anonymity as long as I could, but it wouldn't be long. It was already eight thirty, so time was running out.

Meet me where the beginning foreshadows the end.

Where the beginning foreshadows the end.

The room, fading around me. The thrum of the music, growing more and more muffled. I closed my eyes.

On a night, two years ago.

Two years ago, the five of us—

No. That wasn't right.

Two years ago, there had been six of us.

Fragments of memories, swimming before my eyelids.

A statue. Always that statue, of Richard Sinclair, holding that book, pointing into the distance.

A fire in her eyes. A sickening crack.

Bloodcurdling screams. Her bloodcurdling screams.

Dark blood. Her dark blood.

Jamie. Jamie's screams, Jamie's blood. But no—that was impossible. Jamie was dead. I'd attended her funeral. How could a dead girl be torturing us?

The students whispering, always whispering about the ghosts that walked these halls. Phantoms trapped here, phantoms that couldn't leave even in death. Maybe it was true. Maybe Jamie was one of them.

My phone vibrated in my hand, shocking me so much I nearly dropped it.

Alexander: *Hey, we got to the ballroom. Wya?*
Nancy: *Don't come looking for me.*
Alexander: *What? I thought we were meeting you here*
Nancy: *It's fine. Go on without me*

Alexander must have relayed my message. Not even a second later, my phone blew up with texts from the group chat.

Krystal: *There's only 15 minutes left before 9 PM and we still haven't figured out that clue! Nancy, why are you ignoring us???*
Akil: *Are you hiding something? Why won't you talk to us?*

I didn't bother texting back. My friends would understand, after. That I was protecting them. That I was there at the beginning, when the Proctor took my journal, took my vengeful promise at Junior Honors Night. That I had to be there at the end.

No matter what happened. No matter what it cost.

"Ladies and gentlemen, boys and girls, students of the Richard Sinclair Preparatory School." Principal Bates stood in a navy blue tuxedo on the stage. His bald head glistened with sweat, although at this point, I was pretty sure his head was never *not* glistening with sweat. "This is a special night for which you have all worked tirelessly. I know the last thing you want to do is listen to the rambling words of this cranky old man."

"I want a refund!" yelled Jack Kimball, causing the room to erupt into laughter.

I did my best to multitask, listening to Bates's speech, as well as searching for anyone suspicious, any kind of clue. Everyone was here, packed in this ballroom. The Proctor had to be here. Waiting for me, where "the beginning foreshadows the end."

Moving around without feeling, as though in a dream. Pushing past sweaty students. My feet carrying me slowly, as though in a nightmare.

Principal Bates chuckled. "While this hasn't been an easy year by any means, your achievements are still to be celebrated. So, have fun, students. But not *too* much fun. Remember the values and prestige of the Richard Sinclair Preparatory School. You must strive to uphold and embody them no matter where you are, no matter what you are doing. And as always, remember the words of our founder, Richard Sinclair—"

"*In inceptum finis est,*" the students finished with Bates.

"*In inceptum finis est,*" I said with them.

Like a chant. Like a vow.

"In inceptum finis est," Bates repeated solemnly. Then he motioned toward the DJ, and the beat of a Charlie Puth song thrummed throughout the dance floor.

My eyes bored into the young male DJ, at the sound system around him. *In inceptum finis est,* inscribed on a podium next to the DJ booth.

Maybe it was the DJ? If he commanded the sound system, he could have the ability to disrupt it, use it for his own ends, for "the finale." But no, that theory didn't make sense. I'd never seen this DJ before, and doubted he had any connection to the school and its people. Doubted he had any connection to Jamie, to us, to me.

Sweat trickled down my back, down my arms. The heat of all these students packed here, suffocating me. Burning me up.

In inceptum finis est. Blood, dark and red and thick, staining the floor, my feet.

"Ouch! You stepped on my foot," snapped a girl, jarring me back to the present.

In inceptum finis est, on the colorful balloons that decorated the walls. *In inceptum finis est*, embedded in the students' tongues.

Something, here. Ghosts, here, where the walls had eyes, eyes that were always watching. In the beginning, and at the end.

In inceptum finis est. In inceptum finis est. In inceptum finis est.
In inceptum finis est—there, the words at his feet.

Her, dead, at his feet.

The Proctor wasn't here. Not in this packed room. I knew that, knew it with sudden, shocking clarity, knew it in my bones.

The answer, hidden inside me all along. The answer, with me in the beginning, and at the end.

Blood, seeping through the walls and onto the floor, painting my path forward. I followed it, slipping through the crowd and out the ballroom door. It shut behind me, cutting off the loud music abruptly, as though the speaker had been turned off.

In inceptum finis est. In the beginning, is the end.

Where the beginning foreshadows the end.

That was where we went, Jamie and I. We went there to teach her a lesson. Teach Em a lesson.

There, at the foot of the statue. *In inceptum finis est.* There, where the statue of Richard Sinclair witnessed it all. Witnessed everything when it went wrong.

Em's screaming. A crack. More screaming, our screaming.

And the blood. The blood that dripped from her head. The blood that dripped from Richard Sinclair's hands. His hands, our hands. Her blood, seeping, into the grass. Into the statue, into the walls of the school.

In inceptum finis est.

There, at the beginning, at the end.

There, where we had killed.

"Nancy." Someone grabbed my arm. Jerked me out of the nightmare, out of the reality. No—*this*, here, was the reality. Prom night. "It's you, isn't it?"

I whirled around. It was Peter, face ashen with concern. Peter, holding me back. "Let go!" But he held on, so I wrenched my arm out of his grasp. "I told you to *stay away* from me. How did you even recognize me under the mask?"

"Of course I'd know it's you," Peter said, his voice cracking with some emotion that I didn't want to unpack. Then he added, "Where are you going?"

Of course I'd know it's you. I hated that Peter was the only one who'd recognized me under my mask. Hated that even now, with three minutes left until nine, he was still holding on.

Peter had won our game of back-and-forth. Defeated me soundly. Now, he needed to go. I needed to go. I snarled, "That's none of your business."

"Yes, it is my business. I'm monitoring prom. Students aren't supposed to leave the—Nancy!"

I pulled away from Peter and sprinted down the hall, glad I was wearing flats and not heels.

He didn't pursue me. Good.

My feet carried me on a familiar path down halls I'd walked so many times before. Now, the halls were dark and empty. But I could still hear them. The whispers.

Whispers, following me as I raced through the doorway. Following me as I sprinted down the steps. Across the perfectly trimmed grass. The night black but for the glow of streetlights and the moon.

On a night, as dark as this.

There was no one here. No sign of movement. A pungent, sweet odor entered my nostrils.

"H-Hello?" I called, treading carefully on the slippery, damp grass. Stepping toward the statue of Richard Sinclair. Shivering against a breeze.

On a night, as cold as this.

Then my phone rang, the sound nearly giving me a heart attack. Alexander's name and the time, *the time*, flashed across the screen.

Time.

Time was up.

"Don't come looking for me," I said when I picked up his call.

"Nancy—check Tip Tap." The gravity in Alexander's voice made my heart sink. "Then tell me it wasn't you who did it. I know it wasn't you who hurt Jamie." A pause. I said nothing. His voice cracked as he whispered, "Nancy?"

I didn't respond before hanging up and opening the gossip app. There was a new post from the Proctor.

Want to know who really had it out for Jamie? It was none other than . . . her own "BFF." Hold your friends close, and your enemies closer—isn't that how the saying goes?

A photograph of a note accompanied the post. The full note, written in my handwriting, signed by me.

I WILL END YOU, JAMIE RUAN. MARK MY WORDS.
—Nancy Luo

Texts and messages from friends and strangers began bombarding my phone. Dimly, I knew it was over. Time was up, and the phantoms of the past were here. Here for me. Here to make me pay for my crimes.

In inceptum finis est.

The whispers and the ghosts had come. And here, feeding off our blood, rising out of the dark, the statue of Richard Sinclair came alive.

CONFESSION TWENTY-THREE

Whoever the Proctor is, I hope they're having a good time with their date lmao —Anon

* * * * *

A figure, shifting behind the statue. Stepping into the glow of the streetlights. The outline of long hair and the knee-length skirt of a Sinclair Prep uniform.

Not the statue of our founder coming alive. The ghost of a girl coming alive.

"Who are you?" Although I was terrified, anger steadied my voice. "What do you *want* with me?"

The girl moved gracefully, as though floating. A hunter cornering her prey, enjoying the last moments before she pounced.

"The question is," said the girl—and that voice, I *knew* that voice—"what did *you* do two years ago during freshman year? You must know, since you knew to come here, where the beginning is the end. *In inceptum finis est.*"

The girl stepped fully into view. Light hit her face, but her mask obscured her identity.

"Who are you?" I repeated.

The girl raised her right hand. Slowly, inch by inch, tugged off her mask, and then tossed it aside. Her face caked with foundation, eyes lined with thick black eyeliner. Lips stained red.

The Proctor. Her. But—it couldn't. I'd *spoken* to her half an hour ago. She had no reason, no reason to be behind this. I deserved this punishment, but not from her.

"L . . . Louisa?"

A scornful look twisted her pretty features. "My real name," she said, "is Emily Yang. It's me, Nancy. It's Em."

I stumbled.

Ghosts haunting this school.

This ghost, coming back from my past. Back to haunt me.

"No. That's not possible. Emily Yang . . . Em . . ."

Emily Yang died two years ago. In a tragic accident—as Sinclair Prep ruled. In an incident. The Incident.

Jamie had started the Incident, of course. Jamie always started everything. This time, we helped her finish it.

On a night as dark and cold as this, we helped her finish Em.

APRIL, FRESHMAN YEAR

Emily Yang had transferred to Sinclair Prep a few months into the school year. Right away, we could tell she wasn't like the other freshmen at Sinclair Prep. She didn't ever wear makeup, didn't ever try to stand out. Hung out with the goths and anime nerds. Always carried a journal around with her, scribbling in it so often that some of the juniors started a joke that it was her "Death Note."

But Em *did* stand out where it mattered. She got perfect grades. Won prize after prize for her poetry.

In all our classes, Em was either second to Jamie, or better than Jamie. Everyone else knew not to one-up Jamie. Bad things happened to people who one-upped Jamie. But Em either didn't know or didn't care. She didn't hold back. She was . . . herself.

I admired her. And I loathed her.

In the spring, the Global Youth Leadership Association

announced their annual high school essay-writing contest. The winner would receive $2,500, take a trip to Washington D.C. for a reception and meet-and-greet with the Department of State, and get full tuition to study abroad over the summer.

Jamie and I both applied. Jamie was so sure she was going to win.

But Emily came out on top once again, sweeping the grand prize. Jamie and I were honorable mentions. Which meant we got nothing.

This outcome shocked everyone, Jamie most of all. Nobody denied Jamie anything. What Jamie wanted, Jamie got. It was a law of the universe.

But the laws had changed, now.

"I should have won," Jamie hissed when we found out the results. "There's no way Em can be the winner. There must be some mistake."

"She wrote a better essay, Jamie."

Jamie whirled on me. "It doesn't matter who wrote the better essay. I had Daddy send the judges a bribe. They were supposed to choose me!"

I wasn't surprised to learn about Jamie's admittance. It was just like her. Besides, Jamie hadn't even taken the time to notice I was down about losing to Emily, too.

Emily was a better writer than Jamie. Emily was a better writer than me.

My mother once told me that I had to be the best.

And I had failed.

Em wasn't one of the girls whose life Jamie could ruin by revealing their secrets. She didn't seem to *have* secrets.

I knew there would be trouble when Jamie started being nice to her, really nice to her. Inviting her out to dinners. Taking her shopping. It scared me, too. Scared me because I thought Jamie was replacing me.

Until Jamie took me aside one gloomy spring afternoon, and whispered, "I found out Emily's weakness."

"You did?"

"It's my cousin. It's Peter. She told me she has a crush on him. Ooooh, this makes everything *much* easier." Jamie spoke with a gleam in her eye, with the delight of a child who'd discovered an unopened bag of candy.

"Peter? She likes him?" I tried my best to sound casual, but speaking Peter's name aloud was like a shard to my heart. We'd ended things a week ago. With him going off to Stanford after the summer, and me stuck at Sinclair Prep for another three years, it only made sense. Still didn't make it any easier.

"Yes." Jamie rolled her eyes. "It's that stupid violin. Girls will fall over themselves to hear Peter play that thing. Anyway—I told Em Peter likes her back too, even though he doesn't."

My heart lurched, and then settled in relief after hearing Peter didn't like Em. "Wait, why would you do that?" And then, with a growing sense of horror, I gasped. "No."

"Yes. I'm going to use Em's little crush to humiliate her so badly that she never dares to show her stupid face around here again." A vicious sneer curled Jamie's lips. "I've set it all up. Em trusts me, now. Thinks I'm her friend. I told Em the Golden Trio wants to meet her tonight, because Peter wants to confess his feelings in person. But he's not going to, obviously. He's going to shoot her down—rip her to pieces. I'm going to catch *everything* on camera." Then she giggled, her eyes bulging, and the giggle turned into a laugh.

I forced a halfhearted chuckle, but even that small action made me feel sick inside. Another one. Another life Jamie was about to ruin. How many more times did I have to stand by and watch?

"And you're coming tonight to see the show. Krystal, Alexander, Akil—they're all coming too."

My stomach sunk. I struggled to make up with some excuse, any excuse, not to be there. "Oh, I . . ."

"You're coming, Nancy. All of you are." Jamie's tone was final. A warning that if we didn't obey, there would be consequences. "Quarter to nine tonight, at the Richard Sinclair statue. I told Em to meet Peter and them at nine. That gives us plenty of time to figure out a spot to hide. Remember—eight forty-five."

I showed up at eight forty-five on the dot. Akil was already there, standing next to Richard Sinclair's statue, looking like he'd rather be anywhere else. Jamie, on the other side, smiling, like we were about to do something fun, like there was nowhere else she'd rather be.

"We're only waiting on Krystal and Alexander now. They're both running a little late. Stuck in traffic." Jamie frowned at her phone, as though it had offended her.

"So what's the plan again?" Akil said, breaking the thick silence.

Jamie's eyes scanned the grounds around us. "We can all hide . . . there." She pointed at the large clump of bushes near the front steps. "Let's get into position and wait for Em to show up in ten min—"

"Why are you waiting for me to show up?"

We whirled around at the sharp voice. Em, hands on her hips. Em, glaring, big red splotches on her cheeks.

"Em!" Jamie jumped, and quickly recovered herself. She smoothed her uniform skirt and forced a calm, cold smile. "What are you doing here? I thought I told you Peter said he'd meet you at nine—"

"Yeah, and I didn't believe you. I thought something was fishy. I'm not stupid, Jamie." Em's eyes grew shiny with defiance. And maybe sadness. "I had a feeling you weren't being sincere with me, even though I wished I was wrong. That stuff about meeting the Golden Trio was all made up, right?"

Jamie dropped her smile. Dropped all pretense. Through gritted teeth, she said, "Peter's coming. He'll be here any minute now, him and his friends."

"Yeah, right." Em snorted. "What is this really about, Jamie? Tell the truth. For once."

"How dare you—"

"Is this about me winning the essay contest?"

Jamie's shrieks of rage erupted through the air. "That grand prize should have been mine!"

Em, red-faced and apparently a lot braver than we'd known, shouted, "Do you seriously think you own *everything*? News flash—the judges chose me as the winner, not you. Maybe because, unlike you, *I* have talent, and don't force my way into winning!" Though she was shouting, she backed away as Jamie advanced on her. Then, there was nowhere to go; Em had backed up in front of the statue of Richard Sinclair.

Akil and I exchanged panicked looks. "This is getting bad, really bad," he whimpered.

If Krystal and Alexander were here, too, maybe we could've stopped Jamie. But not with just the two of us. Not when Jamie got out of control like this.

I liked Jamie when she was being nice. But that wasn't the real reason why we were friends. I was terrified of her when she *wasn't* being nice—and that was why we remained friends.

I knew we should stop Jamie. But still there was a tiny, sick, twisted part of me that wanted to see this play out. After all, Em had been beating *me* at all those tests and contests, too. Someone should put her in her place. Yell at her for a bit.

"Nancy! Get over here," Jamie ordered.

My stomach flipped. I didn't want to get involved. But I didn't want to disobey Jamie. Like I said—bad things happened when Jamie didn't get her way.

Shooting Akil a terrified look, I slunk over.

"Let's teach Em a lesson," Jamie hissed in my ear. When I stared at her, the meaning of her words not fully sinking in, she added, "Push her down. Make her remember this lesson permanently."

Em stood right there, her tall, slightly chubby frame shaking. She held her chin up high and stepped toward me. "You always do whatever she says, Nancy, but don't really want to. You know that. Come on. You're stronger than this."

I stumbled back. Was I being weak for always follow-ing along with Jamie's wishes? No. No, I was doing what I needed to do to stay in Jamie's graces, to climb my way to the top.

And in that moment, seeing the determination in Em's eyes, anger consumed me. How dare Em defy the social hierarchy at Sinclair Prep? The rest of us fought tooth and nail for our grades and social standing. Did she really think she could swoop in and worm her way above Jamie, above me, with such infuriating ease?

Shouting came as though from a distance.

"S-Someone's coming!" Akil stammered. "Guys—let's get out of here."

I barely heard him. Jamie and I were going to teach Em a lesson that I'd had to learn over and over again. Nothing in life was easy. Everything came with a staggering price. Tonight, it was her turn to pay.

I nodded at Jamie. Together, we shoved Em back.

And then it went wrong. I must've misjudged my own strength. Or maybe Jamie was stronger than I'd thought.

Em fell backward, screaming, into the stone statue.

A thick, wet crack, like a watermelon splitting on a cutting board.

Em's body, collapsing against the statue. Eyes closed. Unmoving.

And the blood. Blood ran from the back of Em's head onto the ground. Blood everywhere, on Em and on Richard Sin-clair's statue.

"Holy fuck. Holy *fuck*," Akil was shouting over and over. Then he turned around and retched.

Horrified yelling. More retching. Someone pushing me sideways, knocking me to the cold grass.

"Out of the way!" The figure loped over and pressed his head against Em's chest, and I dimly registered that it was Richard. Behind him, the shocked faces of Peter and David. And behind them, Krystal and Alexander, gazing at us in horror.

"H-How is she?" stammered David.

"She's not breathing." Then Richard performed CPR on Em, over and over again, but nothing he did seemed to work.

"I barely touched her," Jamie screamed for all to hear. "You saw, didn't you? Right, Akil?" She shook his shoulders, but he didn't reply. His face had gone bone-white with shock. "She fell on her own! It wasn't me!"

"It wasn't me," I echoed. "It wasn't."

My sobs mixed with Jamie's shrieks mixed with the wails of an ambulance, and maybe in a minute, maybe in a year, help finally came for Em. But by then, it was too late.

The funeral for Emily Yang was held a week after the freshman class returned to the Upper West Side. *A horrible accident*, we were all told. Emily had slipped in the grass and cracked her head on the stone statue.

I'd expected my role in this accident to have ruined my life. I'd expected to go to juvenile detention.

Instead, Principal Bates hushed up what happened. Emily Yang came from a no-name family. Better to destroy the Yangs than the Ruans, who practically had this school in their back pocket. And if Jamie wasn't going to be blamed, then neither would I, the person who'd helped her, who'd helped her kill Emily Yang.

So it went. So long as we held our silence—swallowed this burning secret back into the pits of our stomachs—we had our whole lives ahead of us.

After the funeral, the Yangs moved back to China. Their family business had been struggling for a while. But the real reason for the move, people said, was that they couldn't bear the loss of their daughter, their pride and joy.

With that, Emily Yang was gone. But the memory of Em haunted every one of us. Glued our friend circle together with the horrible, horrible guilt over what had actually happened— what we'd done to her. What *I'd* done to her.

I never imagined Em would come back to haunt us for real.

CONFESSION TWENTY-FOUR

Ngl I've been to funerals that were more fun than this
prom —Anon

* * * * *

I stared at Louisa/Em. Putting together the pieces. "You . . . this isn't possible. But—but you're—you're supposed to be—"

"—Emily," she finished, drawing closer. Gaze never leaving mine. "Say my name."

"E-Emily," I obeyed. "You—You didn't die that day."

"Obviously." Blood-red lips curling into a sneer. "Did you think I was a ghost?"

"So then that funeral . . . *your* funeral . . . was fake?"

"My family wanted to keep our affairs private. They wanted to protect me. Thought it was best if we got far, far away . . . and let everyone think I was dead."

"You don't—you don't look anything like you did before."

The Emily Yang from my memories had been chubby, and had a squashed nose and hooded eyes, for which Jamie had teased her mercilessly. Her hair had been dark brown. She looked nothing like Louisa, who was tall and slim, with a perfectly shaped nose, double-lid eyes, and lighter brown hair.

"I dyed my hair. I lost weight, too—I call it the revenge diet," Em explained. "Then I got plastic surgery when I visited South Korea. Money can be so powerful. Not that you would know about having money." She smiled, and it was a cruel smile, a familiar smile. My smile. Jamie's smile.

"How did you orchestrate all this?" I whispered.

"I had my butler do a lot of the dirty work." Em shrugged, and I remembered the tall, brown-haired man who'd been associated with the Proctor. "The rest wasn't that hard to set up. For a bunch of academic geniuses, you and Krystal and Akil and Alexander sure can be morons sometimes."

I gulped. "What are you going to do to me? I'll—I'll scream."

Em stepped toward me and grabbed my wrist. "You guys tried to bury me two years ago. I came back to return the favor."

"What happened was an accident. Nobody meant to—"

"An *accident*? Do you honestly expect me to believe that?" Em laughed. Though I tried in vain to twist away, her grip around my wrist tightened. The pressure burned my skin, the pain building and building. I gritted my teeth. "I knew you guys—especially Jamie—were threatened by me. If I'd stayed at Sinclair Prep, *I* would've become the top student in our grade. That's why you wanted me dead."

"Nobody wanted you dead," I protested.

"Then why did Jamie and you push me into the statue?" Em's eyes filled with angry tears. That anguish on her face was all too familiar. It was an anguish I knew like the back of my hand—an anguish buried within *me*. "Admit it. You wanted me gone because you were scared of me." Em's tears dripped down her cheeks. "You, and the rest of Jamie's posse, never saw me as a friend."

"Jamie . . . Jamie was the one who—"

"You could have stopped Jamie that night. And instead you helped her."

Em had never done anything to us. And we'd almost killed her.

"I . . . we . . . were scared. We didn't know what to do." The explanation was pathetic even to my ears.

The door banged open behind me. Em's eyes darted toward the sound, and I took the chance to try to wiggle out of her grasp, but she only tightened her death hold on my wrist. "Good. Everyone's here now."

"Nancy!" I heard multiple voices yell in unison.

My stomach sunk. Even before I turned around, I knew what I would see: Alexander, Akil, and Krystal racing down the steps toward me.

"You guys shouldn't have come," I said, ignoring the swell of relief in my chest. "I told you not to come. H-How did you even find us?"

"Peter found me and told me you came this way." Even now, resentment in Alexander's face as he spoke Peter's name. "He said he saw you coming out of the ballroom, saying you didn't look . . . like yourself . . . and then I made the connection, and—"

Alexander stopped, horror dawning over his face as he took in the scene before him. I could practically see the wheels turning in everyone's heads.

"What . . . Louisa? What're you doing?" spluttered Akil, looking bemused.

"Get away from Nancy," snapped Alexander and Peter at once.

"S-So . . . Louisa," Akil said, "you're . . . the Proctor?"

"Her name isn't really Louisa," I said. "It's Emily Yang."

"That's not possible," cried Krystal. "Emily Yang is dead."

A catlike, triumphant smile twisted Em's face. "That's what my family wanted everyone to believe, so I could start over when I returned to the States after getting plastic surgery and a new life. Made it easier to get revenge, too, of course."

"H-How did you know all our secrets?" Alexander demanded.

"Jamie knew everything—well, except the fact that I was Em. After you all abandoned her and I became her closest friend, she sold you out," Em said with a nasty grin. "Showed me photos of your troubled past"—her eyes landed on Krystal, whose jaw clenched—"showed me what she'd been dealing you"—Akil stiffened—"told me all about your convict brother"—Alexander's fists clenched—"and couldn't *resist* telling me about a certain student-teacher scandal."

Em's eyes flicked over to Peter and then burned into mine, but I forced myself not to flinch or look away.

"Jamie couldn't stand that I was better than her, so she got you all to team up against me. I may have been forced to fake my own funeral, and I may have lost *everything*, but I knew my family would be back one day. So I bided my time while my parents slowly rebuilt their fortune. I re-created myself and planned my revenge."

"Okay, what you're saying is . . . really wild," Alexander said, holding his hands up.

Em cut her glare at him. "*You* don't talk to me. Do you know how frustrating it was to always be so fake? To tiptoe around Jamie like I was walking on eggshells, so I didn't upset her and she'd ruin my life? How is it fair that my parents would punish me for *not* being the best, and when I finally became the best, my peers punished me instead?"

"Stop playing the victim here," Krystal spat.

Shame rose within me. If I could go back in time and change what had happened, there was no doubt in my mind that I'd do that. I'd never shove Em into the statue. I'd never even let Jamie bully Em. I'd never let Jamie have her way so easily again.

"Em . . . I know this won't change anything, but . . . I'm so sorry," I whispered. "I know Jamie would be sorry, too."

"You're not sorry. None of you have ever been sorry. Otherwise, you wouldn't have done what you did to Jamie Ruan when the Ruans fell from grace." Em's voice was cold. Unfeeling.

There's that saying—the higher you fly, the harder you fall. The Ruans didn't *fall* from grace, really. They plummeted. They shattered.

"Maybe we're not the best people, but you . . . you *killed* someone, Em," Alexander said in a harsh voice. "You killed Jamie and tried to pin it on us."

Krystal was edging her phone out of her pocket, but Em raised something she'd been clenching in her hands. A stick lighter. "If you call the cops—if you call *anyone*—you're done for. I'll light the grass on fire. I've already coated it with gasoline. Do you think you can outrun fire? Put the phone down, Krystal."

So that explained the vague, sickly sweet odor. The grass beneath my feet, not slippery with dew—slippery with gasoline. My heart thudded, panic clouding my thoughts as I tried to come up with an escape plan. But I couldn't see a way out.

The flame on Em's lighter flickered, casting an orange-yellow glow across her face. The rhythmic sounds of the contraption provided an eerie beat. *Click.* Light on. *Click.* Light off.

Slowly, trembling, Krystal obeyed. "Th-The faculty will be here any moment now," she stammered.

That cruel smile once again. "That's perfect, then. I want to see them. It's been so long, and they've all forgotten Emily Yang. The whole school forgetting made everything so much easier." *Click.* Light. A soft, sad smile on Em's lips. *Click.* Darkness.

"We didn't forget you." Not for lack of trying, though. I'd desperately wanted to erase Em from my memories forever. "We—We had to . . . to move on." Otherwise, the guilt would have consumed us.

Click. Em hissed, "You didn't remember me because you didn't want to remember me. You didn't want to acknowledge what you'd done."

Click, click. Click, click.

"Put the lighter down, Louisa—Emily." Krystal's voice might have seemed calm to anyone who didn't know her, but the slightly higher pitch told me she was scared. "Whatever you want to discuss, we can do without that lighter."

Click. The light was back on, the flame close enough to my face that I jumped back in shock, freeing my wrist from her grasp.

Em staring at us, but not really seeing us.

Out of the corner of my eye, I spotted Akil slowly edging back toward the school, taking advantage of the fact that Emily had taken her eyes off him. Moving seamlessly, wordlessly, Alexander shifted his profile to block Akil out of sight. Akil disappeared around the corner. He was taking the long way around, out of Em's field of vision.

"For all her book smarts, Jamie was so easy to trick in the end. I guess she was so desperate for a friend—a *real* friend, or so she thought. That idiot told me everything, including all of your dirty little secrets." And she was talking more to herself than to us now, musing, face illuminated by the glow of the campus lights. "Jamie was sick. *Really* sick. And instead of helping her, you abandoned her. You're the worst kind of people." She spat the words with a savage satisfaction. "So I thought, rather than getting rid of only Jamie, it'd be best to get rid of the rest of you, too."

"B-But I still don't get one thing." All I could think was that I had to keep talking, keep Em talking, keep her attention on me. Draw out as much time as possible so Akil could get help. "Why would you wait so long to kill Jamie?"

"What fun would it be to just end Jamie's life? Stretching out her suffering to the point of making her want to commit suicide—now, that's a much more suitable ending for her. Plus, I wanted to take my time and ruin *all* of you. First, reveal your secrets and destroy your reputations. Next, end your lives—for good."

"You're sick," Krystal said. "Really, really sick."

Jamie had believed "Louisa" to be one of her only friends in the aftermath of everything that had happened. And all along, "Louisa" had counted on Jamie breaking.

"I might be the Proctor, but I didn't kill Jamie. Jamie killed herself."

"You're lying." Alexander's voice shook, as though he weren't as certain as he tried to seem. "Jamie wouldn't have killed herself. She had everything."

"She had everything, and that's exactly why she killed herself. There's a time limit for one person having so much, you know. Nobody can stay on top forever. And once you've tasted the air at the top—you never want to be away from the throne again. I know. I was there once, too."

A soft laugh. A cruel laugh.

"You're not wrong, though, Alexander. Jamie didn't want to go at the very end. But that's why I was there. To *assist*. I knew she was weakened, mentally and physically. Nobody believed she might have mental health issues, not her parents, not her teachers, not her so-called *friends*, and least of all herself. It was easy to finish the job."

I opened my mouth, then closed it. Words failed me.

Em whirled around and asked sharply, "Where's Akil?"

Time. Time was up once again.

"Stop!" Alexander dove toward Em, but she ducked, then kicked him in the stomach. "Oof!"

Click.

"Stay back," Em warned, holding up the stick lighter. The flame danced in her eyes. Those eyes, burning. Those eyes, black coals, licked with the flame of a long-burning fire. "I'm leaving this shitty life for a better one, and you're all coming with me. Consider it a gesture of mercy."

Run, I urged my feet. Horror rooted me to the spot. This fear, electrifying and all-consuming—had Jamie felt it, too, in her last moments?

Em hissed, a prayer, an oath of revenge: "*In inceptum finis est.*"

And she dropped the burning lighter to the ground.

CONFESSION TWENTY-FIVE

Um . . . is it just me or does anyone else at prom smell
smoke??? —Anon

*****

"No!" I lunged forward to grab the lighter out of the air. If I
could reach it before the flame lit the grass, everything would
be okay.

Unfortunately, Alexander had the same idea. My fingers
collided with his hand. The lighter fell through both of our
grasps. A spark, flickering to life. There—out of the dark. Mes-
merizing. Beautiful.

The gasoline-soaked grass burst into flames.

Flames, blazing. Heat, searing. Screaming. The ancient
school grounds, and all its ghosts, screaming.

Had to move my feet. Had to tear my gaze away from the
glorious sight.

Had to get out—now.

I turned to run, but Em grabbed my hand and tried to drag me back, back toward her and the statue of Richard Sinclair.

"Nancy!" Someone grabbed my hand and yanked me away from Em, toward the school door. It was Alexander.

"But Em—!"

"Hold your breath and *run!*"

Krystal, who'd sprinted ahead, got to the door first. Burning, my lungs. Burning, my legs. Burning, everywhere. And the exit rose in front of me, and so did the flames.

My feet stumbled at the bottom step, and I fell, Alexander's hand slipping out of mine.

The flames spread quickly. Too quickly. My mind grew foggy with panic and lack of breath. I turned around—to see Em's crumpled figure. Crumpled in front of the statue, like two years ago.

Coughing and spluttering, my eyes watery from the force of the fire, I reached for Alexander's hand. The heat threatened to smother me. Pain shot over my body. I held in a scream. Flames licked at my skin, leaving what I knew would turn into ugly scorch marks—even if I survived this.

I *would* survive this. I couldn't die yet. I'd barely begun living.

Faces flashed before my eyes. Mama. Baba. There were so many words left unsaid between all of us. I couldn't die without getting them off my chest. Without hearing the words I deserved from them both.

The air in my lungs had run out. The flames were too high, too fast, too deadly.

Hands reached for me, tugging me away from the brightness

of the fire into a different kind of light. Maybe I'd already died and was crossing over into whatever awaited me next.

"Chief, we've got two more here!" someone yelled, his voice fuzzy and far away. I thought I could see the blurred forms of faculty and firefighters around me.

In the distance, flames licking the sky. Dancing around the stone statue of Richard Sinclair, that stone hand still pointing at the horizon, pointing at something none of us could see.

Burn it. Burn down that statue and this school and everything along with it.

I slumped sideways. The world faded to black.

————

I dreamed that Mama and Baba lived together again. Dreamed I'd gotten into Harvard, and my parents were so overjoyed that they bought me my own penthouse, as fancy and huge as Jamie's.

That was how I knew it was a dream. I never would get into Harvard. Baba would never return to the States no matter how much Mama believed he would, no matter how hard I worked. And my parents would never be able to afford such a nice place.

When I woke up, I was lying in a white room, tucked into clean sheets. It took my groggy brain a few moments to realize that it was a hospital. Then another few moments to process another image—Mama, sitting right next to my bed, fast asleep.

Mama wore her black restaurant hat and uniform. She'd been here for a while, judging from her unconscious state.

"Mama?" I said groggily.

Mama's eyes flew open. She began sobbing. She leaned over and clasped my hand into hers, as if making sure I was real.

271

"Nurse!" Mama yelled. The sound of rapid footsteps answered.

"Where am I?" I groaned as pain traveled up and down my skin. I looked down to find that my arms and legs had been wrapped in stiff bandages. "What . . . happened?"

"You're at the hospital." Mama's tear-filled eyes searched my face. "You . . . were in a fire at the school. Some firefighters rescued you."

I remembered now. I thought I could still feel their hands on me, pulling me to safety.

"The police told me . . . told me it was started by one of your classmates."

At my mother's words, the blurriest of memories returned. The statue. The lighter. Em, waiting for us in the dark.

And the fire. The smoke that choked me. The flames that burned me.

I paused before I could explore the memory further and changed the subject. I wasn't ready to go there yet. "What happened to the others?" My voice was croaky and hoarse from disuse. "Alexander? Krystal? Akil? Peter?" I paused. "Emily?"

"Your friends are alive," Mama said, but her eyes didn't meet mine. "They were taken to the hospital, too. One of your friends called the police and fire department, so they were able to get to you quickly. But . . . there was one . . . who they said . . ." Mama hiccuped, her lip trembling. "They said . . . she didn't make it out."

Emily.

As much as I was horrified by what Em had tried to do to us, I couldn't feel angry at her. Only sad. Frustrated. Upset.

Em had told us she wanted to go, like Jamie had. Yet I couldn't erase the image of how she'd looked right after she'd dropped the lighter, when she'd caught on fire.

That hadn't been the face of someone determined and willing to die. That had been the face of a young, scared girl, one who didn't really know what she wanted, and now would never know.

My chest filled with sadness and grief. Em was dead. And there was nothing I could say or do to bring her back.

A nurse entered the room. "You were very lucky," she said as she examined my skin. "Your wounds are relatively minor, and these burns should heal up within a few weeks."

"What about the others?"

"You were all very lucky," the nurse clarified. "The police arrived quickly. That was some fast thinking on your part to call them so soon."

After running a lot of tests and forcing mountains of paperwork onto my poor mother, the staff released me—on the condition that I took care of my burns according to the doctor's detailed instructions, and came in for follow-up appointments with a burn specialist. She recommended therapy appointments for trauma, too, and insisted I "take it easy" for the next three weeks.

I was pretty sure I didn't know the meaning of "take it easy." But at least physically, I could do that.

Unfortunately, there was no doctor to release me from Mama's imprisonment.

"I'm glad you're going to be okay," Mama told me as soon as we got home. She swallowed hard and brushed a strand of my hair behind my ear. "But you can't do anything like that again. Do you understand, Nancy?"

"I know. I should focus on my studies."

"That's not what I was talking about. I can't bear to lose you, my bǎo bèi." Precious child, a term Mama hadn't used to refer to me in years. She squeezed my hand, her shoulders shaking, the tears flowing forth freely, unabashedly. "You're all I have left. Baba couldn't stand to lose you, either."

"Mama . . ." Tears stung my eyes. I couldn't remember the last time my mother had looked at me with so much fragile emotion in her face. Those eyes that told me I was a real, living, breathing human, with thoughts and dreams of my own, precious to both my mother—and my father, wherever he may be.

"But you are grounded for life," my mother added.

"Grounded *for life*?" I repeated in disbelief. "Since when did we turn into a white family?"

Mama glared at me. I thought I'd crossed a line. But then, amazingly enough, she grinned. "I'm becoming more American by the day, aren't I? Your father . . . he might not recognize me, the day he returns. If he returns." Then she began to laugh, and I joined in.

Mama held on so tightly to my hand, like it was a lifeline. And knowing she was here with me—for the moment it was enough, I was enough.

MARCH, EIGHTH GRADE

The day I was accepted into Richard Sinclair Preparatory School was one of the best days of my life. I told both my parents over text—separately, because they'd been fighting for some time now, and Mama refused to speak to Baba.

Baba sent me a thumbs-up, which was kind of disappointing. He'd never been good with words in the first place.

I started to type: *Can u come home now?*

But then I paused. Thought hard. Shook my head. Backspaced.

Baba wasn't going to come back to the States just because I'd gotten into Sinclair Prep. He had a new life in China. We'd been separated for so long now with so little contact that we were practically strangers.

Maybe all my hard work had, in the end, been for nothing.

Later that night, Mama returned from work holding a large gift-wrapped box in her hands. "For you," she said.

Mama rarely left the restaurant looking so happy, nor did she give me presents. Carefully, I unwrapped it—and gasped. "A MacBook Pro! But these are so expensive." I'd drooled over this laptop for months, dreaming of saving up enough money to buy it one day.

Mama's cheeks glowed. "Do you like it?"

Like it? I loved it. I hugged the box as though it might vanish the moment I let it go. "How . . . I . . . How could you even afford to buy this? It costs over a thousand dollars."

"It's a present to you for working so hard to get into Sinclair Prep. From your father, too."

My throat thickened. Tears welled up in my eyes. I blinked them back. "From Baba?"

Instead of looking angry as she talked about Baba, Mama seemed . . . neutral. Maybe even a little happy. "He's very proud of you."

"You spoke with Baba?" Hope bloomed in my chest. Maybe my parents weren't fighting any longer, and maybe Baba could come here, and maybe we could be a normal family again.

"It was your father's idea to buy you this laptop. You need the best equipment to attend the best school."

A better gift would've been Baba coming to the States, but I decided not to mention that. "Thank you."

"That computer is a reminder not to be lazy," Mama warned, although she didn't look that stern. "You're going to be a student at the best private high school in the country. The next four years will be very difficult."

"I'll work hard," I promised. "I'm not weak."

I eagerly opened the box, while Mama laughed and took pictures of me on her cell phone.

Tomorrow, everything would go back to normal, my initial euphoria overshadowed by everything else I had to do to make Mama proud.

But that night, for the first time in a long while, even without Baba there, we were like a real family. The happy, perfect American family my parents had sacrificed everything to be.

CONFESSION TWENTY-SIX

Unconfirmed: heard from a friend of a friend that the
Golden Trio is gonna be reunited back in UES soon.
—Anon

*****

EXCLUSIVE: "THE PROCTOR" REVEALED TO BE
SINCLAIR UNVEILED'S OWN LOUISA WU

In a series of interviews, six students reveal their
thoughts on recently deceased classmates Jamie
Ruan and Louisa Wu

By: Isabel Lim and Mark Gowain

Going back to school was agony. These dark brick walls, like a
prison.

I hated these walls. Closing in, suffocating me. Hated that I had another year of being stuck in this place.

I hated that even though I hated Sinclair Prep so much, I'd still spend the next year of my life clawing to the top of the class, doing everything I could to get into the best university possible.

The school courtyard burned down, but the firefighters had managed to stop the fire before it reached the buildings, so school was still in full swing. The statue of Richard Sinclair survived, with minimal smoke and heat damage.

The only good thing was that our newspaper club was making a comeback from the brink of irrelevance. On Wednesday, they couldn't distribute the latest issue of *Sinclair Unveiled* fast enough. The students had never been so interested in the school newspaper.

Even better, I could breathe a sigh of relief. Our names were cleared now. For good.

But Jamie and Emily were still dead, and their families would never get their daughters back, and that would never change.

A week after everything that had happened during prom, Sinclair Prep was still all over the news. And not for sending a record number of seniors—fifty—off to Ivy League colleges. Not a day, or even an hour, went by without whispers of Jamie's and Emily's names.

On the outside, Sinclair Prep students and faculty could give the appearance that nothing out of the ordinary had happened. Emily's family wasn't punished for her crimes. In fact, many of their friends were defending Emily, saying she couldn't have possibly been the one who'd killed Jamie.

But something inside the elite college prep school had changed. I could feel it in the air. On the seniors' last day of school on Thursday, all the students were ushered into the huge auditorium for an assembly about mental health awareness. The school board brought on more educators and experts to work on providing counseling services for students who might need them.

It was a start. But I wasn't naïve enough to believe it was going to solve the problem.

The problem started at home. It started with the parents who always pushed for more, more, more. Why were they never satisfied?

The problem lay with this school, with all these institutions. Walls too high to climb, doors shut to all except the most privileged. Lies about not seeing color. Lies about merit-based education, about hard work translating into success.

These ancient walls, taking from us. Stealing our money and our happiness. Stripping us of who we were as they watched us become undone, watched us unwind into nothing. Taking and taking until there was nothing left to give.

Jamie's story went viral. Principal Bates's best efforts to keep student information classified were no match for social media. I read through heated Reddit threads and watched YouTube discussions. There was some push for reform of the education system, but still too many who refused to believe there could be any real, deadly repercussions for mental health.

Too many who still called Jamie—called us—weak.

———

Flames leapt all around me, scorching my hair and clothes and skin. Scorching away the weakness.

An acrid smell of smoke. Invisible hands, closing over my throat. Choking me. Making me. Undoing me.

Burning flesh. Inhuman screams. Was it Em burning? Jamie? Whoever it was, they were in horrible pain. I was in horrible pain. I had to rescue them, but I couldn't open my eyes. The flames suffocated me.

Someone's hands, pressing the life out of me. Jamie. No—Em.

No—Peter.

Everybody was burning.

Nobody was burning, except me.

". . . wake up, Nancy! Le-Le! *Please!*"

I woke, convinced I was on fire, convinced the world was burning.

Mama was shaking me, sobbing, tears rolling down her cheeks. It took me several moments, as my heart hammered madly in my chest, for me to remember where I was: safe in my warm, soft sheets.

"I—I had a nightmare again," I said unnecessarily.

Mama's trembling hands grasped mine. "Was it the same one? The one you've had a few times since . . . ?" Her voice trailed off, letting me fill in the blanks. *Since the fire. Since that girl died.*

"Don't worry about me, Mama. It was a dream. And I'm going to therapy now, remember? Soon, all of this will be in the past." I flashed my mother a smile, which she didn't return. "Wait," I said as I glanced at my bedside clock. "It's already ten. Shouldn't you be at work?"

"I scheduled time off," Mama explained. "It's not good for you if I'm away all the time."

"I can manage by myself—"

"Rest today, okay?" My mother ran her weathered, calloused hand through my hair. "I'm making scallion pancakes. You love scallion pancakes. Get up and eat them whenever you're ready. Don't push yourself too hard, okay, Le-Le?"

Don't push yourself too hard. The permission I'd waited for, my whole life. A long-held sigh, escaping from my lips. Muscles, relaxing. I nodded. "Okay."

An hour later, when I finally couldn't stand the taste of my own breath, I climbed out of bed and threw on my most comfortable old T-shirt. The air filled with the smell of something sizzling. Something that smelled tasty. My mouth watered.

I poked my head into the kitchen. My mother hummed as she attended to the frying pan. I recognized the tune, although I hadn't heard it in many, many years. It was Teresa Teng's "Yuè Liàng Dài Biǎo Wǒ De Xīn," a Mandarin song from the seventies. A song Mama and Baba used to dance to when I was much younger.

"Ah, you're finally up. Feeling better?" Mama said. I nodded and yawned. She gestured toward the kitchen table, from where the tantalizing smell of onions and something savory wafted toward my nose. "Sit and eat your scallion pancakes."

I obeyed. As I sat at the table, I watched the TV in the living room.

". . . amid mixed reactions from the public, the court has made a controversial decision: Jeremy Ruan, former VP of

Matsumoto Technology Corporation, is to be released from his prison sentence in two weeks' time. Ruan was charged with crimes of embezzlement earlier this year . . ."

"What's wrong?" Mama's voice sounded far away.

I turned as my mother came to the table and placed a plate with a pancake slice in front of me. But I'd lost my appetite now. "Jamie's father. He's already being released."

Mama sighed. "When you have that much money and influence, the world is your oyster."

"But . . ." Jamie's father was a criminal. Worse, he'd verbally abused his wife and daughter. "He's really going to walk free?"

It shouldn't have surprised me. And yet still it did. The injustice of it all.

"Life isn't fair. Eat your pancake before it gets cold."

Obediently, I dug into the pancake. An explosion of savory tastes entered my mouth when I bit into it. It was good enough to momentarily distract me from the news of Mr. Ruan's release. "This is really good, Mama."

My mother finished chewing and gave me a pointed look. "It's almost as though I manage a restaurant, or something."

"Are you picking up *sarcasm*?" This was it. Sarcasm. The ultimate proof that my mother was truly getting acclimated to the American way.

Mama laughed. I smiled, but only for a moment. It was hard to smile knowing that Mr. Ruan, an embezzler and someone who'd played a role in Jamie's downfall, would soon be free.

After we finished breakfast, I cleaned the dishes. Mama

left for a few minutes, and when she came back to the kitchen, she was holding some envelopes and a small package.

"For you," my mother said, handing me the flat, rectangular package.

I didn't remember ordering anything. I ripped it open.

And there it was. A pink, worn-down journal. My Diss Diary. There was no return address on the package, but I knew it came from Em.

My hands shook as I picked up the journal. I flipped through it from cover to cover. Aside from the entry Em had ripped out to display on the PowerPoint at honors night, she hadn't tampered with anything. These words, this secret, still mine.

I paused, my fingers tracing the back cover. Em had left one last, final message for me.

If you're wondering how I got this journal, Jamie knew about it all along. She took it the last time she was at your place and gave it to me at the end.

This answer, at last. And this message, along with the return of my journal, was the proof that Em must have known, or guessed, that I might survive prom night. I didn't know what to do with that knowledge. Didn't want to look at the journal that had caused me so much grief.

I shoved it into a drawer, out of sight, and checked my phone. I'd missed a bazillion messages from Krystal, Akil, Alexander, and—

My heart clenched at the name. *Peter.*

As much as I knew I should put Peter and everything we had, or never had, behind me, a small part of me had expected this. Had wanted this. After all, why else would he crop up in my nightmares? We had unfinished business, Peter and I.

Peter: *I know ur upset with me and probably don't want to talk to me again. I get it. The way I handled things was bad. I wanted to check in with you and make sure ur ok tho. I've been really worried since that fire at prom. Shit's been crazy. I've been thinking a lot, and I've decided to resign from teaching at the school. Anyway . . . message me when ur feeling up to it. I wanna know ur ok.*

I stared and stared and stared at the words on my phone screen. The text, shaking. My hands were shaking.

Peter. Peter, and the fire. Both so lovely from a distance. Lovelier as you drew closer and closer. Lovely until you strayed too close, until the flames consumed you.

Enough. Enough of Peter, enough of our mutual destruction. I focused my attention on Alexander's text instead.

Alexander: *Hey, wanted to make sure you're doing all right after what happened*
Nancy: *I'm . . . surviving*
Alexander: *I feel that*
Nancy: *Hey are you free today? I'm around if you wanna chill*

Alexander: *Yeah I don't have to go in to work today, so I'm down to clown*

Nancy: *Yaaaaay* ☺ *How about we meet at the Washington Square Park fountain and go get ice cream or something?*

Alexander: *Sure, meet at 3?*

Nancy: 👍

Alexander: *Quick question tho . . . is this a date?*

Nancy: *Yeah, I guess it is* ☺

Alexander: *Cool, just checking*

A glance at the time showed me it was already almost two. Washington Square Park was about twenty minutes away by train, so I didn't have much time to plan a date outfit. Probably shouldn't have suggested this so last minute, but oh well.

I threw on a simple baby blue sundress from H&M and swiped on a quick coat of lip gloss. When I went to tell Mama I was leaving, I found her fast asleep on the couch. Sleep smoothed the weary lines on her face, making her appear years younger. Tiptoeing around, I quickly wrote Mama a note telling her where I'd gone and that I'd be back in time for dinner.

Then, I headed out to meet Alexander.

CONFESSION TWENTY-SEVEN

Spotted: N.L. and A.L. on a date at Washington Square
Park. Seems like N.L. is more concerned about lip
gloss application than college applications . . . first that
thing with P.S., now she's moving on to A.L.

N.L. and A.L. sitting in a tree, aren't they moving too
quickly? —Anon

* * * * *

After circling the fountain twice, trying to spot Alexander
through the crowds of NYU students and families, I finally
saw him standing in front of one of the benches, waving at me.

I smiled for the first time in what felt like days. Alexander
wasn't wearing anything fancy, just a plain black T-shirt and
blue jeans, which helped me relax. The whole train ride here,
I'd been more nervous than I'd been sitting through any of my
exams.

It was silly. This was Alexander. We'd hung out plenty of times before, studying or working.

"Hey," I said.

We stared at each other for a moment, and then both looked away at the same time.

"So . . . wanna go get that ice cream?" Alexander asked.

"Oh, y-yeah!" Duh. I'd suggested it, and somehow I'd forgotten. "Let's do that. It's crowded today, isn't it?"

"It's always pretty crowded."

"Yeah, that's true . . ."

"Man, I can't remember the last time I had a full day off to relax," Alexander said wistfully, staring up at the sky. I raised my head, too, and noted that it was impossibly blue, the perfect blue. "Like, what do I do with myself outside of studying and working?"

"And catching killers," I added. "Sorry, too soon?"

Alexander snorted. "Let me add that to my resume when I get home. 'Strengths include studying, working, and catching killers.'"

"Harvard would have to be nuts to turn down your applications."

Laughing, we grabbed some ice cream from a place called Van Lee Ice Cream. When I pulled out my wallet to pay for my chocolate ice cream, Alexander smoothly reached over the counter to put his credit card in front of mine. "We're paying for ours together."

"Oh, wait—I couldn't—"

"I'm not letting you pay on the first date, Nancy."

My pulse raced. "Thank you," I remembered to say, smiling down at my shoes.

"You're welcome."

Once we'd left, ice cream cones in hand, I glanced at Alexander out of the corner of my eye. He was smiling, also slightly red in the face, looking pleased with himself.

"Smooth, Alexander Lin. Very smooth," I said.

"Thanks. I've been practicing—I mean, no, not *practicing*, that'd be weird—I mean—ahhh, so much for smooth." He ruffled the back of his messy black hair, his expression now turning sheepish.

"Add that to the resume, too. 'Strengths include studying, working, catching killers, and being smooth.'" That earned a laugh from Alexander, which made me smile.

We walked around for a bit. The sun, beaming down on us. Here, the world at peace. All the stress, all the drama, all the events of the past few weeks simply melted away along with our ice cream.

Soon, though, I couldn't ignore the constant vibrating of my phone in my pocket. As soon as there was a lull in our conversation, I drew it out and glanced at the string of texts I'd received.

Krystal: *Ummm someone posted about you and Alexander on Tip Tap . . . did you forget to tell me that you guys are on a date?!?!*

Krystal: *Nancy WHERE ARE YOU*

Krystal: *WHY DID I HAVE TO LEARN FROM A*

STUPID GOSSIP APP THAT SOME OF MY
BEST FRIENDS ARE ON A DATE
Krystal: *Answer your phone!!!*
Krystal: *Unless you and Alexander are making out then
please DO NOT ANSWER YOUR PHONE*
Krystal: *Not to be dramatic, but I am withering away
and my crops are dying. pls promise you'll tell me
everything soon*

"Who's blowing up your phone?" Alexander asked.

"Krystal. Hang on, let me text her back." Smiling and laughing, I composed a reply to Krystal before she did something drastic.

Nancy: *Yeah I'm out with Alexander rn. We're having
fun 😸 Tell you everything later!*

An incoming text notification flashed on my screen, but it wasn't from Krystal.

Peter: *Alexander Lin can't make you truly happy, and I
think you know that.*

My heart hammered in my chest. I whirled around, searching the crowd, looking for that slim, familiar outline. Peter was nowhere to be found, but there were so many people around today that I couldn't say for sure he wasn't hiding in the crowd somewhere.

Or Tip Tap. Maybe someone had snapped a photo of Alexander and me and posted to Tip Tap, and Peter had seen it.

Whatever. It didn't matter. I wasn't going to let that knowledge spoil this moment.

"Let's, um, let's go closer to the fountain," I said to Alexander.

"Oh, sure."

I grabbed his hand and tugged him into the crowd. Now we were surrounded by stoned students and families with small children, but hopefully we could get some privacy from watching eyes.

Alexander Lin can't make you truly happy, and I think you know that.

Alexander, staring at the fountain. Alexander, no longer smiling, a weary expression on his face. I wondered what was on his mind. I wondered if it was Eric.

I dropped my gaze to Peter's text again. I should block his number. But I couldn't bring myself to do it.

Peter couldn't be trusted. He was good with words. Good with toying with emotions. Good with spinning a web of lies, spinning people—spinning *me*—into traps. Ambitious to a fault. Ambitious, and willing to break the rules to get what he wanted.

But a whisper, a whisper in the back of my head.

Isn't that why you liked him in the first place? Aren't you two more alike than you are different?

Alexander didn't have an ounce of destruction in him. Not like me. Not like Peter.

Krystal's words, gnawing at my insides. *And Alexander—well, I hope you're not going to break his heart one day. Like Jamie broke mine.*

"Are you still talking to Peter?"

Alexander's words startled me, and I nearly dropped my phone. Too late, I looked up and realized he'd seen it. Seen the text.

"I . . ."

"Nancy, you can't have everything," Alexander said. And now, the happiness in his face was replaced with bitterness, with frustration. "I like you. You've got to know that by now. And I've been trying, but it's like . . . you never let me in, and you've got this thing with Peter, and I don't get it. I thought you asking me on this date was you *trying*, but . . ." He shrugged. Then his shoulders slumped. "You're still thinking about him. I guess I shouldn't have expected anything else."

I had no response. No response, because he was right.

"So what do you want to do, Nancy? Because I need to know where we stand with each other."

I wanted to tell Alexander I liked him, too. That he was wonderful. That he deserved the world, deserved better than me.

And Alexander—well, I hope you're not going to break his heart one day. Like Jamie broke mine.

If we took the plunge, I was going to hurt him. I'd already hurt him. And Peter— I still had one thing left to do with Peter, something only he could do for me.

After, if Alexander still liked me, maybe something could

happen. But that was selfish of me, and I wouldn't ask him to wait.

"I . . . I think I need time. And I want to stay friends." There. The answer that was hardly an answer, but the only answer I could give.

Alexander closed his eyes and tilted his face toward the sun. "Yeah, I expected this." Shoved his hands into his pockets. Attempted a rueful smile. "I'm gonna need some time, but I'm good with being friends. And Nancy . . . I hope you know what you're doing with Peter." The smile slipped into a look of disappointment, and something darker. A warning. "Trust me when I say he's no saint."

Peter wasn't a saint, but that was exactly what I was counting on. Peter wasn't a saint, but neither was I.

"If you're going to get involved with Peter and his crowd again, you should at least know what they're *really* capable of."

And Alexander leaned in, and he whispered a secret in my ear. The secret that changed everything. The secret that would give me everything.

———

The date ended quickly after that. I watched Alexander leave, taking long strides through the park, disappearing into the crowd. He didn't turn back. It bothered me that he didn't turn back, though I knew I had no right to feel bothered.

I swallowed the painful lump in my throat. I'd made my choice, now. There was no way but forward.

Once more, into the fire.

Once more, but this time I wouldn't be burned.

I reached for my phone and dialed his number.

He picked up instantly. He'd been waiting. "Nancy."

"I hate you."

"You don't mean that."

No, I didn't. I wished I did, but I didn't. Hating Peter would make everything easier. Like hating Jamie would have made life so simple. And so boring.

"Listen up, asshole. Here's how it's going to be." I reveled in speaking this way to Peter, in turning his own words against him. In his silence as he listened on the other end. "You once said that you'd give me everything, and I'm going to take it now. We're going to appeal to the Board of Trustees and erase the suspension from my permanent record, using your family's influence. You *will* make it happen, even if it means telling them the truth—that it was *you* who approached *me*. You owe me that much." I paused. Quiet on the other end, but for Peter's steady breaths. "You're going to meet me, but somewhere public, and *only* to talk about how we're going to strike this thing from my record. Understood?"

A pause. Then: "I'm impressed, Nancy. You've become more interesting than ever. What happened on prom night?"

A small part of me sang at Peter's praise, but I tried my best to squash the feeling. "Peter. Your answer."

"What makes you think I'd be willing to go to the board and say *I* was the one who started everything?"

"Because." And power, a surge of power pulsed through me. My hands, shaking from adrenaline. "Because I know *that* secret about the Golden Trio. And I'll let everyone know about it if you don't cooperate."

This time, the silence stretched. Finally, Peter said, "Tell me when and where to meet you."

I thought fast. "The Green Bottle Coffee near the school, at ten sharp tomorrow morning."

"See you then."

I hung up before Peter could. And then I glanced toward the sky. And I said, "I'm sorry."

Sorry I could not be the good girl Alexander, and my family, and this world wanted me to be. I could not chain myself to the safety of the ground when I knew I was born to fly. Born to burn fast and hot and bright.

One day, Alexander would understand. They would all understand. I would make them understand, make them see me, the real me.

This fire that burned loveliest, right before destroying everything in its path.

––––––––

PLOT TWIST: Looks like A.L. ditched N.L. at the WSP fountain. F in the chat for N.L., boys. But good for A.L. Sometimes you gotta walk away before you get burned . . . —Anon

IN INCEPTUM FINIS EST

ACKNOWLEDGMENTS

Seven years ago, a one-line story pitch entered my mind. An Asian American high school student is found murdered, and her high-achieving friends become the prime suspects. Seven years and many life-changing experiences later, *How We Fall Apart* is now a real book to be found in real bookstores. I never dared to dream that a global publisher would one day take on such an emotionally raw, dark academia thriller with an Asian American main cast. I am so grateful for the many people who have made this day possible.

Thank you to my superhero agent Penny Moore, who has advocated tirelessly on behalf of me and my stories. Thank you for finding the best publishers for my work. I started out writing young adult novels back in 2011, and a decade later in 2021, my first traditionally published young adult title is finally hitting shelves. Publishing YA fiction is a lifelong dream, and I couldn't have done it without you. Thank you from the bottom of my heart, and I look forward to many more proudly Asian YA titles in our future.

Thank you to my acquiring editor Hali Baumstein, who saw the possibilities in a much rougher version of this story, and took a chance on me. Thank you to my brilliant editor Sarah Shumway Liu, for challenging me to make this book so much more than I could've imagined it could be. The work was brutal while we were both going through it, so much of it done during the bulk of a pandemic, but I'm so proud of the finished copy and how much we've achieved together. Thank you for pushing me to make *How We Fall Apart* shine.

Thank you to my wonderful publishing team at Bloomsbury, as well as the editorial freelancers who helped proofread: Donna Mark, Jeanette Levy, Oona Patrick, Michelle Li, Jeff Curry, Nicholas Church, Alexa Higbee, Lily Yengle, Erica Barmash, Faye Bi, Beth Eller, Jasmine Miranda, Alona Fryman, Teresa Sarmiento, Jo Forshaw, and Tom Skipp. You've been so supportive and enthusiastic about these dark, angry teenagers, and I'm very grateful to you all for giving me the chance to write Asian dark academia. From publishing my debut middle-grade fantasy *The Dragon Warrior* to my debut young adult thriller *How We Fall Apart*, you've been in my corner championing my books from the beginning. Words can't express how grateful I am for your support.

Thank you to the book blogging community, everyone from Bookstagrammers to Booktubers, to whom I owe so much. Thank you to the members of the #SinclairStudents street team who shouted about my book from the rooftops, as well as to those who weren't members but showed so much support regardless, including but not limited to: Tiffany (ReadbyTiffany), Lili (UtopiaStateofMind), Alyxandria (AlyxandriaAng), Izzy (BookishlyIzzy), Sam (Never_Ending_Novels), Emmanouella (Em.Booknook), Julia (Julias.Booknook), Aashi (That_Brown_Bibliophile), Abigaëlle (Boohoo.Books), Catherine (CathsBookshelf), Krisha (BookathonBlog), Sofia (The_Technicolour_Bookshelf), Hanna (HannaKimAuthor), Jordan (ReadingWithFaeries), Mike (TheLasagna), Sara (LyricalReads), Anandi (SleepyDoe), Shenwei (TheShenners), Blake (BlaketheBookEater), Tabassum (WhatIrinReads), Rameela (stars.brite), Leticia (BooksWith_Elle), Kajree (Paperbacksandpen), Katie (WhisperingofPages), Divyaa (DivReadsBooks), Karina (AFirePages), Aliya (LiyaReadsYA), Kate (Kates.lit), Rachel (LetMeintheLibrary), Minju (SchreavingThroughPages), Ace (PeachnAce), Juliana (TomesandThoughts), Delphine (DelphReads), Sai (ZanyAnomaly), Chloe (TheElvenWarrior), Sidhant (UpontheBookTower), Isabella (SolaceinReading), Cossette (TeaTimeLit), Rick (NekutheBookLocke), Krupali (MusingofSouls), Daphne (daphne.reads), Charvi (ItsNotJustFiction), Marloes (SubtleBookish), Areli Joy (WhatPollyReads), Katherine (kb._.reads), Maria (MariaHossainBlog), Cody (CodyRoecker), Artie (ArtieCarden), Saynab (SaynabReadsBooks), Eleanor (CosyBookCorner), Kayleen (BookaPlenty), Isabelle (Isabellestonebooks), Mika (ArinasLibrary), Avery (BforBookslut), Sabrina (SabsLibrary), Sagarika (Sagarific), Lay (BookshelfSoliloquies), Francesca (AHealthyDoseofFran), Virag (Nerdy.bookdragon), Alexis (EvilQueenReads), Hayley (Hay.Reads), Brittany (ScienceOwlReads), Deepika (DeepinaBook), May (The.Mixed.Pages), Jackie (FabledFolklore), Nidhi (LailaofSerra), Haadiya (HerBookishObsession), Sara N., Sandra (BookBlubbs), Meghana (Sunflowers_andstories), Rosa (Rosaredss), Izzy (Teen_Writing_101), Ahaana (WindowstoWorlds), Nora (NovelsWithNora), McKenzie (Cravebooks), Safa (Tea.books.magic), Katherine (Kat.Reads), Jordyn (RedThisstle), Caitlyn (TheCaitlynintheRye), Hallie (BookLoaner),

Luna (BlogsLattesandJournaling), Kailey (IntheLandofPages), Bella (RainstormReads), Leeann (GeometryofStories), Raquel (PoisonBookNerd), Mari (MacnBooks), Paola (ANotSoWickedWhich), Birdie (BirdiesBooktopia), Saika (BooksWithTsai), Astrid (BookLoverBookReviews), Heaven (HeavenlyBibliophile), Kau (KoosReviews), Bianca (YourWordsMyInk), Noorain (NerdGurll), Naadhira (LegendBooksDary), Jacob (JacobRundle), Megan (BookBirds), Prutha (PruthaReads), Isabelle (ThisBelleReadsToo), Taylor (TaylorReads), Nihaarika (Svnshine.Reads), Michelle (musingsbymichelle), Thya (WiltedPages), Arin (TomesofOurLives), Ari (ReadingUnderStreetlamps), Aria (BookNookBits), Riv (DearRivarie), Kristi (ConfessionsofaYAReader), Grace (BooksWithGraceAnn), Mary Roach, Jordan (TheHeartofaBookBlogger), Jayati (ItsJustaCoffeeAddictedBibliophile), Ramnele (bookdragonism), Sophie (MindofaBookDragon), Marcella (MariaMarcellaW), Ja-Mel, Lily (SprinklesofDreams), Jen (PopGoestheReader), Tammie (TammieTriestoRead), Veronica (KollabSF), Rachel (RecItRachel), Paola (Gurerrerawr), Shealea I (ShutUpShealea), Khyati and Daman (BrownGirlsRead).

The above is not a full list, and by the time *How We Fall Apart* is published, there will certainly have been more book bloggers and influencers who have supported this book than at the time I'm writing these acknowledgments. So let me thank you all, every last one of you, from the bottom of my heart. You know who you are. Writing is a solitary experience. Releasing novels, especially as a new author, *especially* without in-person events, can feel like flinging your work into an abyss. Without reader enthusiasm for my books on social media, I would have felt so unbearably alone. Thank you for shouting about *How We Fall Apart* from the rooftops. I can't thank you all enough, really and truly.

Finally, a most heartfelt thank-you to my family, and to my wonderful writer friends for supporting me throughout my journey. To Amélie Wen Zhao, Becca Mix, Grace Li, Aly Eatherly, Kianna Shore, Elora Cook, Francesca Grandillo, Lyla Lee, Andrea Tang, Aneeqah Naeem, Britney Shae, June Hur, Jamar Perry, Elinam Agbo, Diana Urban, Stephan Lee, Victoria Lee, and the many, many more friends who have been there for me from the start, or who I've found along the way—thank you for reading my words and letting me read your beautiful words in turn. I am the luckiest author to get to embark on this writing adventure with the best people in my corner. I can't wait to keep sharing my stories with you.